Final Sail

Also by Elaine Viets

Dead-End Job Mystery Series

Shop till You Drop
Murder Between the Covers
Dying to Call You
Just Murdered
Murder Unleashed
Murder with Reservations
Clubbed to Death
Killer Cuts
Half-Price Homicide
Pumped for Murder

Josie Marcus, Mystery Shopper Series

Dying in Style
High Heels Are Murder
Accessory to Murder
Murder with All the Trimmings
The Fashion Hound Murders
An Uplifting Murder
Death on a Platter

Final Sail

A DEAD-END JOB MYSTERY
• • • • • • • • • • • • • • • •

Elaine Viets

AN OBSIDIAN MYSTERY

OBSIDIAN
Published by New American Library, a division of
Penguin Group (USA) Inc., 375 Hudson Street,
New York, New York 10014, USA
Penguin Group (Canada), 90 Eglinton Avenue East, Suite 700, Toronto,
Ontario M4P 2Y3, Canada (a division of Pearson Penguin Canada Inc.)
Penguin Books Ltd., 80 Strand, London WC2R 0RL, England
Penguin Ireland, 25 St. Stephen's Green, Dublin 2,
Ireland (a division of Penguin Books Ltd.)
Penguin Group (Australia), 250 Camberwell Road, Camberwell, Victoria 3124,
Australia (a division of Pearson Australia Group Pty. Ltd.)
Penguin Books India Pvt. Ltd., 11 Community Centre, Panchsheel Park,
New Delhi - 110 017, India
Penguin Group (NZ), 67 Apollo Drive, Rosedale, Auckland 0632,
New Zealand (a division of Pearson New Zealand Ltd.)
Penguin Books (South Africa) (Pty.) Ltd., 24 Sturdee Avenue,
Rosebank, Johannesburg 2196, South Africa

Penguin Books Ltd., Registered Offices:
80 Strand, London WC2R 0RL, England

First published by Obsidian, an imprint of New American Library,
a division of Penguin Group (USA) Inc.

First Printing, May 2012
10 9 8 7 6 5 4 3 2 1

LIBRARY OF CONGRESS CATALOGING-IN-PUBLICATION DATA:

Viets, Elaine, 1950–
    Final sail: a dead-end job mystery / Elaine Viets.
      p. cm.
    "An Obsidian mystery"
    ISBN 978-0-451-23674-6 (hardback)
    1. Hawthorne, Helen (Fictitious character)—Fiction. 2. Women detectives—Fiction. I. Title.
    PS3572.I325F53 2012
    813'.54—dc23   2011045363

Set in Bembo
Designed by Elke Sigal

Printed in the United States of America

PUBLISHER'S NOTE
This is a work of fiction. Names, characters, places, and incidents either are the product of the author's imagination or are used fictitiously, and any resemblance to actual persons, living or dead, business establishments, events, or locales is entirely coincidental.
    The publisher does not have any control over and does not assume any responsibility for author or third-party Web sites or their content.

For Victoria,
who really should kill
people—on paper.

ACKNOWLEDGMENTS

Final Sail would have been totally at sea without the help of Victoria Allman. She's a yacht chef who writes as well as she cooks. Many of the meals aboard the fictional *Belted Earl* came from Victoria's two cooking memoirs: *Sea Fare: A Chef's Journey Across the Ocean* and *SEAsoned: A Chef's Journey with her Captain* (NorLightsPress). The recipes are fabulous.

Victoria's captain is also her husband, Captain Patrick Allman. His help was invaluable. Gina Soacat, the yacht's head stewardess, taught me the finer points of yacht cleaning, including running the vacuum cleaner in the tracks.

One mystery still remains: Victoria, Captain Patrick and Gina would not reveal their yacht's owners.

A very special thanks must go to my editor, Sandra Harding, for her insights and her patience, and to the ever-helpful Elizabeth Bistrow at NAL. Writers love to complain about copy editors, but this one saved my hide. Thank you!

My agent, David Hendin, gave excellent advice, and my husband, Don Crinklaw, is my first reader and best critic.

Old salt and sailboater Barry Talley steered me across the treacherous Gulf Stream and mystery writer Marcia Talley provided photos and other information about the Bahamas.

I am deeply grateful to my friend and former newspaper editor Dick Richmond for his help.

Tom Adair, a retired forensic scientist, helped with the forensics. Enjoy his blog at forensics4fiction.wordpress.com. Mystery writer Joanna Campbell Slan told me how the rich really advertise for household help. Sue Schlueter gave wardrobe advice for my yacht-goers.

Mary Lynn Reed, when she isn't providing Phil with fake references, is a real friend. Valerie Cannata gave me her name for my TV reporter. Nancie Hays let me turn her into a lawyer.

Suzanne Schoomer is a fine chef who generously lent her name in return for a large donation to a worthy cause.

The real Margery Flax is much younger but just as crafty as the fictional Margery—and both love purple. She does wish the Coronado landlady drove a hotter car, but it's a Florida law that anyone over age seventy must drive a large white car.

Helen still works those dead-end jobs, but now that she and Phil have their own private eye agency, she takes them to solve cases. Private investigator William Simon gave invaluable information about this business. Detective R. C. White, Fort Lauderdale Police Department (retired), is also working on his PI license. He gave me the benefit of his insights and information.

Rick McMahan, ATF special agent and one heck of a writer, helped. MarySue Carl and author Eileen Dreyer assisted with hospital procedure. Fort Lauderdale attorney Vladimira Libansky, Esq., helped with the legal issues. Luci Zahray, internationally known poison expert, uses her powers only for good—and to help mystery writers like me.

Like the song says, I get by with a little help from my friends. They include Karen Grace, who spent many hours discussing these characters and their motivation, Alan Portman, Molly Portman,

Doris Ann Norris, Kay Gordy, Jack Klobnak, Robert Levine and Janet Smith. Mary Alice Gorman gave me promotional advice. I can't forget supersaleswoman Carole Wantz, who could sell beer at a temperance meeting.

Boynton Beach librarian Anne Watts lent me her six-toed cat, Thumbs, for this series. Once again, I am grateful to all the librarians who helped with this book, especially the staff of the St. Louis Public Library and Broward County Library. Librarians are the original search engines.

I'm grateful to the booksellers who recommend my novels to their customers.

To the sources who can't be named, I appreciate your legal, medical and tax information.

Thank you, blog sisters. I rely on the advice and encouragement of the wise women in the Femmes Fatales (www.femmesfatales.typepad.com). You'll enjoy what they have to say, too. Stop by our blog.

Finally, any errors are my own. You can tell me about them, or better yet, tell me you enjoyed this novel, at eviets@aol.com.

Final Sail

CHAPTER 1

"That woman is murdering my father," Violet Zerling said. "We're sitting here while he's dying. And you— you're letting her get away with it."

Violet Zerling jabbed an accusing finger at attorney Nancie Hays. Violet was no delicate flower. She was twice the size of the slender lawyer and obviously upset.

Nancie wasn't intimidated by the large woman. The lawyer was barely five feet tall, a hundred pounds and thirty years old, but tough and adept at handling difficult people. She had faced down—and successfully sued—a slipshod homicide detective and the small South Florida city that employed him. She'd fought to keep an innocent woman out of jail. Now she didn't back away from Violet.

Nancie was all business, and so was her office. The carpet was a practical dark blue. Her plain white desk was piled with papers and folders. A workstation with a black computer, printer and fax machine was within rolling distance of her desk. Seated next to the workstation were the two partners of Coronado Investigations, Helen Hawthorne and Phil Sagemont. Nancie had called in the husband-and-wife PI team to help her new client.

Helen felt sorry for Violet, sitting rigidly in the lime green client chair. Her beige pantsuit was the same color as her short hair. The unflattering cut and drab color turned her face into a lump of dough.

Violet's clothes and shoes said she had money and spent it badly. Despite her sturdy build, she seemed helpless. Helen thought Violet could be pretty. Why did she work to make herself unattractive?

I'm not here to solve that mystery, Helen told herself. We have to save a man's life.

Nancie did not humor her client. "Violet, we've discussed this before," she said, her voice sharp. "Your father did not leave any medical directives or sign a living will. In fact, he doesn't have any will at all. Your stepmother—"

"That witch is not my mother," Violet said. "She is Daddy's second wife. She married my father for his money and now she's killing him. She wants his ten million dollars. He'll be dead soon, unless you do something. I need to save Daddy. Please. Before it's too late."

Violet burst into noisy tears. Helen had seen women turn weeping into an art form, shedding dainty droplets as if they were Swarovski crystals. Violet's tears seemed torn from her heart. Helen would bet her PI license those tears were genuine.

Nancie, Helen and Phil waited out the tear storm until Violet sat sniffling in the client chair. Then Phil handed her his pocket handkerchief. Helen loved her husband for that old-fashioned courtesy.

Violet liked it, too. She dabbed at her reddened eyes, then thanked Phil. "You don't meet many gentlemen these days," she said. "I'll have this laundered and return it to you."

"Keep it," Phil said. "That's why I carry one."

Violet stuffed Phil's handkerchief into a leather purse as beige and shapeless as its owner. The ugly bag was well made. It would probably last forever. Unfortunately.

"May I ask a question?" Phil asked.

Violet nodded.

"How does the rest of your family feel about your fight to keep your father alive?"

"There is no one else," Violet said. "I'm an only child. Daddy is the last of the Zerling family. He doesn't even have distant cousins."

"And you're not married, I take it?" Phil asked.

"I'm divorced," Violet said. "My husband married me for my money and the marriage was not happy." She looked down at her smooth, well-shaped hands. They belonged to a woman who did not work for a living.

"I might as well tell you," Violet said. "You and Helen are detectives. You'll find the whole sordid story of my divorce on the Internet. My marriage was miserable. My ex-husband drank and beat me. I had no idea he was like that when I fell in love with him. I was only twenty-one. Daddy opposed the marriage, but I had a trust fund from my grandmother, and I was determined to marry. My ex slapped me around on our honeymoon, and the marriage went downhill from there.

"I tried to hide the bruises, but I couldn't fool Daddy. He knew why I wore heavy makeup and long sleeves in August. He never said 'I told you so.' But he was there for me. It took me more than a year to walk away from my marriage. After my ex put me in the hospital, I got the courage to leave him.

"He wouldn't let go of his meal ticket without a fight. He accused me of living a wild life. We were tabloid material for months. I couldn't have made it without Daddy. I changed my name back to Zerling after the divorce.

"My family's money never brought me happiness. I can't trust my judgment about men. I've set aside that phase of my life."

"Oh!" Helen said. She was a new bride and couldn't imagine life without love, though her first husband had been a disaster.

"It's better that way," Violet said. "I can't make any more mistakes."

Now Helen understood Violet's dowdy appearance. It hid a badly wounded woman.

"We aren't here to talk about me," Violet said. "I have to save my father."

"Violet, I wish I could do more," Nancie said. "Legally, Blossom is Arthur's next of kin. He's being given the best possible care, but he had a heart attack and he's in a coma."

"No! He was poisoned," Violet said. "She did it. That's why he's in a coma."

"There's no proof," Nancie said. "Your father's housekeeper, Frances, accused Blossom of poisoning Mr. Zerling. Fran took two samples to the police. They were analyzed. The so-called poison turned out to be harmless spices, turmeric and cumin."

"Fran was right to be suspicious," Violet said. "That woman never even scrambled an egg. Suddenly, she decided to fix Daddy a spicy curry dinner. A meat-and-potatoes man like Daddy, eating curry. Guess what? He got deathly ill after he ate it. Fran said she made a big pot of curry, but there wasn't a crumb left. That woman dumped it down the disposal."

"After her husband took sick?" Nancie asked. "You couldn't expect her to eat it."

"It disappeared before Daddy was sick."

"Blossom ate the same meal as your father," Nancie said.

"She poisoned Daddy's dinner," Violet said. "That's what I told the police. They didn't listen."

"They can't," Nancie said. "Not after Fran. The doctors said he had a heart attack. They didn't see any symptoms of poison."

"They didn't look. That woman's got a boyfriend," Violet said. "She left Daddy's house to meet a man. Fran saw her."

"Fran never actually saw Blossom with a man," Nancie said.

"That woman left at midnight," Violet said.

"She could have been going for a drive," Nancie said.

"Dressed in a short skirt and a low-cut blouse?" Violet asked.

"Fran reported that woman's suspicious behavior to the police. Blossom fired my father's housekeeper. Threw poor Fran out of her home."

"Can you blame her?" Nancie asked. "Let's look at the facts: Mr. Zerling has a heart condition. He uses nitroglycerin pills. He also took Viagra. That's not recommended for a man with his health issues. I'm surprised his doctor prescribed it."

"He didn't," Violet said. "His Fort Lauderdale doctor refused. Daddy got the blue pills from India. That woman told him he was a stud and he believed her."

"It's not illegal to encourage your husband to take Viagra," Nancie said.

"You didn't see the way she flaunted herself at him," Violet said. "I did. Daddy was taking twice the recommended dose. I know he'll pull through if I take care of him. Daddy is a fighter."

"What else could you do for him?" Nancie asked. "The doctors are doing everything they can. They say there's almost no chance of recovery. According to Blossom, your father said, 'If anything happens to me, pull the plug. I don't want to be a vegetable.' She wants him to die with dignity. Your father is an old man who's had a massive heart attack."

"He's only eighty-four," Violet said. "That's not old, not in our family. His father, my grandpapa, lived to be ninety-seven. His mother passed away at a hundred and two. Daddy could go on for another ten, twenty years if he hadn't married that woman. She murdered him."

"Mr. Zerling is still alive," Nancie said gently.

"Not for long," Violet said. "He's on a ventilator. My father is unconscious, wrapped like a mummy in tubes and wires. That machine makes the most horrible sound. I tried to see Daddy in the ICU, but that woman won't let me in his room. She says I give off bad vibes."

Helen saw tears welling up in Violet's eyes again.

"That's her right," Nancie said. "Unfortunately, the law is on Blossom's side. The judge denied your petition for guardianship."

"If I may interrupt," Phil said, "I find it hard to believe that a businessman like your father didn't have a will or a medical directive."

"Daddy hated lawyers," Violet said. "After my divorce, he set up a trust to run his companies if anything happened to him, and settled half his personal wealth on me. Then he made even more money. Daddy said he'd make a will when he was old."

"But he was eighty-four," Phil said.

"That's not as strange as it sounds, Phil," the lawyer said. "Even smart people aren't rational about wills. They're afraid if they sign one, they're signing their death warrant. They put it off until it's too late. Mr. Zerling is an amazing man, but he is old."

"Daddy is strong," Violet said. "He will get better."

He will recover—he won't. Helen rode that same seesaw during her mother's last illness. Her heart couldn't accept what her mind knew.

Nancie turned toward Violet and her voice softened. "Violet, dear, I know this is hard for you to hear, but you must prepare yourself for the worst. Your father may not recover."

From the depths of her beige purse, Violet pulled out a photo of a white-haired man on a glossy black stallion and handed it to Helen. She saw a square-jawed older man with a straight back and strong hands gripping the reins. He looked fit and muscular. Helen handed the photo to Phil.

"Look at him! Is this the photo of a man who would give up?" Violet's eyes burned with fanatic fire and her pale skin was tinged with pink. For a moment, Helen got a glimpse of the vital woman she could be.

"That's my father on his eighty-fourth birthday, three months before he met her," Violet said. "He barely looks sixty. Blossom has reduced him to a thing on a machine. Soon Daddy will be nothing at all. He'll be dead and she'll have his millions and spend them on her boyfriend."

"Violet," Nancie soothed, "you must be careful what you say. That statement is actionable."

"I'm saying it to you in your office," Violet said. "These detectives work for you, right?"

"Yes," Nancie said. "When Helen and Phil work for my firm, their investigation is protected by attorney-client privilege. Also, under Florida law, client communications with private investigators are protected. They can lose their licenses if they breach confidentiality."

"Good," Violet said. "That means I'm doubly protected. I want to prove she's killing Daddy. Then I can be in charge of his care."

"Violet," Nancie said, "your father may not live long enough for that to happen."

"If you can't save my father, I want her in jail for murder. I have the money to get what I want.

"His millions may kill my father," she said. "I want my money to save him."

CHAPTER 2

"*I have the money to get what I want.*"

Violet's sentence sounded sweet to Helen: Nancie's new client had just handed their struggling PI agency an unlimited expense account. Her reasons sounded noble: She wanted to save her father.

But Helen also detected discordant notes: Violet had used "I" twice, plus "money" and "want." She'd packed a lot of ego into nine short words. She'd mentioned her father's millions and her own money.

If Violet solved her problems by throwing money at them, she could give Helen and Phil's newborn agency a healthy cash infusion.

But that sentence also signaled Violet could be difficult, demanding and determined to get her way. She was so eaten with hatred that she could not say her stepmother's name. It was an unnerving pattern. Violet didn't mention her ex-husband's name, either. She'd erased the man, if not the damage he did to her.

Violet was in the grip of powerful emotions. Her desire for revenge could hinder their investigation.

You've spent years in retail, Helen told herself. This isn't the first difficult person you've had to handle. Phil has enough charm for both of us, and Nancie stood up to a whole city and got her way. We can handle one rich, wounded client.

"I know how we can get that woman," Violet said.

Phil caught Helen's eye and raised an eyebrow at that *we*. He knew that was client code for *you*.

Nancie leaned forward in her desk and gave Violet a gunslinger's stare. "We'll be happy to consider any ideas you might have," she said. "But I am in charge of any inquiry, and Coronado Investigations works with me. We will not do anything illegal or unethical."

Violet sat back slightly, as if the force of Nancie's statement made her retreat. She fumbled with her purse strap while she carefully chose her words and softened her voice. "I'm worried that woman will try to kill my father in the hospital," she said. "She could smother him with a pillow or pull the plug on the ventilator. Then Daddy will never get a chance to recover." A fat tear escaped and slid down her pale cheek.

Nancie seemed to suppress a sigh. Very slowly, as if she were explaining a complex subject to a small child, she said, "There's no evidence your father is receiving improper treatment—or that he's been poisoned. We need facts. All we have is his housekeeper's bungled attempt to get Blossom arrested and an imaginary boyfriend."

"He's real," Violet said. "She's cheating on Daddy. My father needs protection, and I can't be there to help him. That woman won't let me into his ICU room, but she'd have to let in Daddy's spiritual adviser."

"Your father has a minister?" Helen asked.

"Yes," Violet said. "You."

Her words detonated a deafening silence. Violet rushed to fill it. "Daddy wasn't religious. I don't think he's been in a church since Mama was buried. But that woman has been with Daddy such a short time she doesn't know if he has a Baptist minister or a Buddhist monk."

Phil said the name Violet couldn't bring herself to pronounce. "Is Blossom from Fort Lauderdale?"

"That woman says she's from California," Violet said, "but who knows? Her maiden name—though I doubt she's been one for years—is supposed to be Blossom Mae. We had dinner together after she and Daddy came home from the cruise. It was awkward. Watching my father slobber over her almost made me lose my dinner."

Violet suddenly seemed aware of how bitter she must sound. "I guess you think I have issues with my father remarrying. I don't. I want Daddy to be happy. But she's pure evil."

More tears trickled from her reddened eyes. Violet fished Phil's handkerchief out of her purse and blotted her eyes, but she couldn't stop weeping. Helen felt sorry for her. Violet seemed sincerely worried about her ailing father. But was she right about Blossom?

"I tried to get her to talk about herself," Violet said. "Everyone likes to do that. She wouldn't. All that woman would say was she grew up in San Diego and she went to work for the cruise line. I couldn't pry another fact out of her, which I thought was fishy. I know she's hiding something. She wouldn't even tell me what year she graduated from high school."

"Maybe she's hiding her age," Phil said.

"Then that's all she's hiding," Violet said. "She definitely flaunted her goodies. Daddy's eyes crossed when she leaned over to pass the cream. I'm guessing she's about thirty-five. Her name is flaky enough that she could be from Moonbeam Land. Daddy is a sucker for flower names. Mother's name was Honeysuckle and my name is Violet. He calls that woman his Little Flower."

Violet snorted. "Little Flower, my eye. Clinging Vine is more like it. She's wrapped herself around Daddy and hung on tight. Now she's strangling the life out of him.

"That woman came from nowhere. She never mentions her family. I don't know if her parents are alive or if she has brothers or sisters. All I know is she was a masseuse on a cruise ship and met Daddy while he was on a world cruise.

"Heaven knows what kind of massage she gave him. Daddy said it was a full-body massage." Violet rolled her eyes. "Full body, indeed. She threw her body at him. I thought that cruise line was respectable."

" 'Full body' is a type of therapeutic massage," Phil said.

Violet looked like she'd swallowed something sour and continued. "Daddy called me from the cruise ship and said he was marrying her. He'd only known that woman for two weeks. I told him she was after his money."

"You said that before you even met her?" Helen said.

"It wasn't tactful, I know," Violet said. "I probably made things worse. Daddy said he was old enough to know his own mind and I'd never seen her, so how could I criticize her?

"I wanted to fly in for the wedding, but he said there wasn't time. They were marrying on the beach the next day, when their ship reached the Maldives. Those are islands off the coast of India."

Nancie and the two detectives nodded like bobblehead dolls.

"That woman had signed a contract to work for the cruise line for a whole year. Daddy bought it out and paid to have a substitute massage therapist flown in at the next port of call. They spent their honeymoon on the ship where she'd been an employee.

"They were only home three weeks when Daddy had that 'heart attack.' "

Helen could hear the quotation marks around those words.

"He was popping Viagra like candy. The last time I saw Daddy, he was swaggering around like a teenager. He bragged that they hadn't left the house in four days and made it clear they'd spent it in bed."

"Wow!" Phil said. "That's pretty impressive."

Violet seared him with an angry look. "She was wearing nothing but a negligee at four in the afternoon."

Phil started to say something, then stopped himself.

Violet rushed into the silence. "That's why you could get into Daddy's hospital room, Helen. You could say you were his minister. She never bothered learning anything about him except he had a big bank account. If you went to the hospital, you could sit in the ICU and watch over him. I want you to be his bodyguard at night. That's when I worry most about Daddy, when there isn't much activity in the hospital. If you were there, she couldn't harm him."

"But I'm not a minister," Helen said.

"You could be," Phil said. "Our landlady, Margery, is a minister in the Universal Life Church. You can get ordained online for free."

Helen glared at her husband. She didn't like being rushed into this.

"Is that church legal?" Violet asked.

"I sure hope so," Phil said. "Margery married us."

"The ordination is legal," Nancie said, "as long as Helen uses her real name."

"Let's do it now," Violet said. "Helen could get ordained by your office computer."

"Wait a minute," Helen said. "Even if I do get ordained, why would Blossom let me in to see Mr. Zerling? She's kept you away from your own father."

"Because she wants everyone to think she's a sweet, concerned wifey," Violet said. "She's painted me as a jealous, possessive daughter."

And you helped with that portrait, Helen thought.

"That woman bribes the hospital staff," Violet said. "She doesn't give them money, but she brings in gourmet sandwiches and pizza. There's always a huge hundred-dollar box of Godiva chocolate at the nurses' station. They love her. The nurses don't like me because I'm too proud to buy friends."

Too bad, Helen thought. We're going to cost a lot more than chocolates and sandwiches.

"Now will you get ordained?" Violet asked. "Please?"

Helen was a lapsed Catholic. A casual ordination made her feel uneasy. "What about Phil?" she asked. "He could be a minister."

"I have other plans for him," Violet said.

"Perhaps you'd care to share them with us," Nancie said, her words sharp and clipped. "Please remember Helen and Phil will take no action without my approval. Now, let's hear your idea for Phil."

"He could be that woman's estate manager," Violet said. "She's advertising for one in the newspaper. That's what she's calling the job: estate manager. Have you ever heard anything so pretentious?"

"How big is the estate?" Phil asked.

"It isn't an estate," Violet said. "It's a comfortable house with eight bedrooms and twelve bathrooms. It does need looking after. Daddy had Fran. What that woman wants is a houseman, or a handyman, or even a caretaker. Those are the right terms. But she's new rich, so she inflated the title to estate manager."

"Would I have to keep the books?" Phil asked.

"No," Violet said. "Daddy has an accountant. You'll deal with the household staff, the pool service, the lawn service, the security service and various repair people. You'll have to make sure the property is well maintained."

"I could do that," Phil said. "Am I qualified?"

Helen bristled as she watched Violet run her eyes up and down Phil's body. Violet lingered over his broad shoulders and stopped at his striking silver hair, which Phil had pulled into a ponytail.

"Oh, you're qualified," Violet said, laughing too loudly. "You've got everything she'll want. Right between your legs."

"That's enough, Violet," Nancie said. "That's sexual harassment and I won't permit it in my office."

"Phil is married," Helen said. "To me."

"I'm not that kind of guy," Phil said, and attempted a laugh, but he was embarrassed.

So was Violet. She'd turned a blotchy red. "I apologize," she said. "I was out of line. I've been upset since Daddy got sick. I hope you'll forgive my coarse remark. I meant the job as estate manager would get you into my father's house. Then you can find out who is that woman's boyfriend and get the evidence to prove she's trying to murder Daddy.

"She is killing him," Violet said. "You have to believe me. I'll spend every nickel I have to prove it."

CHAPTER 3

The Reverend Helen Hawthorne had been a minister for three minutes, and she didn't like it. Helen believed women had the right to perform pastoral duties. Now the click of a mouse on a lawyer's computer made her a minister. She could baptize, bury and legally marry couples in all fifty states.

It didn't feel right. The power to preside over life's major milestones should be given in a solemn ceremony, she thought. Being a minister was a sacred duty, even to the nonreligious Helen.

Nancie and Violet applauded when the online ordination was complete, but Helen didn't feel like celebrating.

"You'll have an e-mail verification in twenty-four hours," Nancie said. "I'll forward it."

"Congratulations, Reverend," Phil said, and kissed her cheek.

"May I speak to my partner in private, please?" Helen asked.

"Use the conference room next door," Nancie said.

Helen dragged Phil into the room, yanked two tall gold-upholstered chairs away from the oak table and said, "Sit."

Phil sat. He looked puzzled. Helen sat across from her husband.

"Did I say something wrong?" Phil asked.

"Yes," Helen said. "Don't ever volunteer me for something again without asking. I'm your partner in our agency. You trapped me into that farce of an ordination."

"I didn't think you'd care," Phil said.

"You could have asked," Helen said. "And for the record, I do care. Being a minister is a serious business, even to someone like me."

"I'm sorry," Phil said. "I thought it was part of going undercover. I'm working as a fake estate manager for Blossom and you'll guard Mr. Zerling as a minister. Your ordination gives your cover authenticity."

"Point taken," Helen said.

"Something else is wrong," Phil said. "What is it?"

Helen stared down the long expanse of polished oak and tried to find the right words. She wondered if the frugal Nancie had bought the overgrown dining set with the stiff, gold-plush cushions second-hand and recycled it for her conference room. Its ornate style was so different from the lawyer's own practical office.

Phil interrupted her thoughts. "Helen, we left Nancie and Violet waiting on us. What else is wrong?"

"I don't like this," Helen said.

"This what? This case? This client? Do you think Violet is lying?"

"No, I think she's telling the truth," Helen said. "As she sees it. I also think she has a knack for making trouble for herself. She insulted her father's bride before she even met the woman."

"When a much younger woman marries a very old man, the main attraction is usually his money," Phil said.

"I know that," Helen said. "But not always. Sometimes a woman is attracted to qualities that transcend age—a man's vitality and creativity. Violet never bothered finding out. She branded Blossom a gold digger and treated her father as a randy old fool. I suspect if she'd been a little nicer to those ICU nurses, they might have let Violet see her father."

"The hospital has rules," Phil said. "Blossom left those instructions, and the nurses have to follow them."

"A busy nurse could look the other way if Violet wanted to visit her father," Helen said. "They could convince themselves they were being compassionate. But none of them did. I'm betting Violet has ticked them off, too."

"It's true she won't even say Blossom's name," Phil said. "She radiates anger."

"I'd be angry, too, if I thought someone was killing my father," Helen said. "But I'd try to control my feelings better."

"Really?" Phil said. "I seem to remember that you attacked your first husband's Land Cruiser with a crowbar, Ms. Cool."

"I surprised Rob while he was having sex with our next-door neighbor," Helen said. "That was different."

"If you say so," Phil said. "Dying in the saddle is a good way to go. At least old Arthur will die happy."

"And before his time, if Violet is right," Helen said. "Do you think Blossom poisoned him?"

"Can't tell," Phil said. "Blossom's sudden urge to cook sounds strange. And she might have a lover. We're certainly not getting the full picture from the daughter, and the housekeeper messed things up further. At least we work for an ethical lawyer. Nancie won't treat Violet like a cash cow, milking the woman until her money runs dry. She must think Violet has some credibility or she wouldn't have called us.

"Let's take the case and investigate further," he said. "You can check out Blossom when you're at the hospital and get a feel for what she's like. I'll find out more about her if I get the job as estate manager. I'll also do a background check on her."

"I can interview the housekeeper," Helen said. "Maybe she saw something useful."

"It's pretty clear she never saw exotic spices before," Phil said. "I'll tail Blossom and find out if she's meeting a boyfriend." He held up his right hand. "And I solemnly swear I'll consult you first on all major decisions for our agency."

"Deal," Helen said, and kissed Phil.

"Are you going to wear a Roman collar to the hospital, Your Holiness?" Phil asked. "That would look hot."

"That's overdoing it," Helen said. "I'll go ahead with this investigation and see if we turn up anything. I don't want to be mercenary, but Violet is willing to pay."

"We're supposed to be mercenary," Phil said. "We're running a business. Violet is racking up more billable hours in Nancie's office while we talk."

"Then let's rejoin them," Helen said.

As she entered Nancie's doorway, she heard the lawyer say, "Yes, they are new, Violet. They've been in business only a few months. But Phil was a private investigator with a multinational agency for many years. I have absolute confidence in Coronado Investigations. I've worked with them before and—hi, Phil and Helen. I was telling Violet about your qualifications. I hope you're taking her case."

"We're ready to start," Helen said. "When do you want me at the hospital?"

"Five o'clock tomorrow," Violet said. Her tears had dried, but her face was still red and blotchy. "Some of Daddy's friends are keeping watch for me in shifts. I told them I'd have someone in place by tomorrow evening."

"I could start sooner," Helen said.

"No, they love Daddy and they"—her voice wobbled—"want a chance to say good-bye."

"Do they think Blossom poisoned your father?" Helen asked.

"They're staying neutral," Violet said. "They want to sit with their old friend and they don't believe he'll recover." She rushed through that sentence before her voice broke. "Bob, one of Daddy's partners, has the last shift tonight. Will you wear a Roman collar?"

"I discussed that with Phil," Helen said. "It's best to keep it simple. I'll wear a plain gray suit, black pumps and a small silver cross. I can carry my mother's Bible."

"Helen, what will you do if that woman tries to hurt my father?" Violet asked.

"I'll ask her firmly and loudly what she's doing," Helen said. "I'll yell if I have to. We'll be in the ICU. There will be staff all around. I'm not afraid of some little blond trophy."

"She's not blond," Violet said. "She's a brunette with rather extravagant hair. That woman is definitely not little. She's nearly your height—about five feet ten—and she does yoga and Pilates. I think she's too thin, but Daddy calls her willowy. I doubt she'll cause you any trouble, Helen. Sneaking up on a sick, helpless man is more her style."

"I'd like to talk to the housekeeper as soon as possible," Helen said. "How do I reach her?"

"Fran is moving into a condo in Coconut Creek," Violet said. "I'll call her now."

Violet found her cell phone and speed-dialed a number. "Hello, Fran, it's me. I've hired a detective for Daddy. . . . Would you be willing to talk to her today? Good. Her name is Helen Hawthorne. . . . I'm sure she understands."

Violet punched END and said, "She'll see you at four o'clock, but she says her condo is still a mess." She smiled. "Fran has her professional pride." She wrote on a small pad and said, "This is her address and cell phone number. Then you'll report to the hospital tomorrow and stay with Daddy until he's well enough to come home."

"Violet," Nancie said, drawing out her name. "Remember what I said. You realize there are extra charges if Helen is on duty more than twelve hours at a time in your father's room?"

"I told you I don't care about money," Violet said. "I want to save Daddy." Her voice cracked into sobs. Helen felt sorry for the distraught daughter.

"Phil, will you call that woman and apply for that ridiculous estate-manager job this afternoon?" Violet said. "My friend Mary Lynn Reed will give you a good reference. Here's the information about Mary Lynn's property for your job interview." She pulled an envelope from her massive purse and handed it to Phil.

"What am I looking for if I get hired?" he asked.

"Evidence of murder."

"Attempted murder," Nancie corrected.

"How do you think Blossom killed—uh, attempted to kill your father?" Phil asked.

Violet didn't hesitate. "Poison," she said. "Fran says she poisoned him. She's no expert on spices—she thought cumin and turmeric were poison—but she's smart. Fran recognized that woman's behavior was suspicious. She just picked the wrong things off the counter. Poison is a woman's weapon."

"Not always," Phil said. "I've known women to shoot, stab and strangle."

"You don't know that woman," Violet said. "She's sly. She knows how to ingratiate herself. Somehow she flattered her way into my father's life on that cruise ship."

Even a smart man can have a weakness for a beautiful woman, Helen thought. Especially if he's a lonely widower. Why can't Violet see that?

"That woman has sailed to India and Asia," Violet said, "places famous for exotic poisons. I think she brought some home. So does Fran."

"Poison isn't always from the exotic East," Phil said. "I could find enough at Home Depot to wipe out half of Lauderdale. Blossom could kill your father with his own medication, like giving him too much blood thinner."

"My father doesn't take blood thinner," Violet said. Her voice softened into a plea. "Fran knows that woman poisoned Daddy. So do I. We want you to work at her house and find the evidence. We think she used a poison that doesn't show up on normal tests. That's why the doctors can't find it."

"Violet, if Blossom used something from your father's medicine cabinet, there may be no way to trace it," Nancie said.

"If Daddy should die, I want that poison found during the autopsy," Violet said, her voice rising.

"There won't be an autopsy if your father dies," Nancie said.

"And why not?" Violet was standing now.

"Because if he dies, he'll be in a hospital under a doctor's care," Nancie said. "The law says there is no need for an autopsy. Autopsies are expensive."

"I can pay for one," Violet said.

"You still can't do it," Nancie said. "Blossom is next of kin. She'll have to give permission, unless there is compelling evidence of a homicide."

"That's what I'm paying these investigators to find," Violet said.

CHAPTER 4

· · · · · · · · · · · · ·

Frances Murphy Sneed was proud of her new condo, a corner unit overlooking a lake. She answered her door in a white polyester uniform. "Come in, Helen," she said. "Don't mind the uniform. It's still good, even if I don't work anymore."

Helen wondered if the housekeeper with the crinkly gray hair had lost her identity as well as her job. "Thanks for seeing me, Mrs. Sneed," she said.

"Call me Fran. Anything for Mr. Z. I need a cigarette and coffee. What about you: coffee, water, Coke?"

"Coffee's fine," Helen said.

Fran was a plump, comfortable woman. Helen guessed her age at sixty-something. From her work-worn hands, she could tell they'd been hard years.

The housekeeper's condo building could fit inside the Zerling mansion, but it was light, airy and livable. Helen followed Fran into a beige-tiled kitchen with cardboard boxes piled in a corner. She poured two mugs of coffee and told Helen, "Sugar and creamer's on the counter."

Helen carried her coffee carefully across the living room's pale blue carpet. Fran patted a pillowy white sofa wrapped in thick plastic as if it were a pet.

"Delivered this afternoon," she said. "I had a furnished apartment at Mr. Z.'s. When that witch Blossom fired me, I wanted to rent a furnished place, but Miss Violet wouldn't hear of it. She bought me this condo."

"Violet bought this?" Helen asked. And never mentioned it, she thought. She gave the woman points for her secret kindness.

"And the furniture," Fran said. "That girl has a good heart, like her parents."

Fran slid open the doors to a screened-in porch with white wicker. "This is my favorite room," she said. "It's the only table until my new kitchen set arrives. Let's have our coffee out here."

Fran sat down with a small, tired sigh and lit a filter-tip cigarette. Golden sun slanted through the green trees by the lake. Graceful white birds foraged in the lush grass.

"It's like a painting," Helen said.

Fran looked pleased. "Some condos, like Oak Hill, don't have an oak or a hill. But White Egret has real egrets."

She sipped her coffee, then asked, "What do you want to know?"

"Tell me about Blossom and Mr. Zerling," Helen said.

Fran's faded blue eyes hardened with dislike. "She killed Mr. Z. Not a doubt in my mind. I worked for the Zerlings for thirty years. I ran the place and did the cooking. Nothing fancy, just good home cooking—fried chicken, steaks, chops.

"Violet's mother hired me, and no finer lady walked this earth. Mr. Z. was lonely after she died. He said everything reminded him of Honeysuckle and he needed a change of scene. That's why he took that cursed cruise.

"He called me all the way from India and said he was getting married. I was happy for him. But when I saw his bride, my mouth dropped open. She was fifty years younger than him. He was crazy about her. She acted like she was in love, but that's what it was—an act. She'd flinch sometimes when he touched her. Poor Mr. Z. never noticed.

"Blossom tries to act like a lady, but she makes little slips."

"Like what?" Helen asked.

"I fixed salmon steaks for dinner and she didn't know what a fish fork was. Drinks her tea with her pinkie extended. Pretends to be fancy when she's common as dirt.

"Blossom wanted rid of me from day one. She complained about my cooking. Said it was fattening. 'I need vegetables,' she says. So I made a pot of green beans with new potatoes and a nice ham bone. 'The beans are overdone,' she says. 'I like them al dente.' That's half-raw. It ain't healthy.

"One night I brought a crown roast into the dining room and Mr. Z.'s face lit up. I was going back for the baked potatoes and sour cream and chives, when she whispered, 'If I keep eating like this, I'll be as fat as Fran.'

"That hurt my feelings. I'm no size two, but I'm strong and healthy."

Helen tried not to stare at Fran's swollen ankles and the purple veins worming through her legs.

"Mr. Z. shushed Blossom. After dinner, he dropped by the kitchen for a cookie and slipped me a hundred dollars. 'Buy yourself a little treat, Fran,' he says. That's the kind of man he is.

"Blossom kept on about my cooking until Mr. Z. let her get rabbit food special-delivered from some chef. But he still wanted me to cook for him. She never went into the kitchen, not even to make tea.

"That's why I got suspicious when Blossom said she was cooking Mr. Z. a special dinner. 'I'm making chicken curry,' she says. 'Arthur likes spicy food.'

"'Since when?' I says. Mr. Z. let me speak my mind, though I tried not to take advantage of it.

"She says, 'Since our cruise. That's where Arthur discovered curry.' She turns to Mr. Z. and says, 'You like it spicy, don't you, sweetie?' She gives him a goopy look and he grins at her like he doesn't have a brain in his head.

"The next day she took over my kitchen and shooed me out, except when she couldn't find a pot for the rice. The kitchen counter was covered with strange stuff she'd bought herself. A bunch of leaves she called coriander. It looked like parsley and I saw no harm in that. I recognized the bay leaves, garlic, cinnamon, poppy seeds, gingerroot and cayenne powder. But there were two other powders I never saw before: one yellow-green and the other one orange.

"I asked straight out what they were. 'Spices,' she says. I didn't trust her. I snuck a pinch each in a Baggie, just in case. That was my mistake. I should have thrown it all out. I'd still be fired, but Mr. Z. would be healthy. But I let her serve that foreign slop and now he's dying."

"Was any curry left over?" Helen said.

"No," Fran said. "That's suspicious, too. She made a big potful. After dinner, she cleaned the pot and washed both their plates, then left the rest for me to clean up.

"Mr. Z. took sick during the night and she called 911. The next day I went to the police with those Baggies and—" Fran stopped, her face pink. "Made a fool of myself. But that curry was poisoned."

"You still think that?" Helen asked.

"I know it. I saved the wrong part, that's all. I'll tell you something else, too." Fran leaned forward and lowered her voice. "Blossom has herself a boyfriend."

"Did you see him?" Helen asked.

"No, but I saw her going out at midnight all dressed up. She wasn't wearing her regular rich-lady clothes. She had on a skintight skirt and a blouse cut to her navel. She was clickety-clacking across the drive to her car when she set off the security lights. That woke me up. I saw her plain as day, dolled up and wearing false eyelashes. She never dressed like that around Mr. Z.

"I mentioned it when I brought her morning tea. She says real casual-like, 'Oh, yes, I couldn't sleep. I went for a drive.' She was dressed for a man, not a midnight drive."

"Did Blossom ever call a man from the house?" Helen asked.

"No," Fran said. "I'd hear her ordering things from stores and talking to Mr. Z.'s friends when they called. She didn't have any friends of her own.

"She fired me after she found out I went to the police. Next time I saw Mr. Z., he was in the ICU in a coma. I sneaked in when his partner Mr. Roger sat with him. One look and I knew Mr. Z. was dying, but I can't say that to Miss Violet."

"She believes he'll recover," Helen said.

"She hasn't lived as long as I have," Fran said.

She finished her coffee, then said, "Here's something else about Blossom. She won't let anyone clean her dressing room. Cleans it herself. There's something in that room she doesn't want me to see."

"Did you search it?" Helen asked.

"Too afraid," Fran said. "She was looking to can me. Now she has."

The housekeeper was quiet now, as if she'd exhausted the subject and herself.

Helen thanked Fran and drove home. She parked the Igloo in front of the Coronado Tropic Apartments, pausing briefly to admire the building's sweeping Art Moderne curves in the fading light. The Coronado was built in 1949, when their landlady was a bride.

Helen and Phil rented half the units in the L-shaped apartment building. Their Coronado Investigations office was upstairs in apartment 2C. They lived downstairs in an odd arrangement: After their marriage, Helen and Phil kept their same small apartments next door to each other. They slept mostly at Phil's.

Helen thought slipping into Phil's bedroom to spend the night made their legal love feel illicit. But Phil sometimes retreated to his place to play loud music and Helen occasionally read alone in her apartment. Her cat, Thumbs, didn't mind the arrangement as long as he was fed.

The palm trees in the courtyard rustled like old-fashioned petticoats. Helen heard laughter and found Phil, Margery and their neighbors Peggy and Pete sitting by the pool for the nightly sunset salute, a Coronado tradition.

Their landlady wore a filmy lavender caftan and a swirl of cigarette smoke. A stylish seventy-six, Margery wore her gray hair in a swingy bob and her wrinkles as marks of distinction.

She raised her glass of white wine and said, "You look tired, Your Holiness. Take a pew. Have a drink." She poured Helen a cold glass from a box labeled "White Wine." Even the grapes in the photo looked plastic.

"Hi, Helen," said Peggy, a redhead with a dramatic nose. Her little black dress skimmed her figure and showcased her pale good looks.

"Hello!" said Pete. The Quaker parrot had emerald green feathers and a sober gray head. He was perched on Peggy's shoulder.

"Hi," Helen said. "You're dressed up for a poolside party, Peggy."

"I'm going to dinner with Danny," Peggy said. "Phil said you were ordained today. Congratulations. Should I call you Reverend Hawthorne?"

"No," Helen said. "I was ordained in the line of duty and it doesn't feel quite right."

"You'll make a better minister than most seminary graduates," Peggy said. "We're also celebrating your agency's two new jobs."

"Just one," Helen said. "Phil is working undercover as an estate manager."

"Not yet," Phil said. "The lady is talking to me tomorrow afternoon. If I don't get hired, we'll have to rethink this investigation. Meanwhile, I found us another job when I stopped at a restaurant on Seventeenth Street. I had a burger at the bar and got talking to a yacht captain at the next seat."

"A lot of yacht crews hang out in that area," Peggy said.

"Turns out the captain is looking for a detective. His name is Josiah Swingle."

"Josiah sounds like a good name for a sea captain," Helen said.

"He's from an old New England family," Phil said. "Josiah captains a luxury yacht docked on the New River. Says the owners mostly cruise the Caribbean. On the last trip they went to Atlantis in the Bahamas."

"The fancy hotel and casino on Paradise Island?" Peggy asked.

"That's the one," Phil said.

"I've seen the photos," Helen said. "Atlantis looks gorgeous."

"You may get to see it in person," Phil said. "The captain is worried there's a smuggler aboard his yacht and wants to hire a detective to find him. It has to be a woman. You can work it."

He added quickly, "If you want, Helen. I said we'd only take the job if you approve."

"How will I watch our client's father?" Helen asked.

"I don't think he's long for this world," Phil said. "But if he lasts, Margery can babysit him."

"I'm a minister, too, you know." Margery grinned and exhaled an unholy amount of smoke.

"Tell me about this yacht," Helen said.

"The captain says it's got a cool sky lounge, a Jacuzzi and a dining room big enough for a dozen people. You'll be one of the crew."

"Doing what?" Helen asked.

"You'll find out tomorrow morning at seven thirty," Phil said. "That's when the captain will be in our office. This job comes with an awesome ocean view."

CHAPTER 5

J osiah Swingle was born to be a yacht captain—at least Helen
thought so.

He had the right build: a compact muscular body with
strong arms. A white polo shirt set off his broad chest nicely.

Josiah had the right look, too: neatly trimmed sandy hair and the
sun-reddened complexion of a fair-skinned man. Helen liked the
sun wrinkles around his eyes.

He was the right size. Josiah was about five feet nine. That made
him tall enough to command, but not so tall he'd perpetually bump
his head in the ship's low-ceilinged passageways, or whatever sailors
called them.

Josiah had an air of calm confidence. I wouldn't follow you into
hell, Captain, Helen thought. But I'd obey your orders if the ship
was in trouble. And I'd expect you to get us out of it.

Josiah had knocked firmly on the door of Coronado Investigations the next morning. Helen checked the office clock and was
impressed by his punctuality: seven thirty on the dot.

Phil opened the door to their office, 2C, upstairs and across the
courtyard from their apartments.

"Morning, Captain," Phil said. "This is my partner and my wife, Helen Hawthorne."

The captain shook hands with both Phil and Helen, another point in his favor. She liked his firm handshake and calloused hands. They belonged to someone who worked hard.

Josiah surveyed the Coronado office and nodded approval. "This is how a detective agency should look," he said. "It's a working office, not some decorator's showcase."

Almost right, Captain, Helen thought. Those gunmetal gray desks and file cabinets have been battered by years of work—but not our work. We bought them used.

Phil beamed when Josiah admired his framed poster of Humphrey Bogart as Sam Spade, her husband's tribute to the romance of their trade. Then Josiah sat down in the yellow client chair, ready to tell his story. Helen and Phil sat across from him in their black and chrome chairs.

Josiah's voice was low, but distinct. "I captain a 143-foot motor yacht called the *Belted Earl*," he said.

"Interesting name," Helen said. "Is the owner British royalty?"

"No, an American with a sense of humor," Josiah said. "Before I tell you the family's name, I need you to promise that you'll keep it confidential, even if you don't take my case."

"You have our word," Phil said. "Unless you're doing something illegal that we're required to report."

"I'm not," the captain said. "I'm trying to catch someone breaking the law. That's why I need detectives. This is my first job as captain and I don't want to lose it. I like the owner and the ship. Word can't get around that there's trouble aboard the *Belted Earl*."

"We understand," Helen said, wondering who owned the yacht: a movie star? A superathlete? A rocker or rapper? Maybe an A-list comedian?

"The yacht is owned by a man from Chicago," Josiah said. "Earl Grantham Briggs."

"I never heard of him," Helen said. She tried not to sound disappointed.

"Most people haven't," the captain said, "and Earl likes it that way. Mr. Briggs is well-off and he knows money attracts trouble."

"Where did his money come from?" Phil asked.

"Something smart and simple," Josiah said. "He invented a heavy-duty belt for a lawn mower. Every time a riding mower needs a new one, Earl gets a chunk of change. He enjoys his yacht and makes sure it has the best of everything. He spent more than a million dollars upgrading the sound system."

"That's astonishing," Helen said.

"Not in his world," the captain said. "Earl has money, but he's a quiet guy. He's sixty-two and married to Beth, a former fashion model. She's younger than Earl and very attractive. They have no kids, unless you count Mitzi, Beth's miniature white poodle. Beth treats that dog like a child—even pushes it around in a stroller."

Helen had seen women wheeling their dogs around the Fort Lauderdale malls. She felt sorry for them, but this was no time to discuss canine child substitutes.

"Earl and Beth enjoy entertaining," the captain said. "They live in a perpetual party, and some of their friends are, uh, well, flamboyant. The Briggses entertain at their co-op on Lake Shore Drive in Chicago and their villa in Tuscany. Their yacht is a floating mansion with marble floors, art glass and custom-built oak cabinets."

"They live well," Helen said.

"Comfortable, for their society. The ship is relatively small by yachting standards. It's not some five-hundred-foot tub that can't turn around in the Lauderdale yacht basin. It has two fourteen-foot tenders, a Yamaha cruiser, WaveRunners and the usual toys. But it doesn't have a submarine or a helicopter."

Poor Beth and Earl, Helen thought. Phil caught her eye and she swallowed her snarky comment.

"We cruise mostly to the Bahamas and other Caribbean islands," Josiah said. "Earl and his friends like to gamble, especially at Atlantis. The wife, not so much. She and some of the lady guests power-shop instead.

"The ship usually has a crew of ten. We lost one crew member on the last trip. Our new stewardess took off with a dude she met at Atlantis. Earl didn't want me to call a Lauderdale crew agency and have one flown to the Bahamas. He said it was only a thirteen-hour trip back. The other two stewardesses could pick up the slack and I could hire someone when we reached port.

"I wasn't happy about sailing shorthanded, but he's the owner. When we left the Bahamas, I was worried about the wind. It wasn't dangerous, but it would make the trip uncomfortable. Earl didn't want to wait for it to die down. He wants to go when he wants to go. So we left.

"Before we passed Chub Cay in the Berry Islands, I did a walk-around to make sure everything was secure. I left the first mate on the bridge watching out for other boats. I went past the bosun's locker and heard something sliding around inside. That's where we store the cleaning equipment, the shammies and deck cleaners, along with the rope, fenders and hooks. I opened the locker and saw a gray tackle box behind some rope, sliding around the deck. It hadn't been stowed properly. The box was plastic and didn't look like one of ours. I popped it open."

The captain shifted uncomfortably in his chair. "At first, I couldn't believe it. The tackle box was filled with emeralds."

"Real ones?" Phil said.

"Real good ones. The bigger ones, about the size of postage stamps, were stored in the tray. The smaller ones were tossed in the lower compartment. About two hands full."

"Rough stones or cut?" Phil asked.

"Cut," Josiah said.

"Somebody knows what they're doing," Phil said. "Emeralds can have major flaws that only show up during cutting. Get one of those and a gemstone goes from priceless to worthless."

"I'm no expert," Josiah said, "but these looked like the fine emeralds I've seen displayed in the jewelry shops at Atlantis. The colors ranged from blue-green to deep green."

"Any other gemstones in the box?" Phil asked.

"Just emeralds," Josiah said.

"How do you know a yacht guest didn't stash the box in the bosun's locker?" Phil asked.

"If any guests were in that area, we'd know it," the captain said. "We keep track of them and the staff stays in touch by radio. A crew member would have reported it, asked if the guest needed help and steered the person back to the salon or stateroom or other guest area. Besides, the crew carried on the guests' luggage and nobody had a cheap one-tray tackle box. Our guests have expensive luggage."

"So who uses the bosun's locker?" Phil asked.

"The whole crew has access to it, but mainly the guys use it. Yacht work is divided into old-school his-and-her duties. Men do the outside work, including washing the boat every day. The engineer changes the zillion filters and handles the air-conditioning and other mechanical problems. Women do the serving and cleaning. They're called stewardesses. We do have a woman chef.

"I should have confiscated the emeralds, but I wanted to catch the smuggler and get rid of him. We had a rough crossing over the Gulf Stream. The guests and owners were seasick and stayed in their staterooms. Most of the crew was seasick, too, but the two stewardesses had to work anyway, cleaning up after the guests and serving them soup and ginger ale.

"The next time I checked the locker, the emeralds were gone. I did a quiet search of the crew cabins and found nothing. The smuggler has to be a crew member. The guests and owners were too seasick to remove that box. Only the crew was moving around during the time it disappeared."

"Who do you suspect?" Phil asked.

"Three people," the captain said. "The chef, the chief stewardess or the first engineer."

"How long have you known them?"

"I took command of the ship in February," Josiah said. "The other crew was already in place. They've been with the yacht for at least three years. That's a long time in this business. They were hired through reliable crew agencies. The crew work hard and don't cause trouble."

"How old are they?" Phil asked.

"The first engineer is thirty. The chef is twenty-eight and the chief stewardess is twenty-nine."

"Any money problems?" Helen asked. "Major changes in their lives? Late twenties is when people may decide to settle down."

"Not that I know," the captain said. "We're paid well for our work. No one's been talking about getting married or wanting to quit."

"What about drugs or gambling?" Phil asked.

"I don't allow drugs on board," the captain said. "That's a firing offense and they know it. Even the owners' friends aren't users. Nobody has any gambling debts that I know about. But I don't go drinking with the crew."

"Where do you think the smuggler sells the emeralds?" Helen asked.

"Miami or New York," he said. "I've been on guard for drugs. I never expected emeralds. I shouldn't be surprised. The Bahamas are a smugglers' paradise."

"Where are the emeralds coming from?" Phil asked. "Colombia?"

"That would make the most sense. I want this person found fast. If the yacht's boarded by the Coast Guard or searched by the island authorities, it could be impounded."

"Why would you be searched or boarded?" Phil asked.

"Lots of reasons. Somebody has a bite against the smuggler. Somebody wants a bigger cut. Anything happens and I lose my license and my reputation."

"But you didn't do anything," Helen said.

"Makes no difference," Josiah said. "I'm in charge. It's my ship and my responsibility. I want to hire you, Helen, to be the new stewardess. Have you had any experience working in a hotel or as a housekeeper?"

"I was a hotel maid at a tourist hotel here," Helen said. "I cleaned twenty-eight rooms, seventeen toilets and the honeymoon Jacuzzi each day."

"Good," he said. "You have a passport, right?"

"Just got it," Helen said. She didn't add that she had a passport, a credit card and a driver's license since she'd cleared up her troubles with the court. Helen had some things in her past that had to stay buried.

"The owner wants to cruise to Atlantis again," Josiah said. "We'll have the same crew. When you work with them, you'll hear things that I never will."

"When do you sail?" Helen asked.

"In two days," the captain said.

"Good," Helen said. "I'll be ready by then."

I'll spend the next two days trapped in a sad domestic drama, she thought. Then I can pursue a smuggler on a luxury yacht.

Helen could almost taste the sea air—and the adventure.

CHAPTER 6

S tranahan Medical Center was built in the 1950s as a small community hospital. When air-conditioning made the brutal Sun Belt summers endurable, the hospital spread like the tumors it claimed to cure. Stranahan's main hospital, in downtown Lauderdale, now sprawls over six city blocks and sends its tentacles into the surrounding neighborhoods, turning pleasant family bungalows into cramped Stranahan doctors' offices. Four more Stranahan hospitals have spread to the city's richer suburbs.

The medical center is named after Fort Lauderdale settler Frank Stranahan. Its billboards proclaim STRANAHAN—PIONEERING MEDICINE! and feature white-coated, white-skinned male doctors.

The medical center never mentions that Frank Stranahan committed suicide during the Depression, after he lost his money when a real estate deal went sour.

Helen thought poor Frank's death foretold Fort Lauderdale's future. Residents continue to try to survive the city's real estate boom and bust cycles.

Helen parked her white PT Cruiser in the hospital garage, adjusted her prim gray suit and checked that her silver First Communion cross was visible at her neck. Then she picked up her mother's well-worn Bible and her black video-camera purse and clip-clopped across the pedestrian bridge into the hospital in her sensible heels.

Helen was greeted by a blast of cold air, a medicinal odor and a bored security guard.

"I'm a minister," she said. "I was told that Mr. Arthur Zerling is gravely ill in the ICU." On the drive to the hospital, she had carefully chosen her words so she told only the truth. Helen couldn't bring herself to say that Arthur was in her congregation.

The guard yawned, snapped Helen's photo and issued an ID badge for Rev. Helen Hawthorne.

"The ICU is on the second floor," the guard said. "Take the elevator and follow the signs."

Helen was packed into the elevator with a harried mother and her crying baby, two skinny teenage boys who kept elbowing each other, a staffer in scrubs balancing a container of soup and a large soda, and a worried older woman carrying an African violet. Helen was grateful she had to endure the scents of soup, unchanged diaper, teenage feet and cloying perfume for only one floor.

She dashed out of the elevator and into the ICU. A short, sturdy nurse barred her way. Once again Helen recited, "I'm a minister. I understand that Mr. Arthur Zerling is gravely ill."

"His wife is with him in Room Two," the nurse said. "I'll ask her if you can see him."

The nurse bustled off on her mission, leaving Helen to get her first look at the couple together. She switched on the video camera in the shoulder strap of her purse and pointed it toward the ICU room. The light was so low, she guessed the Zerlings would be recorded in black and white instead of color.

Helen was shocked by the dramatic change in Arthur Zerling. The vital, vigorous old man photographed on horseback was gone. Arthur had shrunk to a skin-covered skeleton with limp rags of white hair plastered to his skull. Tubes and wires snaked out of his wizened body. A pole hung with six IV bags stood by his bedside like a tree bearing exotic fruit.

Blossom Zerling was reading a *Vogue* magazine beside her dying husband. She held the magazine on her lap. She'd slipped one arm through the tangle of plastic tubing to hold Arthur's clawlike hand.

If she was playing a dutiful wife, Helen gave her points for that tender gesture.

When the nurse hurried into the room, Blossom let go of her husband's hand, gave it a soft pat and greeted the nurse with the smile of someone who expected to be liked. She stood up, towering over the nurse by some six inches. Her crisp white blouse and Escada jeans were well tailored but not tight. Blossom wore her long, glossy brown hair brushed back from her face. Pink lipstick seemed to be her only makeup. She looked like the girl next door—if she lived in an eight-bedroom home.

Prickly, plain Violet was up against a formidable adversary, Helen thought, if Blossom was faking concern for Arthur Zerling.

Blossom tucked the magazine into her pricey Birkin bag and walked briskly out to Helen. "I'm so glad you're here," she said. Her words were softly pleasant and carefully enunciated. "Nurse Abbott says you're Reverend Hawthorne."

"You can call me Helen."

"I'm Blossom Zerling. I know we've just met, but could I ask you a favor? Would you sit with Arthur for a little while, please? I live nearby on Hendin Island. I've been here at the hospital since six o'clock this morning."

Eleven hours in that room, Helen thought, then felt a flash of panic. "What if your husband takes a sudden turn for the worse while you're gone?"

Blossom looked toward her husband's still form. Helen thought Arthur looked like one of those creepy wax saints in glass cases in old churches.

"The doctor said he could be that way for another day, or a

week, or even months," Blossom said. "His daughter—do you know Violet?"

"Yes," Helen said. "I've met her."

Blossom sighed. "May I speak to you in confidence, as a minister?"

Something stirred uneasily in Helen. This wasn't right. She was hired to prove that Blossom was a killer and now the woman wanted spiritual counseling. She nodded yes, unable to say the treacherous word.

"Let's sit in Arthur's room a minute," Blossom said.

Helen took the big turquoise visitor's chair and put her purse on the windowsill, where the video camera had a clear view of Arthur. Blossom sat on the edge of a small, spindly chair out of camera range. The microphone would still pick up her voice. The blinds were drawn, but Helen could make out Blossom's earnest face.

"I know I can't be a stepmother to Violet," she said. "I wouldn't even try. It would be an insult to her own mother. Besides, I'm young enough to be her daughter. I try to get along with her, but she's been hostile from the day Arthur announced we were getting married. I've tried to understand. I invited her to dinner when we came back from our honeymoon. Violet acted like a spoiled child. She accused me of marrying her father for his money.

"It's true I knew Arthur had money," Blossom said. "It's no secret that I met him while I was working on a cruise ship. All the passengers were comfortably off. There is an age difference, but I never think of Arthur as old. As least, I didn't until he had his heart attack. He is—was—such an active man. He loves life. He loves me. He loves Violet, though she's . . ."

Blossom toyed with the zipper on her Birkin bag. "She's difficult. And furious at her father for marrying me. Arthur and Violet had a terrible fight during our homecoming dinner, and she left before dessert. They made up later, but she's never pretended to like me.

"When Arthur had his heart attack, Violet wanted to take over his care. She marched in here and accused me of killing her father. Right in the ICU. She screamed so loud, the nurses had to ask her to leave. As security escorted her out, Violet shouted that she would get a lawyer and take me to court. There was no reasoning with her. Well, she filed a petition for guardianship, but it was denied. The doctors said I've done everything to ensure he has the best possible care.

"Look at my husband," Blossom said. Her voice trembled as if she was on the verge of tears.

Helen could see Arthur was a sad ruin. His ravaged frame made a pathetic mound in the hospital bed. His thin arms were bruised from needle sticks and his hands were crisscrossed with tape for the IV lines.

"You knew my husband when he was healthy," Blossom said.

Again, Helen's lie made her feel uneasy. She'd never seen Arthur Zerling except in a photograph.

"Arthur has lived life to the fullest," Blossom said. "He wouldn't want to be a mindless thing kept alive by machines. He told me. I don't want that for him, either. Violet loves her father, but she needs to let go and accept that there is no hope."

"You're right," Helen said. "Violet does love her father. She wants to say good-bye to him. Please let her."

For a moment, Helen thought she saw something hard and feral flicker in Blossom's eyes. Then it was gone, if it was even there.

"I can't," Blossom said. "Violet made such a scene last time, it upset her father. Arthur became restless and thrashed around. He can't communicate, but she disturbed him. You could feel her hatred for me when Violet walked into this room. It was like another person . . . like a demon. That sounds fanciful, I know, but it took two nurses to calm Arthur, and the doctor had to order a shot so he could rest. Ask Nurse Abbott."

"I wish you would consider this," Helen said. "It would mean a lot."

"So does Arthur's peace of mind," Blossom said. "I'm sure this isn't the first difficult family situation you've encountered. Now, if you'll excuse me, I'd like to slip out while Arthur is resting comfortably. I want to freshen up and eat food that doesn't come from a hospital cafeteria. I won't be gone long. Here's my cell phone number if there's any change in Arthur's condition. The nurses have it, too. You don't have to do anything but sit with him. Please? I don't know anyone in Florida."

"I'll do it," Helen said. She wondered what Blossom would think if she knew Arthur's daughter was paying her to be in that room.

"Thank you so much," Blossom said. "Do you have any questions?"

Lots, Helen thought, but she only asked one. "I thought Mr. Zerling would be on a ventilator. Did the doctor remove it?"

"No, I asked that Arthur be taken off that horrible thing," Blossom said. "I want him to be comfortable."

CHAPTER 7

Arthur Zerling looked like a corpse in a hospital gown. His scrawny chest barely moved. Helen thought the machines attached to him seemed more alive. They beeped softly and produced squiggly lines and colorful numbers on multiple monitors.

She was grateful he was still breathing. She had kept the final vigil by her mother's deathbed. In a crisis, those machines would flash, screech and summon a medical army. Then Helen would be sent packing.

She could hardly believe this shriveled man had incited such strong passions. Arthur had courted death with a potent cocktail of vanity and Viagra to love his beautiful wife. Was he an old fool or a man grasping at a last chance for a full life?

His daughter, Violet, seethed with jealousy and hatred after her father's marriage. She believed her father would get well if she took over his care. Helen didn't. She was no expert, but Arthur looked nearly dead. She agreed with Blossom: Arthur would not recover.

And Blossom—what about her? How could a young woman have sex with this wreck? Helen thought of her own honeymoon with Phil and tried not to imagine this bag of bones in her bed. Was Blossom really attracted by Arthur's strength and vitality—or to the possibility that she would soon be his wealthy widow?

Arthur, you are a man of mystery, Helen thought. But she was here as his minister as well as his bodyguard. She had to pray for Arthur Zerling. She paged to the back of her mother's Catholic Bible and found the section on the seven sacraments: Baptism, Confirmation, Confession, Marriage—that one got Arthur into this mess.

She skipped over Holy Communion, averted her eyes when she saw Holy Orders and riffled through more pages until she found the Sacrament of the Sick.

"Formerly known as the Last Sacrament or Extreme Unction," Helen read. "The priest anoints the suffering person with olive oil."

I don't have any olive oil, she thought. But it is a heart-healthy oil. Maybe I could find some in the hospital cafeteria. Helen derailed that train of thought, disgusted with herself. She wasn't a priest and she sure didn't feel like a minister. She was here to pray for the sick man. Anyone could do that. She didn't need olive oil.

Helen read, "The Sacrament of the Sick commends those who are ill to the suffering and glorified Lord, that he may raise them up and save them."

She took Arthur's limp hand and tried to pray: "God, please save Arthur, if that's possible. Or give him a peaceful death and forgive his sins, if he has any. Of course he has sins. Forgive mine, too, while you're at it."

That wasn't a good prayer. It was too much about her and not enough about him. Helen tried again.

"Please let Violet, his daughter, feel her father's love. Make the hatred that torments her go away. Comfort his wife—unless, of course, she killed him. Then give her the justice she deserves."

Still not a satisfactory prayer, but at least it was about Arthur. What a fraud I am, Helen thought. I can't even pray properly.

Arthur's hand twitched and then was still. The machines continued their monotonous missions while Helen searched for a better prayer. She finally settled on the Our Father. That was comfort food for the Christian soul, she decided. She recited the timeless prayer. Duty done, she pulled an Agatha Christie paperback out of her surveillance purse to read an old favorite, *The Body in the Library*.

She found her own comfort in Miss Marple's observations about the evil in everyday life. She enjoyed the old woman's gentle rebuke to the police that most people "are far too trusting for this wicked world."

The ding of the elevator and the hiss of the medical machinery blended into a soothing background symphony.

Just as Miss Marple was unmasking the killers at the seaside resort, Helen was startled by a loud announcement from a stern female voice. "Visiting hours will be over in five minutes at eight o'clock," the voice said. "Please turn in your ID badges at the front desk. Good night."

Was it really going on eight o'clock?

She stood up and stretched. The tall-backed turquoise visitor's chair failed to give the comfort it had promised. Helen felt like she'd been sitting on a stone. And where was Blossom? She'd been gone almost three hours, long enough for a hot shower and a meal.

Helen walked to the nurses' station. Nurse Abbott was still on duty, making notes in a thick chart. Helen studied the woman. Her short graying hair gave the nurse a mature, serious look. She had an air of competence and confidence that made Helen want to trust her. But should she? She remembered Miss Marple's warning as if the old woman had been knitting in Arthur's room.

Nurse Abbott reached into a box of Godiva chocolate the size of a silverware chest. Helen remembered Violet saying that Blossom had bribed the nurses with a lavish assortment. Helen estimated the box held more than a hundred pieces of light, dark and white chocolate. Her stomach growled loudly.

Nurse Abbott looked up and asked, "May I help you, Reverend?"

"Just taking a break," Helen said. "I thought Blossom would be back by now."

The nurse unwrapped a dark chocolate and bit into it. Helen watched the caramel ooze out. Her favorite. There was another loud rumble from Helen's stomach.

Nurse Abbott ignored it. "That poor thing needs a little time away," she said. "She sat with her husband for eleven hours straight. Caretakers must take care of themselves, too. If you need a short break, I'll keep an eye on Mr. Zerling."

"I would like a cup of coffee," Helen said. "I'll be back in half an hour."

She ran down the stairs to the courtyard. The concrete was littered with cigarette butts and the air was thick with stale smoke. Most of the smokers wore hospital scrubs. Didn't the staff know cigarettes caused cancer?

Helen fished out her cell phone and found a message from Phil. He was practically crowing. "You're speaking to an estate manager," he said. "Blossom hired me. It's six thirty. I start work at nine tomorrow morning. I'll stop for dinner before I go home. See you when I see you. I love you."

Poor wilted Blossom went home and found enough energy to interview a new estate manager? She'd hired Phil an hour and a half ago. Helen wondered if her hot, silver-haired man had given Blossom a new interest in life—and frisky ideas.

Surely not. But where was she? Blossom had had enough time to eat, shower, even take a nap.

Helen called Phil's cell phone. No answer. She left a message that she was still sitting with Arthur Zerling and waiting for Blossom to return to the hospital. Next she called Nancie and gave her report.

"Did the wife let you in his room?" the lawyer asked.

"Blossom couldn't wait to get out of the ICU," Helen said. "Not that I blame her. She'd been sitting with Arthur since six this morning. She said she needed a shower and food. She ran home and hired Phil."

"I know," Nancie said. "He already checked in. How does Arthur look?"

"Bad," Helen said. "And our client didn't tell us everything."

"They never do," Nancie said. "What do I need to know?"

"Violet made such a scene in the ICU that security had to escort her out. She accused Blossom of murdering her father."

"Terrific," Nancie said. "Blossom could sue our client for slander if she decides to go after Violet."

"She'll probably win," Helen said. "Blossom has looks and charm."

"Any more bad news?" Nancie asked.

"I'm no doctor, but Arthur looks like he hasn't much time left. If I hadn't seen that photo, I wouldn't believe it was the same man. Blossom said the doctors told her Arthur could die any time now. She had him taken off the ventilator."

"Like I said, that's her right as next of kin," Nancie said.

"Arthur is still breathing on his own, but who knows how long he'll last," Helen said.

"I'd better tell Violet," Nancie said. "If the wife's not there, she might be able to get in and see her father one last time."

"Don't get her hopes up," Helen said. "The nurse on duty doesn't like Violet."

The hospital cafeteria was closed. Helen had a cup of vending machine coffee and a sandwich made with stale bread, gray meat and soapy-tasting cheese. By eight thirty, she was back in the ICU. There was still no sign of Blossom.

"No change in Mr. Zerling," Nurse Abbott said briskly. Helen saw a golden mound of candy wrappers by her computer. She longed for a chocolate to take away the taste of her awful meal.

Helen settled into the iron embrace of the visitor's chair and took out her paperback. Miss Marple would have to get her through the night. At eight fifty-five, Helen heard a woman shout, "Please! You have to let me in. I must see my father before it's too late." She recognized Violet Zerling's tearful plea and ran out to see her client arguing with Nurse Abbott.

The two sturdy women stood nose to nose. Violet looked like she was wearing a sackcloth pantsuit. She couldn't get around the roadblock in scrubs.

"I have my orders, Ms. Zerling," Nurse Abbott said. "You are not allowed to see Mr. Zerling."

"But he's dying," Violet cried. "I want to see my daddy before he dies. I want to say good-bye."

Helen stepped between them. Violet backed off. Nurse Abbott didn't move.

"Please, Nurse, I'm asking as the family minister. Is there any way Violet can visit her father to say good-bye?"

"Orders are orders and she's not allowed," Nurse Abbott said. She seemed to savor her power as much as the chocolate.

"You can't refuse this request," Helen said.

"I can and I will," Nurse Abbott said. "This woman disturbed the whole floor last time. She's banned from the ICU."

"She's Arthur's only child," Helen said.

"She's hardly a child," Nurse Abbott said, and glared at the large woman.

"At least call Mrs. Zerling and ask if she'll change her mind," Helen said. "Please." She watched the nurse punch in the number for Blossom's cell.

"No answer," Nurse Abbott said, not bothering to hide her triumph.

"How do I even know you called her?" Violet said.

"Then you try," Nurse Abbott said.

Helen took out her phone, punched in Blossom's cell number and heard, "This is Blossom Zerling. Please leave a message."

"Voice mail," she reported.

"This is Helen Hawthorne," she said into her phone. "Violet is at the ICU with me and she wants to say good-bye to her father. I'll stay with her in the room. Please, in the name of charity, let Violet say good-bye to Arthur."

"Told you," the nurse said, her voice triumphant. "Do you want to see Mrs. Zerling's *written* orders? I have them."

Violet opened her mouth, but Helen cut her off. "That's not necessary."

"None of this is necessary," Nurse Abbott said. "I have critically ill patients to care for. I'm going to do you one more favor, Ms. Zerling. I won't call security if you leave now."

Violet erupted into quiet tears. Helen put her arm around the weeping woman and led her out of the ICU toward the elevator.

"I wanted to say good-bye," Violet said, sniffling and blinking back more tears. "I wanted Daddy to know I love him."

"He already knows," Helen said. She pressed the elevator button for Violet. "I have to go back to the ICU. You go home and rest. I'll keep you posted."

Nurse Abbott tried to justify herself as Helen passed her desk. "I really couldn't let her in," she said, popping another chocolate into her mouth. "I'd lose my job."

Helen didn't answer. She sat down in the visitor's chair and took out her book. At nine seventeen, she heard Arthur's breathing change dramatically. First it was deeper and faster—then it stopped altogether and started up again. Helen's mother had sounded that way before she died. Arthur's room was alive with beeping and shrieking alarms. Helen ran for Nurse Abbott, but she'd already called "Code Blue."

"In the hall," she commanded, shoving Helen out of her way. Staff flooded into Arthur's room. Someone issued terse commands. The privacy blinds on Arthur's window snapped shut, blocking Helen's view.

Helen called Blossom's cell phone. Still no answer. "Your husband has taken a turn for the worse," Helen said. "Please hurry."

With that, Helen heard footsteps running down the hall and Blossom came flying through the ICU door.

"What's wrong?" she said, fast and frantic. "Why aren't you with Arthur?"

"I tried to reach you," Helen said.

"I was caught in traffic on I-95," Blossom said. "There was a terrible accident. What's going on?"

"I'm afraid the news isn't good," Helen said, trying to prepare her.

Nurse Abbott came out of the room, looking shell-shocked. She took Blossom's arm and started to lead her to the family lounge. "I'm very sorry, Mrs. Zerling. Your husband—"

Blossom screamed before the nurse finished her sentence.

CHAPTER 8

· · · · · · · · · · · · · · ·

Blossom's scream stopped abruptly, as if someone had hit a switch. Helen found the sudden silence shocking. Blossom swayed slightly, then suddenly pitched forward.

Nurse Abbott caught the new widow before she hit the floor and held her in a strong grip. Blossom's head drooped and her face was lily-white.

"Nice catch," Helen said.

"Years of practice," the nurse said. "I'm good at spotting when they're going to drop."

Helen realized her comment wasn't very clerical and tried to make amends for her insensitivity with a concerned question. "Is Blossom okay?"

"I think so. Low blood sugar and stress, most likely," the nurse said. "I'll check her vitals. Grab that wheelchair there and we'll take her to the family lounge. If something's really wrong, we can wheel her straight to the ER."

Nurse Abbott gently lowered Blossom into the chair and rolled her toward the lounge.

Helen thought its mournful shades of mauve and gray were the perfect place to take a new widow. The blaring TV added to the depressing atmosphere. Helen found the remote and turned down the volume.

Blossom started to come around as they entered the lounge. She shook her head, then ran her fingers through her long brown hair and sighed.

"Welcome back," Nurse Abbott said, helping her onto a mauve couch.

"I'm sorry to be so much trouble," Blossom said. "I know you're busy."

"Your husband just passed away," Nurse Abbott said. "You don't have to apologize for being human." She pulled a flat hospital pillow and a thin blanket from a cabinet and settled the woman comfortably on the couch. Then she checked Blossom's pulse and blood pressure.

"Both normal," she reported. "How do you feel now?"

"Fine," Blossom said. "No, I'm not fine. I feel terrible. Arthur's dead. I should have been with him when it happened." A single tear slid down her cheek. Her face looked like it had been dusted with flour. "Because of me, my poor husband died alone."

"He wasn't alone," Helen said. "I was with him. Arthur had a peaceful passing."

She remembered Nurse Abbott pushing her out of the way and the staff running into Arthur's room and wondered if that was true.

"He didn't feel any pain," Nurse Abbott said. "He wouldn't have known if you were there."

"But I know," Blossom said. "I failed my husband in his final moments."

"Nonsense," Nurse Abbott said. "You need some food."

Blossom wept quietly. Helen handed her a fistful of tissues from a box on the side table, then patted Blossom's cold hand. The silence stretched between them. Helen wished she could say something comforting but couldn't find the right words.

She was relieved when Nurse Abbott rushed in with two packs of graham crackers and a cold container of orange juice. "Drink the orange juice," she commanded. "It will help your blood sugar. Would you like a sandwich?"

"No, thanks," Blossom said, and started weeping again. "I ate dinner. How could I eat when Arthur was dying?"

"You have to keep up your strength," Nurse Abbott said. "Life goes on."

"Can I say good-bye to Arthur now?" Blossom asked.

"We're getting him tidied up," Nurse Abbott said.

"Was he"—Blossom hesitated—"hurt?"

"Not at all," Nurse Abbott said. "But we want to disconnect the IV lines and monitors and clean him up a little. As soon as he's ready, you can be with him."

"Thank you," Blossom said. "You've been so good to me—to us." Her voice wobbled.

"Just doing my job," Nurse Abbott said. "Reverend, if you'll stay with Blossom, I have to get back to my patients."

She marched briskly out of the lounge, leaving Helen and Blossom in the gloomy room with the television. A screaming red BREAKING NEWS banner interrupted the ten o'clock local newscast. An aerial view of a massive traffic jam on I-95 appeared on the screen. An overturned tractor-trailer sprawled across the highway. Flames were devouring the cab as firefighters sprayed it.

"There it is," Blossom said. "That's the accident that kept me away from Arthur."

She reached for the clicker on the coffee table and turned up the sound. The announcer said, "The driver of the truck escaped injury. But the highway remains blocked from Sunrise to Commercial Boulevard. The Broward County Sheriff's Office urges drivers to seek another route until the highway is cleared. We'll bring you more live updates on News Channel . . ."

Blossom turned down the TV and said, "If only there hadn't been that accident. I was stuck for over an hour, frantic to get back to the hospital. I tried to get around the cars by driving in the breakdown lane, but the police wouldn't let me. They forced me back in line." Her voice seemed to fade away.

"You need to keep eating," Helen reminded her. "Nurse's orders."

"Right," Blossom said, absently. She crunched on a graham cracker, then said, "Finally, the traffic moved enough so I could get off at an exit, but then I had to drive through downtown and that took more time."

She finished the graham cracker and struggled to open the orange juice container with shaking fingers. Helen gently took the juice from her, peeled back the foil top and handed it to her. Blossom sipped daintily.

"You did the right thing," Helen said. "Arthur wouldn't have wanted you to get in an accident." She was enjoying passing out platitudes. They seemed to work when Nurse Abbott said them.

"You think so?" Blossom said, sniffling.

"Absolutely," Helen said.

"You've been so good to me," Blossom said. "Would you conduct Arthur's funeral? I know he'd want that."

"I'd be honored," Helen said as she felt another stab of guilt. Arthur didn't want Helen. He'd never met her.

"I'll have to find out when the hospital will release Arthur's—" Blossom teared up, then made an effort to steady her voice. "Will release Arthur."

"Do you know where he will be buried?" Helen asked.

"Yes. My husband was so thoughtful," Blossom said. "Arthur told me he bought a funeral plan when his first wife died. I can't remember her name. I'm so upset."

"Honeysuckle," Helen said.

"That's right," Blossom said. "He wanted to be buried next to

Honeysuckle. He asked me if I'd mind. Wasn't that sweet? I told him that was fine. She had him longer than I did and she is the mother of his child. Did you conduct Honeysuckle's funeral service?"

"That was before I knew Arthur," Helen said, truthfully.

"He bought the plan at the Dignity Forever Funeral Home on Federal Highway. The one with the white columns."

Helen thought all Fort Lauderdale funeral homes had white columns, but she nodded.

"Then you'll do it?" Blossom said. "Please?"

"On one condition," Helen said. "Violet must be allowed to attend her father's funeral."

"But—" Blossom started to object.

"I will not be a party to a family feud," Helen said. "I know you and Violet have had your differences, but you must set them aside for Arthur's sake. Violet can be difficult. I won't deny that. But I think she can help you."

"Help me how?" Was there a slightly surly sound in Blossom's voice—or did grief give it an edge? Helen couldn't tell.

"Arthur Zerling was a successful man," Helen said. "He lived in Fort Lauderdale all his life. Do you know how to contact all his friends, family and business associates?"

"I have his address book," Blossom said.

"But do you know which ones are family and which are friends? Do you know his colleagues and his staff?" Helen asked.

"No," Blossom said.

"Violet will," Helen said. "We can put her to work contacting them."

"She's impossible!" Blossom said. "We can't be together two minutes before she starts a fight."

"You won't have to deal with her," Helen said. "You won't even see her. She can make the calls from my office."

Blossom took a deep breath and blotted her eyes. "Okay, I'll do what you want. But what if she makes a scene at Arthur's funeral? You can't believe how she carried on here in the ICU."

"I will personally guarantee her good behavior," Helen said. "I'll watch her myself."

"How can you?" Blossom asked. "You'll be conducting the service."

Blossom was right. Helen knew asking Phil to accompany Violet was out of the question. The Reverend Hawthorne wasn't supposed to know Mrs. Zerling's new estate manager. And Blossom wasn't supposed to know Coronado Investigations was hired to prove she'd murdered her husband. Helen needed someone strong to keep Violet in line, but she couldn't insult their client by hiring a muscle head in a black suit.

Then she thought of the perfect solution: someone strong who could look dignified and blend in as an ordinary mourner. Helen thought her idea was inspired.

"I'll make sure she attends the funeral with a family friend, Margery Flax," Helen said.

"Is this Flax woman a bodyguard?" Blossom asked.

"Better," Helen said. "And far more forceful."

CHAPTER 9

A rthur Zerling was buried under white flowers. His polished dark wood casket was heaped with washed-out lilies, waxy camellias and rubbery roses. The sweet sickly scent of the hothouse blooms made the Reverend Helen Hawthorne slightly dizzy. The newly minted minister prayed she wouldn't pass out. This was her first time presiding at a funeral. She wanted Arthur to have the solemnity he deserved.

Helen steadied herself at the funeral home podium and surveyed the mourners. The room's candy-box colors—pink walls and spindly gold chairs—were overwhelmed by the dark tide of mourners.

Arthur's wife and his daughter sat on opposite sides of the aisle. Blossom looked like a noir widow in a black high-collared suit and dramatic wide-brimmed hat. Helen thought she needed a cigarette holder to complete the outfit.

Violet was upholstered in some shiny, lumpy black material. Her heavy black veil couldn't hide her glare. She aimed it with laserlike intensity at the woman she'd accused of killing her father. Margery sat at Violet's side, her face half-hidden by the glamorous swoop of her lavender hat. She rested one purple-gloved hand lightly on Violet's arm, as if she was comforting Arthur's grieving daughter. Helen knew Margery's hand would clamp down if Violet acted on her hostility.

She wished Phil were there, but Blossom didn't want her new estate manager attending the funeral. His job was to prepare the funeral reception. Phil would deal with the caterers, bartenders, valet service and florists while Helen handled the funeral.

Helen gave Violet credit. After Blossom agreed to let her attend her father's funeral, she worked hard to give Arthur a proper service. She still refused to speak to Blossom. Instead, Nancie had to act as mediator. The lawyer conveyed Violet's information to Blossom's attorney, who passed it on to the widow. Helen couldn't begin to calculate what this diplomacy-at-a-distance cost, but it kept the peace.

Violet had done a good job of assembling Arthur's friends and colleagues at the Dignity Forever Funeral Home. They filled every gilded chair in the massive room, lined the walls and spilled into the hall. Most were white-haired men and women. Helen saw a sprinkling of sun-blasted workingmen. Helen remembered the photo of the vital Arthur on horseback and wondered if they were ranch hands.

She recognized Fran. The housekeeper's gray curls were topped with a small, flat black hat. She'd tucked herself in the back where Blossom couldn't see her. Fran was not going to risk a scene at her beloved Mr. Z.'s funeral.

Helen scanned the crowed for the troublemaking Uncle Billy. Violet had warned her about him. "Uncle Billy is not my father's brother," she'd explained. "He is Daddy's best friend. The uncle title is honorary. He and my father were in college together and he introduced Daddy to my mother. Uncle Billy drinks too much. I know he'll have a snootful and say something embarrassing at Daddy's funeral."

"Can we sort of not invite him?" Helen had asked.

"He'll barge in anyway, and make a bigger scene," Violet had said. "I don't know if I can stand it, between that woman and Uncle Billy."

"I'll keep him under control," Helen said.

"You can't," Violet said, sounding hopeless. "Nobody can."

Helen prayed that Uncle Billy would stay away and quietly blessed the dead man for requesting a closed casket. She'd dreaded seeing Arthur's wasted body in an open coffin.

She opened the service with the Our Father, a prayer Violet and Blossom had both approved, then launched into a short speech.

"Arthur Zerling was one of those rare businesspeople who cared about his family, his friends and his colleagues," she said. "You've had the pleasure of knowing him longer than I have. Mrs. Zerling has asked that you share your memories of Arthur today. She will begin with hers."

Helen sat next to the podium where she could watch Violet. Arthur's daughter had already refused to talk about her father. "I loved Daddy," she said. "But I don't think I could say anything without crying."

Blossom rose gracefully, took the podium's microphone and said, "I knew my husband for less than a year. Arthur was kind, loving, generous—"

Violet made some sort of sound—a sniffle? A snort?

Helen wasn't sure what it was, but she saw Margery's gloved hand grip Violet's wrist. Blossom did not seem to notice. She continued smoothly, "I thought that fate, which brought us together, would allow us more time. But that was not to be. I—" She stopped, dabbed her eyes with a black lace handkerchief and said, "I am too sad to say any more. But your memories of Arthur will be a comfort to me."

The widow glided softly back to her seat. Helen wondered if she should sympathize or applaud that speech. Where the heck did she get a black lace handkerchief?

Two sober-suited businessmen followed Blossom. Bob, a portly man with a face like a slab of rare roast beef, praised Arthur's integrity.

Roger, the second one, said, "I agree with Bob. Arthur was a man of integrity in the boardroom—and on the golf course, where even the best men are tempted to cheat. Arthur played by the rules. You've seen those hospital billboards that say, 'Outlive your golf foursome.' Well, I've outlived my golfing partner of twenty years. I'll miss you, buddy." He slapped the casket as if it were Arthur's back. The waxy flowers trembled.

As Roger sat down, a man in an ill-fitting brown suit, white shirt and striped polyester tie nervously took the microphone. At first, he mumbled, but his voice grew stronger as he spoke. "Name's Jack," he said. "I worked for Mr. Zerling for fifteen years."

Jack looked nervously at the crowd, gulped twice and said, "When my missus got cancer, I was having trouble making the co-pays. I was going to sell the house to raise money for her treatment, when the cancer doctor's office called and said not to worry about those payments. Mr. Zerling had paid for her treatment. My wife is alive today because of him. Thank you, Mr. Zerling, for saving my Leann."

Jack sat down next to a thin woman in a ruffled black dress with a purple silk rose at the neck. She patted his hand.

Helen felt a flutter of panic when she saw a dark-haired man push his way up front. This had to be Uncle Billy, the man Violet had warned her about. Uncle Billy looked exactly the way Violet had described him. He was five eight with suspiciously black hair, a self-important manner, a potbelly and a perpetual smile, even at a funeral.

He was still elbowing his way to the podium. Blossom seemed

oblivious to the approaching disruption. Violet leaned forward in her seat, tensed for trouble. Helen caught Margery's eye, and the landlady gave a single nod. She was ready.

Violet had predicted that Uncle Billy would "wear something awful like mustard golf pants or an orange plaid jacket."

She was right. His red Hawaiian shirt was a riot of blue parrots. His shirt matched the grog blossoms on his nose. Lime green shorts exposed knobby knees and varicose veins. Uncle Billy's outrageous outfit seemed to shout at the somber funeral-goers.

He grabbed the microphone and hung on to the podium as if he were seasick. Helen could smell the alcohol fumes from where she sat.

The microphone gave a shrill blast of feedback. He waited it out, then said, "I never thought I'd see old Art lying down on the job." Uncle Billy grinned and paused for laughter. The stony silence would have stopped a more sensitive—or sober—person. He steamrollered ahead.

"When Art called me from India and said he was getting married, I told him, 'Go for it.' I'd introduced him to Honeysuckle at Florida State. He loved her. We all knew that. He took care of her when she was sick. I told him, 'Art, Honeysuckle has been gone for two years now. Life goes on.'

"When he got back from that cruise, I saw the new Mrs. Zerling. I had no idea Art had bagged a looker. He had to pop Viagra like popcorn to keep her happy."

Helen heard gasps from the audience. Blossom sat frozen. Violet started to get out of her chair, but Margery held her back.

Helen stepped forward to pry the microphone from Uncle Billy's hand before he said anything worse, but he was too quick.

He gave a hideous grin, then said, "Art died riding a great little filly. No man could ask for more."

"Thank you, Billy," Helen said, pushing him toward the aisle.

Bob and Roger, Arthur's friends and partners, stepped forward and escorted Uncle Billy back down the aisle as if he were a felon. They shoved him into a seat, then stood next to him.

Most of the mourners were shocked into silence, but Helen heard a few gasps. Blossom looked as if she'd been turned to stone.

Helen ended the service with Psalm 90 and the hopeful words: "'Make us glad according to the days wherein thou hast afflicted us, and the years wherein we have seen evil. Let thy work appear unto thy servants, and thy glory unto their children.'"

Margery had a comforting arm around Violet. The big woman leaned against Helen's landlady. Blossom seemed oblivious to anything but her own grief.

"Mr. Zerling will be buried at Evergreen Cemetery," Helen said. "The service is private. Mrs. Arthur Zerling hopes to see you all at her home for the reception."

The pallbearers advanced to carry Arthur Zerling to the hearse, as the undertakers dismantled the quivering mound of flowers. Blossom followed the casket out of the room, head bowed. The mourners filed out behind her.

Helen followed them, Margery and Violet at her side. The funeral director steered them toward the waiting limousine. Helen collapsed gratefully into her dark leather seat and closed her eyes. Her head ached from the strain and the raw emotions.

Margery and Violet slid onto the bench seat across from her and the door closed with a quiet click. "What did I tell you?" Violet said. "I knew Uncle Billy would pull one of his stunts."

"Helen handled him beautifully," Margery said.

"And that woman—"

"Was on her best behavior," Margery said.

"My daddy's dead," Violet said, her voice filled with wonder. "He's not coming back. I knew he was dead, but I really felt it at the funeral when I saw his casket."

"That's how grief works sometimes," Margery said, patting Violet's hand.

"It hurts," Violet said. "I miss him so much. It's like a physical pain."

"It may take a while," Margery said. "But you'll start remembering all the good things you did together. Then his loss won't hurt so much."

"It will stop hurting when that woman is in jail for Daddy's murder," Violet said.

CHAPTER 10

Arthur Zerling's polished casket was slowly lowered into the yawning grave by a machine. Instead of a hymn sung by the mourners, the machine hummed softly while Helen read a verse from Saint Paul. She wondered how many times his Epistle to the Philippians had been read at a burial in Evergreen Cemetery.

"Finally, brethren, whatsoever things are true," she read, *"whatsoever things are honest, whatsoever things are just, whatsoever things are pure, whatsoever things are lovely, whatsoever things are of good report; if there be any virtue, and if there be any praise, think on these things."*

Violet kept her head bowed. Helen hoped she was remembering her father, but suspected she was plotting revenge against Blossom. Arthur's widow also kept her head bowed, but tension radiated from her slender form.

A stone angel watched from a nearby grave, wings folded in sorrow. Arthur would rest under a cool shade tree, next to his first wife, Honeysuckle. Helen hoped that Fort Lauderdale's oldest cemetery would not see one more family feud.

"Please grant Arthur Zerling eternal rest," she said. The casket mechanism stopped. "Give him peace."

Deliver us from the two warring women at his grave, Helen thought.

Violet stayed calm, though her hands were clenched and her body was rigid in its shiny black cocoon. Margery stood resolutely at Violet's side, poised to prevent a fight. Arthur's surviving golf partners lined up beside Violet's purple-clad guard.

Across the gulf of the open grave was Blossom, the grateful ranch hand and his rescued wife, Leann. The woman Arthur had helped save sniffled into a tissue. The housekeeper was not at the burial, but Helen had no doubt Fran was mourning the loss of her employer.

Four dark-suited undertakers stood discreetly behind lichen-covered tombstones. They had strict orders to head off Uncle Billy if he barged into the burial service. Helen didn't think they'd have to look hard to spot him. Billy's shirt was loud enough to wake the dead.

The funeral director handed Blossom a single white rose. She delicately tossed it into the grave. The rose landed soundlessly on the shiny casket lid. Next, the funeral director solemnly presented Violet with a sheaf of flowers the size of a shrub. Helen studied the tendrils escaping from the ribbon-wrapped bundle and realized this was a huge bouquet of honeysuckle and violets.

Violet would never be accused of subtlety.

She dropped the flowers into the grave. The heavy bouquet landed with a graceless thud, smothering Blossom's single rose.

Helen thought if Violet could have fallen on Blossom and squashed her, she would have. Margery must have felt the same way. She laid a restraining hand lightly on Violet's arm after the bouquet toss.

"We will conclude the burial service with the Twenty-third Psalm," Helen said. *"The Lord is my shepherd, I shall not want. . . ."*

As she recited the comforting words, another, secret burial in her homctown of St. Louis flashcd through her mind. Helen couldn't block out that awful scene. Death stared her in the face, reminding her of her own sins.

Helen knew that obsession, greed and blazing hatred led to misery and untimely death, but she couldn't tell anyone, not even Margery or Phil. An innocent person's future depended on her silence.

"He maketh me to lie down in green pastures," Helen read. *"He leadeth me beside the still waters."*

For seventeen years, Helen had been a well-paid executive on the corporate fast track. She'd lived in suburban St. Louis and thought she had a happy marriage. Her husband, Rob, was looking for work, but couldn't find a job equal to his talents. Then she came home early from her office and caught Rob cavorting naked with their neighbor. Blinded by rage, Helen had smashed her husband's beloved SUV to smithereens, then filed for divorce.

"He restoreth my soul," Helen read. *"He leadeth me in the paths of righteousness for his name's sake."*

There was nothing right—or righteous—about the divorce judge's decision. As Helen expected, he split the house between Helen and Rob, even though she'd bought it. But then the judge awarded half of Helen's future income to the unfaithful louse. Helen had tossed her wedding ring into the turbulent Mississippi River and taken off in a crazy-mad journey around the country until her car died in Fort Lauderdale. She wound up living at the Coronado Tropic Apartments, with Margery as her landlady.

"Yea, though I walk through the valley of the shadow of death, I will fear no evil: for thou art with me. Thy rod and thy staff they comfort me."

Helen found comfort in her friendships at the Coronado while she lived as a fugitive from the court and worked low-paying jobs to stay off the law's radar. But Rob pursued her relentlessly, determined to get his money. She figured if her ex ever caught up with her, he wouldn't be interested in her miserable income. She'd underestimated Rob's greed.

"Thou preparest a table before me in the presence of mine enemies," Helen read. *"Thou anointest my head with oil; my cup runneth over."*

When Rob sailed off with a wealthy widow, Helen thought he was gone from her life. But the widow threw Rob overboard with a million-dollar good-bye gift. Rob ran through that money and tracked Helen down at her sister Kathy's house in St. Louis, where he demanded the money the court had ordered her to pay. When Helen refused, Rob had grabbed her arm and twisted it. Helen's ten-year-old nephew, Tommy Junior, saw Rob threatening his aunt and swung his ball bat so hard, the boy knocked out Rob. The dazed Rob had refused treatment, then died suddenly.

Helen was grateful that Tommy had been sent to his room after he hit Uncle Rob. The boy had no idea he'd accidentally killed the man.

Helen had wanted to go to the police and take the blame for Rob's death, but Kathy refused. She feared Tommy would confess that he'd whacked Uncle Rob and the boy's life would be blighted. Instead, Helen and Kathy had wrapped Rob's body in plastic and buried him in the gravel for the foundation of the church basement. The next morning, concrete was poured over his unmarked grave.

No one looked for the missing Rob, which Helen thought said a lot about her ex-husband. But someone had seen the secret burial. So far, this person had blackmailed Helen and Kathy for fifteen thousand dollars. Helen expected more demands for cash.

She tried to live with the burden of Rob's death. She tried to pretend the awful incident had never happened. She'd married Phil and they'd started Coronado Investigations. The two private eyes were paid to uncover other people's secrets.

Helen had to keep hers buried. She couldn't share her guilty secret at the expense of her nephew's future.

She longed to tell Violet and Blossom the damage that hate and greed caused. But she couldn't say a word. She could only pray that Rob's body was never found.

"Surely goodness and mercy shall follow me all the days of my life," Helen said. *"And I will dwell in the house of the Lord forever."*

"Amen," chorused the mourners.

"That was lovely," Blossom said, patting Helen's hand. Helen studied the widow's pale face under the glamorous hat for signs of guilt. She saw only weariness, lightly touched with makeup. "You will come back to the house for the reception, won't you?"

"I have another appointment at three o'clock," Helen said.

"Then you'll have a couple of hours," Blossom said. "I'd like to ask you for a favor. Would you sort through Arthur's things? I want to give them away."

"Today?" Helen said, struggling to hide her surprise.

"As soon as possible," Blossom said.

"I know you must think it's too soon. I'm not getting rid of Arthur's things because I don't love him. It's because I loved him too much. They're a constant, painful reminder of my loss. I'm hoping you'll take them to a charity for me. Arthur has some lovely clothes. They won't do any good sitting in his dressing room."

Helen couldn't believe her good fortune: Blossom was letting her search Arthur's personal possessions. She also didn't believe the widow's excuses. She couldn't wait another day to get rid of her husband.

"I'm sure you'll find something useful," Blossom said.

"I certainly hope so," Helen said.

CHAPTER 11

W as that a house or a hotel? The Zerling mansion was a monster even in a millionaires' ghetto like Hendin Island. Helen hoped she was pulling into the right driveway. The wrong choice could land her in hot water. The rich regarded lost strangers as potential burglars and were quick to call the cops.

Blossom's directions had sounded simple. "Turn right onto Hendin Island Road," she'd said. "There's only one road on the island. We're the fourth house on the left with the big ficus hedge."

But all the Hendin Island mansions had towering ficus hedges. Ficus never got that big in Helen's hometown of St. Louis. In the Midwest, they were scrawny houseplants struggling to survive in uncaring offices and drafty apartments.

Burly Florida ficus grew into impenetrable hedges that had to be trimmed with chain saws. The fourth house on the left had twelve-foot hedges cut into sharp angles. Helen counted the houses twice, then decided that one had to be the Zerling mansion.

It was barely noon, but Helen felt like she'd spent an eternity with the Zerling women.

After Arthur's burial, the limo had driven Helen, Margery and Violet back to the funeral home parking lot.

Once they were inside the limo again, Violet's control snapped. She unleashed a bitter stream of invective against Blossom. "She didn't even invite me to my father's funeral reception," she'd said. "Not that I'd go. I don't want to be in the same room with that woman."

That's when Margery lit up a Marlboro.

"Please, Margery. Do you have to smoke that in here?" Violet asked.

"Let's make a deal," Margery said. "We'll agree that you hate Blossom and I'll put out my cigarette."

She stubbed out her cigarette in the ashtray and Violet sat slumped in silence. Helen sighed with relief when the limo stopped in the parking lot. She climbed into the Igloo and headed to Arthur Zerling's funeral reception.

The mansion wasn't even marked with a house number. That was the only discreet thing about the frantic swarm of turrets, towers and arched colonnades, painted face-powder pink and topped with red barrel tile. It was Spanish mission style on steroids.

The sumptuous black wreath on the dark, arched door was the only sign there was a funeral reception at the home. Helen left the Igloo with the valet. A uniformed Hispanic maid opened the massive door before Helen could knock. She heard string music and subdued conversation drifting from the back of the house.

She followed the maid's bobbing white apron bow through dimly lit rooms and corridors to Arthur's reception, grateful she had a guide. The Zerling home could have been a set for *Sunset Boulevard*. Rooms and corridors were crammed with mahogany chairs upholstered in dark fabric, faded dull brown tapestries and twisted candlesticks. Silk fringe, fat tassels and swags of braid clung to lampshades, cushions and couches. Bulbous gold frames gripped dark oil paintings.

Thick Oriental carpets smothered Helen's footsteps. Velvet curtains shut out the subtropical sun. The curtains were looped with ropes of braid and hung with tassels like golden fruit.

Helen could not imagine herself relaxing on those braided, tasseled velvet sofas with a book and a glass of wine. She'd be searching the shadows for serial killers. She felt the weight of the home's heavy fabric and dark furniture, as if money was a burden. She itched to open the windows and let in the light.

When she turned the last corner, she was nearly blinded by the sunlight. The reception was in a stark glass annex that led to a pool the size of an inland sea. The funeral reception could have been an exclusive gallery showing. The crowd was subdued, mostly seventy and over, and spoke in murmurs. The harsh light revealed thinning hair, wrinkles and tight, face-lifted skin. She scanned the faces but saw no sign of Phil.

Servers circulated with trays of champagne and mineral water. Hungry mourners lined up at cloth-draped tables along the east wall for a buffet. A chef cut thick bloody slices off a round of roast beef. Another carved a roast turkey and a pink ham. There were mounded platters of fruit, vegetables and shiny glazed pastries. A whole table was devoted to a tower of oysters, shrimp and lobster tails crowned by a silver bowl of caviar.

The cloying scent of waxy white flowers overpowered the luscious food.

A black-clad string quartet sawed delicately on their instruments. In an alcove, a slide show flashed on a tall screen. Helen paused to watch Arthur's life unfold in photographs: first, as a curly-haired baby cradled in his mother's arms. She gazed at her son as if he were a newborn god. Next as a sturdy toddler on a rocking horse, then a serious young scholar in a blazer and tie. The photos of Arthur's school years ended with an exuberant college graduate throwing his mortarboard into the air.

Helen thought young Arthur was movie-star handsome. He

played tennis in a white polo shirt that displayed his tanned arms, stood on the deck of a yacht, his hair tousled by a sea breeze, and rode a brown stallion with a white blaze. He donned a business suit and gradually aged into a strong, snowy-haired man. Helen saw the photo Violet had shown her of the white-haired Arthur on the black horse. That was followed by Arthur and Blossom at their wedding. He wore a well-tailored navy jacket. Blossom was a sophisticated bride in strapless white satin clutching a huge white bouquet of roses and orchids. The new bride and groom kissed with the setting sun as a dramatic backdrop. The next photo showed the couple at home, lounging by the same pool sparkling outside the reception room. Blossom held Arthur's hand and smiled into his eyes. Then the slide show started again with chubby baby Arthur held by his proud mother.

Arthur's life was bookended by adoring women. Helen noticed that photos of Violet and Honeysuckle Zerling were conspicuously absent. Blossom may have let Arthur sleep beside his first wife in the prepaid cemetery plot, but she wouldn't acknowledge the woman and her daughter were part of Arthur's life.

"Helen!" Blossom called, and sailed over. The chic black hat was gone and the widow had freshened her lipstick. Her black suit accented her creamy skin.

"Would you like a drink? How about some food?" Blossom asked.

"No, thanks," Helen said. "I have to leave for an appointment at three o'clock. Do you still want me to sort through Arthur's belongings?"

"You'd be doing me a huge favor," Blossom said. "Let me take you to his dressing room."

She ducked through a service door near the alcove and said, "We're going up the back stairs. Otherwise, people will keep stopping us to talk."

The gray-carpeted service stairs opened onto another long,

gloomy corridor. Arthur and Blossom's bedroom looked suitable for the procreation of a dynasty. The four-poster bed had columns like tree trunks. The floor was cushioned by a dark Oriental rug the size of a small country. Maroon curtains blocked the light. Everything was festooned with tassels, even the key to the mahogany secretary.

Helen wondered if Blossom wore tasseled bras.

"This really isn't my style," Blossom said. "I was planning to redecorate after Arthur and I settled in." Her voice quavered. Then she steadied it and said, "Arthur's dressing room is this way."

Helen followed her through a master bath the size of her Coronado apartment. The bathtub was encased in shining mahogany. Next to it was a marble Jacuzzi. The commode was tucked behind another door.

Arthur's dressing room was a man cave with dark wood, brass fittings and forest green walls. Neckties and suits were arranged on motorized carousels. Dress shirts were displayed by color on wooden hangers. Polo shirts were folded on shelves. Two shelves were devoted to cowboy hats, including a white Stetson with a crocodile band.

Six shelves held well-shined shoes from wing tips to cowboy boots. Only Arthur's deck shoes were comfortably scuffed and battered. Helen noticed a bronze statue on a chest of drawers—a beautifully rendered cowboy on a bucking horse. She checked the signature at the base and saw a name she recognized: St. Louis artist Charles Russell. That dressing room decoration was worth at least six figures.

On another chest of drawers was a photo of the bridal Blossom with her white bouquet.

"Arthur's cuff links, watches and other jewelry are in these cases," Blossom said, patting the tall chest under the Russell bronze.

Helen opened the top drawer and saw four watches on velvet. From her years in retail, she guessed she was looking at more than a hundred thousand dollars in timepieces.

"These are good quality," Helen said. "Are you sure you don't want to keep them or give them as mementos to Arthur's friends?"

"No, give them to charity," Blossom said. "I would appreciate a receipt for taxes. Please take them away today."

Blossom paused, then said, "Arthur's clothes and things could help people if they went to a charity. I'd like them put to good use. I know Arthur would, too."

"Any particular charity?" Helen asked.

"No, I'm new to Lauderdale," Blossom said. "You're a minister. You must know some good ones."

Helen eyed the floor-to-ceiling rows and racks of clothes and shoes. "There's a lot for me to carry," she said.

"I'll send my man," Blossom said. "He's taking a break in the kitchen. I had him get packing boxes. He can carry them out for you. His name is Phil."

"Good," Helen said. Phil and I can search this room together, she thought.

"May I make a donation to your church?" Blossom asked.

"No, thank you," Helen said. "I'm happy to do this for Arthur." And I'm already paid by his daughter, she thought. The ethics of this situation made her a bit queasy.

"I'll leave you to it, then," Blossom said. "I have to get back to my guests." She held out her exquisitely manicured hand and shook Helen's. "Thank you for your help," she said. "I know you've had a long day. Please find a good home for Arthur's clothes."

Blossom paused, then said, "I don't want you to think I'm getting rid of Arthur."

Helen said nothing.

Blossom kept talking. "Every time I walk by this room, I seem to see him. Not the smart, strong man I first met, but the dying Arthur. I don't want to think of him that way. I don't want to face what I lost one more day."

Face what you lost—or what you did? Helen wondered.

CHAPTER 12

Helen could see Blossom's dressing room on the other side of the bedroom. Arthur's wife had barred the housekeeper from that room. Now Fran was fired and Arthur was dead and Blossom boldly left the door open.

It was an invitation to snoop. That's what Helen was, and she knew it: a paid snoop. A professional investigator. I really shouldn't do this, she thought. I've just buried the owner of this house.

Who may have been killed by his wife. Helen quickly tossed aside her few reservations, like a stripper's flimsy costume. She stalked across the half acre of posh rug and stood in the doorway to Blossom's dressing room.

I could get caught, she told herself. But I don't expect Blossom back soon. She has her duties at Arthur's funeral reception.

Helen slipped into Blossom's dressing room. It was as organized as Arthur's, but definitely feminine. Helen caught the scent of some light, spicy perfume. The walls were a flattering pale peach and the well-lit full-length mirror was slimming. The only art was a gold-framed photo of Blossom as a bride carrying that lush white bouquet.

Helen would love to have these finely crafted shelves in pale, golden wood. She'd like to have the clothes and shoes to fill them.

Well, some of the clothes. There seemed to be two Blossoms: the sedate wife that Helen knew and a sexy woman who wore daringly cut clothes in come-hither colors—red, sapphire blue and vibrant emerald green. Helen had never seen that side of Blossom, and she examined a carousel of gaudy evening dresses.

Cocktail dresses and long gowns glittered with sequins, rhinestones and bugle beads. As the dresses whirled slowly around, Helen saw flirty ruffles and frisky feathers.

Each dress was protected by a clear plastic zipped bag. They must look spectacular on Blossom's well-toned figure. A red velvet number with a plunging front and back looked like the fabled "gownless evening strap" worn by a Hollywood starlet.

When did Blossom wear clothes like these with her elderly husband? And where? Certainly not at any soiree given by the staid silver hairs downstairs.

Helen slowly watched the dresses on the carousel until she came to a section of subdued silver and black gowns. Some were strapless, others had long sleeves, but all were elegant and tasteful. These were suitable for Arthur's friends. So were the two racks of black, gray and pale peach suits.

Blossom's casual clothes showed the same split personality: risqué halter tops with deep-cut necklines and V-cut backs. Blouses with sexy lace-up fronts, provocative corset styles and wisps of leopard prints with barely enough spots to cover the vital spots.

Club clothes, never meant for daylight. They contrasted oddly with schoolmarmish tailored skirts, pants and clamdiggers from Tory Burch, Brooks Brothers and Talbots, designed for a rich man's wife.

Blossom's shoes ranged from modest ballerina flats to an outrageous pair of purple cage sandals with six-inch stiletto heels. How did she walk in those? Helen wondered. She picked up the heel for a closer look. The strappy purple shoe weighed at least three pounds and the skinny heels looked lethal.

"Drop that weapon now," said a voice behind her.

Helen jumped and the heel went flying across the peach carpet. She turned and saw her husband leaning against the doorframe, laughing.

"Phil!" she said. "I ought to stab you with that stiletto."

"What are you doing in Blossom's dressing room?" he said. "She could catch you poking around in her things."

"She's busy," Helen said. "Why are you wearing white shorts and a blue polo shirt instead of your jeans?"

"The lady of the house gave me this uniform," Phil said. He did a model's turn in the dressing room.

"Shows off your buns nicely, Cabana Boy," Helen said. "Where did she send you to buy that outfit?"

"She didn't," Phil said. "She guessed my size and had it waiting for me."

"She's been observing you closely," Helen said. "When did she have time to run to the store and buy uniforms? She hired you the night her husband died."

"Maybe she missed being at Arthur's deathbed because she was uniform shopping," Phil said.

"Maybe our client should suspect her stepmother," Helen said. "Blossom said she was caught in the traffic from that accident on I-95."

"Which isn't on the way to the hospital," Phil said. "But it is the fastest way to several malls. If Violet and Fran are right and Blossom poisoned Arthur, we've got a hell of a job. I checked out the place this morning while helping set up the reception. Besides the eight bedrooms and twelve baths, there are two dining rooms, a six-car garage and a pool house. I lost track of the halls, sitting rooms and living rooms."

"Find any poison?"

"Lots," Phil said. "Enough rat poison in the garage to kill everyone on Hendin Island."

"They have rats?"

"In a big old house on the water? Sure. But I don't think Arthur showed symptoms of that kind of poisoning. Where do I start?"

"Here," Helen said. "The room Blossom wouldn't let Fran enter. The housekeeper said Blossom was hiding something."

"Then let's find it," Phil said. "You look through the clothes. I'll check the drawers. Hurry. In case she comes back."

Helen poked through the pockets and felt the hems of Blossom's clothes. Phil searched the drawers, prying through sheer scarves and flimsy lingerie, probing behind and underneath the drawers. Phil looked in the air-conditioning vents. Helen crawled along the molding, feeling for hiding places. She tried to pull up the carpet, but it stayed securely nailed to the floor.

"Nothing," Helen said. "Maybe she's already used the poison."

"If it existed anywhere but in the mind of her housekeeper," Phil said.

"Maybe she was hiding those outré outfits," Helen said. "Some of these clothes are costumes. How do we find the real Blossom? Aren't you doing a background check on her?"

"I've been too busy working here," Phil said. "I should have asked. How was Arthur's funeral?"

"I got through it," Helen said, and shrugged. "Had a slight problem with a drunken uncle. Violet was well behaved, except for an outburst against her stepmother in the limo after the burial, and nobody but Margery and me heard that. Violet doesn't have Blossom's charm, but we shouldn't discount what she says."

"She's not getting a discount," Phil said. "She's paying full price." He kissed Helen slowly, backing her against a chest of drawers while he unbuttoned her blouse. Helen kissed him back, then pushed him away.

"Not here," she said, buttoning her blouse again. "What if

Blossom finds her minister and her estate manager in a steamy embrace? We're not supposed to know each other."

"We're not getting a chance to know each other," Phil said. "You leave tomorrow on the yacht and I won't see you for a week."

"Then let's hurry and pack Arthur's things," Helen said, "so we can be together tonight. I have to tour the yacht at three." She thought that sentence sounded romantic.

She led the way to Arthur's dressing room. A foot-high stack of flat boxes and packing supplies was piled on the carpet.

Phil unfolded a box and taped the bottom while Helen pulled suits off hangers.

"These look handmade," she said. "Amazing details. Even the cuff buttons have real buttonholes. They aren't stuck on the sleeves for show. The fabrics are gorgeous." She lined the box with tissue paper, folded each suit neatly and packed it between more paper while Phil taped a second box.

"Blossom said I could choose the charity," Helen said. "What about a homeless shelter?" She labeled the first box "Men's Suits" and Phil taped it shut while she filled the second.

"Many shelters don't take clothes," Phil said. "They're swamped with cast-off clothes. Florida has lots of old people and their clothes are donated when they die."

"Too bad," Helen said. "The city could have homeless men in hand-tailored suits and Turnbull & Asser shirts. Look at this." She held up a shirt with a white collar and pale pink pinstripes.

"Good way to get the homeless hassled by the police," Phil said. "Why don't we give the clothes to Out of the Closet? They're a chain of thrift stores. The proceeds help people with AIDS."

Six boxes later, the suits and shirts were packed and Phil was emptying Arthur's underwear drawers.

"Was Arthur a boxers or briefs man?" Helen asked.

"Boxers." Phil held up a pair of dark blue boxers and read the label: "Hanro Fishbone cotton boxers."

"He had good taste for an old guy," Helen said.

"Or a young one," Phil said.

"Those boxers sell for about seventy-five dollars each," Helen said.

"I just packed a thousand dollars' worth of men's underwear," Phil said. "They didn't feel like plain old tightie whities. On to the socks."

Phil opened a narrow drawer and whistled. "Look at these. Paisley, striped and tartan. Socks with clocks."

"Beautiful," Helen said. "Your socks are so plain. You either wear black or white."

"Reflects my view of the world," Phil said. "They're easier to pair if I stick to two colors. Matching up these patterns would make me dizzy."

"I doubt Arthur did his own laundry," Helen said. "Did he make his money or inherit it?"

"Blossom told me this is his childhood home, so I guess he came from big bucks and made more," Phil said. "Hey, look what's under these paisley socks."

He lifted out a wedding photo in a mother-of-pearl frame. The groom was a twenty-something Arthur Zerling. The bride wore white satin with shoulder pads and carried a bouquet of honeysuckle.

"I'll bet she's Violet's mother," Helen said. "Honeysuckle was a pretty thing. She and Arthur made a handsome couple. I wonder why Arthur hid that wedding picture. Did he still love his first wife—or regret his second marriage?"

"Honeysuckle was a major part of his life," Phil said. "Maybe he didn't want to hurt Blossom's feelings by displaying his first wife's photo."

Helen opened the top drawer of watches. "They're all at two o'clock," she said. "Someone kept these old-fashioned watches wound. Look, Phil, this platinum Rolex Oyster is engraved on the back. It says: *To my love on our first anniversary. We have all the time in the world—HZ.* That's so sweet. HZ has to be Honeysuckle. I'm giving this watch to Violet. She should have this memento of her parents."

"Does Blossom know you're doing that?" Phil asked, packing more socks into the box.

"She said I could dispose of the watches any way I wished," Helen said.

"Really?" Phil lifted one eyebrow.

"She never said I couldn't give that watch to Violet."

"But you didn't ask, did you?" Phil said.

"No." Helen's eyes shifted away.

"Because you were afraid she'd say no," Phil said.

"I can't predict what she'd say," Helen said, and looked her husband straight in the eye.

"Ever study the spirit versus the letter of the law, Reverend?" Phil asked.

"Didn't have time," Helen said. "I was ordained in the click of a mouse."

"If you give Violet that watch," he said, "what will you do when she runs and shows it to Blossom?"

"Violet's not getting the watch until this case is closed," Helen said. "If we prove Blossom killed her father, it will be her parting gift."

"And if we don't?" Phil asked.

"Then it's a consolation prize," Helen said.

CHAPTER 13

"Ahoy!" Helen called, as she stood at the back of the yacht. Was that the right way to hail a ship's crew?

From the rear, the *Belted Earl* was about thirty feet wide and looked like a triple stack of elegant porches. The lowest deck was tea-colored teak with rattan furniture upholstered in the colors of the Caribbean Sea: light blue, azure, turquoise and navy. A clear plastic railing was a shield against the workaday world.

Half a dozen white yachts were anchored at the concrete dock on a branch of the New River, protected by an open metal-roofed shed. Helen saw uniformed staffers polishing brightwork and carrying cases and crates aboard. She thought the sleek *Belted Earl* made the other yachts look tubby.

"Hello? Anybody home?" she tried again.

The deck doors burst open and a slim blonde in white shorts and a polo shirt waved and said, "Hi! Are you Helen?"

She flashed a cheerleader's smile, ran lightly down the gangplank and held out her hand. "I'm Mira, chief stewardess of the *Belted Earl*. I'll show you where you'll be working and sleeping—if you get any time to sleep. We cruise at nine tomorrow night and the captain will see you at seven thirty."

Mira had small, doll-like features and a muscular, compact body. Her blond hair was pulled back with a two-toned silver barrette. Helen followed her along the narrow teak deck until Mira opened a door. Helen stepped over the raised threshold into a kitchen bigger than her own.

"The galley is the chef's domain," Mira said. "Suzanne cooks for the owners and crew. We eat well."

"She must have a terrific view from this window when you're at sea," Helen said.

"She's so busy, I doubt if Suzanne has much time to admire the view," Mira said. "When we're in port, you can see the crew washing the boat next door. They're pretty scenic." She winked. "And single."

"I've got one, thanks." Helen had removed her wedding ring for this assignment. Her finger felt naked without it.

"Just because you're on a diet doesn't mean you can't look at the menu," Mira said.

She giggled, then turned serious. "This is the dining room and wet bar. The main salon is beyond the oak divider."

Helen liked this floating mansion better than the gloomy barrel-tiled monstrosity on Hendin Island. The yacht's rooms were comfortably roomy, not dark, intimidating caves. They were brightened by big windows and warm honey-colored wood.

"Beautiful wood," she said.

"Custom-carved oak," Mira said. "You'll dust and polish it twice a day."

Now Helen noticed the room was unnaturally dust free. "I guess I'll vacuum this carpet, too," she said.

"The captain said you've worked as a hotel maid, so you're an experienced cleaner," Mira said. "You know to stay in the tracks."

"Tracks?"

"We don't run a vacuum over the carpet every which way," Mira said. "We vacuum the way you mow a lawn, so there aren't random tracks."

Mira opened a door off the main salon. "This is the on-deck head," she said. "We have ten heads for the guests, including their stateroom baths." This one made the Coronado bathrooms look like outhouses. The commode was a beige sculpture. The granite sink had gold fixtures. Two fluffy hand towels embroidered with THE BELTED EARL hung on a brass rack.

"The heads are cleaned after each use," Mira said. "That will be mainly your job."

"Every time?" Helen tried to hide her disbelief.

"Yes," Mira said. "I'm sure you cleaned toilets at the hotel."

"Yes," Helen said. She doubted the men on the yacht had better aim than the hotel guests. If they missed on land, how steady would they be on a shifting ship?

"You'll also clean the sink, the counter, the mirror, and empty the wastebasket. The toilet paper has to be folded into points after every use. It's stowed under the sink."

She opened the carved oak cabinet doors to show stacks of TP, towels and bars of deliciously fragrant Bvlgari soap.

"The labels on the toilet paper rolls should face out on the shelves," Mira said. "Towels are changed every time. They're kept folded with their labels facing the same way. Most guests use the liquid soap, but if a bar is used, we put out a fresh one."

"Bvlgari is twenty dollars a bar," Helen said.

"Fifteen," Mira corrected.

"What happens to the used bar?"

"The crew gets it," Mira said. "One of our perks. Don't expect to load up on fancy soap. You'd be surprised how many people don't wash their hands."

"How do you know if a guest has used the head?" Helen was proud she'd remembered the nautical term.

"We keep in touch by radio." Mira pulled a two-way radio off her belt. "You'll get one, too. If I'm serving in the main salon and you're doing laundry, I'll radio you, 'Guest X is coming back, used the on-deck head,' and then you'll clean it.

"The master stateroom and baths are forward on this deck," she said.

Helen wanted to sink into the depths of the cushiony azure bed piled with dark blue pillows. It faced a sixty-inch television. Who'd watch TV when they had a bed like that? she wondered. She caught herself before she said anything. Mira didn't know she was a newly-wed.

"Most rich people's homes are either fussy or gaudy," Helen said. "I could actually live here."

"All you need is twelve million for the yacht and another million a year to run it," Mira said.

"I'd better start buying lottery tickets," Helen said.

"Let's go downstairs," Mira said. "The crew quarters and guest rooms are on the lower deck."

Helen was grateful they walked down an ordinary tile staircase instead of climbing a ship's ladder. "This room is the crew mess and galley," Mira said.

A beige wraparound booth and table took up the port side. Above it, a wall-mounted TV was tuned to the news. The dock and the yacht interior were displayed on four screens.

Across the room was a small galley. Mira opened a fridge stocked with food, soda and bottled water. "What do you drink?" she asked. "I run on Red Bull."

"Water's fine," Helen said.

"We've got a whole shelf," Mira said. "Help yourself. Any allergies or food you don't like?"

"Liver," Helen said.

"Never serve it."

"Do you really care what I like?" Helen asked.

"When we cruise, you may work twenty hours a day. If the owners come home at four a.m., we have to be ready to serve them drinks and sandwiches or an early breakfast. It's a demanding job. We try to keep you happy in little ways."

Two stacked washer-dryer sets churned and hummed next to the galley. Helen noticed the washers were on the bottom and stifled a groan. She'd have to stoop to load them.

"We do laundry from six a.m. till midnight," Mira said.

"I guess so, if you change the towels after one use," Helen said.

Mira barged ahead. "We also do the guests' laundry and ironing, including their underwear."

"You iron underwear?" Helen didn't own an iron.

"We have to stop washing and drying at twelve so the crew can sleep," Mira said.

How am I going to find an emerald smuggler if I'm working twenty hours a day? Helen wondered. If my heart sinks any lower, I'll need a salvage company.

"You must carry a lot of water to wash clothes eighteen hours a day," she said.

"The yacht makes its own freshwater," Mira said. "It pumps seawater." She turned a metal wheel about the size of a steering wheel. "The secret passage and crew quarters are through this hatch."

Helen followed her into a narrow, windowless hall. Mira slid open a door. "You'll share this with Louise, the second stewardess." The cabin was big enough for two bunks and a three-drawer cabinet. The narrow bathroom was no bigger than Helen's, but much cleaner.

"Who cleans our rooms?" Helen asked.

"We do," Mira said. "Some of the boys pay a stewardess to clean for them."

The passageway grew smaller and lower. Helen bumped her head on a wheel in the ceiling.

"Ouch." Mira winced. "Are you hurt?"

Helen shook her head no.

"You found the escape hatch," she said. "It leads to the bosun's locker. If there's an emergency, that's how we get out belowdecks."

The bosun's locker, Helen thought. Where the captain found the emeralds.

Mira climbed a metal ladder and twisted the hatch and Helen followed. She saw a gray-painted area the size of a toolshed with neatly stowed boat gear.

They backed down the ladder. Now the narrow passageway made a slight jog. The port side was lined with white plastic caddies and cleaning equipment. "You'll have your own caddy. Here's where we go through the looking glass."

Mira opened a door to a hallway with thick beige carpet. Helen saw the other side of the door was a gold-framed mirror. "That way the guests don't see us," she said.

The four staterooms named for Bahamian islands—Andros, Paradise, Bimini and San Salvador—were almost as luxurious as the master suite. Mira opened a louvered door in the Bimini stateroom and said, "You'll help unpack the guests' luggage and put away their things."

Helen saw enough towels in the guest baths to stock a linen store. "Do we clean these baths after every use?"

"Same routine. If the guests take a shower, we wipe down the stall, clean the bathroom, change the towels and soap. We hate people who shower more than once a day. We also restock the soda and bottled water in the guests' fridges, labels facing out.

"The beds are turned down at night and we put on the sleeping duvet," Mira said. "The sheets are changed every two days."

"Good," Helen said. "That will save a little work."

"Not much. We iron the sheets on the bed so they look fresh. We dust the hangers and make sure they all the face the same way."

Helen raised an eyebrow. "Dust the hangers?"

Mira shrugged. "The owners want it."

Helen said nothing. She couldn't. She'd not only walked through the looking glass—she'd fallen down the rabbit hole.

"You'll see the rest tomorrow night when you start work. Wear your dress uniform. Remember, no flirting, no nail polish and no makeup."

"Not even pink lipstick?"

"Nothing."

Helen realized Mira's face was makeup free. She didn't need it with her clear skin.

"And no jewelry," she said.

"What about your silver barrette?" Helen asked.

"That's allowed. It keeps my hair out of my eyes, and when I serve dinner, I put my hair up in a twist."

"Mine slips out of a barrette," Helen said.

Mira unclipped her distinctive barrette with the slashes of smooth and frosted silver. "Try this one," she said. "It's a Ficcare. About forty bucks online at Head Games."

Helen whistled.

"You'll save the money on makeup," Mira said. "You're not to compete with the women on the yacht. It can cause problems with the guests. This is the serious part, so listen carefully."

Mira locked eyes with Helen. "The guests are always right. That's why you're getting nearly forty thousand dollars a year for an unskilled job. You cannot make a scene. If one of the men gets handsy, let me know. Some of the women can turn nasty."

"How nasty?" Helen asked.

"These are the wives and girlfriends of rich men. The men give these women everything—except freedom. They feel angry and helpless. The only power they have is to lash out at the stewardess. They may insult you or scream at you."

"What do I do?" Helen asked.

"Nothing. These women live in pain and pass it on. You're paid to take it."

CHAPTER 14

H elen burst through the door of Coronado Investigations and found Phil frowning at his computer screen, barricaded behind a stack of foam coffee cups. His gray metal desk was awash with printouts. All signs her partner was working. But Helen was facing a week of hard labor. She felt trapped and resentful.

Phil smiled when he saw her. "How is the job with the ocean view?" he asked.

"Some view," Helen said. "The only water I'll see is in a toilet bowl. I'm working twenty hours a day washing clothes, scrubbing, vacuuming carpets. I have to stay in the tracks. You can wipe that smirk off your face, Phil Sagemont. Unless you want to sleep alone on our last night together."

She paced their office in tight, angry circles.

"Come here," he said, softly. "Sit down and talk to me."

"I can't sit," Helen said. "I'd rather keep moving."

"I'd rather hold you." Phil caught her as she passed him, and pulled her onto his lap. She struggled briefly, then stayed there, enjoying the comfort of his strong arms. She inhaled his soothing scent of coffee and sandalwood and sighed.

"Tell me what you'll be doing on the yacht," Phil said, "and why you're vacuuming in the tracks, whatever those are."

Helen explained, detailing her duties. "Talk about pointless work. If these people were any cleaner, they'd live in plastic bubbles. How can I find a smuggler when I'm a seagoing Cinderella?"

"A well-paid Cinderella," he said, kissing her eyelids. "I'll be your prince." He kissed her nose next.

Helen pushed him away. "I didn't tell you the best part. I'm supposed to be a verbal punching bag for bimbos. I won't take it."

"Easy there," Phil said. He held her tighter and rocked her slowly, kissing her neck. "It's only for a week. When you work undercover, you'll hear lots of things you won't like. As long as you're not doing anything illegal, you put up with it for the job."

Helen's dying anger flared up again. "You want me to be a spineless wuss?"

"No," Phil said. "I want you to be a detective and get that smuggler. There's nothing spineless about it. While you've started tracking down the smuggler, I've been working on Arthur Zerling's case."

"When did you get away from his funeral reception?" Helen asked.

"The last guest left at two o'clock. I supervised the cleanup and Blossom let me leave early, about three thirty."

Helen realized Phil was wearing his soft blue shirt and jeans. "Where's your Cabana Boy uniform?"

"I left it at the Zerling house."

"Really? Did she supervise the removal?" Helen raised one eyebrow.

Phil laughed. "You're jealous. I like that." He kissed her again, a lingering kiss this time. "I changed in the pool house. Blossom gave me six uniforms. She offered to have the staff do my laundry, but I said I could do my own wash."

"Anything else she offered?" Helen was still suspicious.

"No," Phil said. "She wanted to nap. She was exhausted."

"From what? Ordering around the staff?" Helen asked.

"Grief is exhausting," Phil said. "So is maintaining a facade. As soon as I got to our office, I did a background check. I hit pay dirt. And I do mean dirt. Blossom is no fragile flower."

"Was this a legal or illegal search?" Helen asked.

"Strictly legal," Phil said.

"Like those 'Find anyone, anytime for $29.99' offers that pop up when I'm trolling the Net?"

"Those are a good way to throw away thirty bucks," Phil said. "Their information is hopelessly outdated. One still has me married to Kendra, and we've been divorced for years. Since you're my trainee, Grasshopper, I will tell you a secret: No reputable investigator uses those databases."

"You found out fast," Helen said. "I thought you'd use the old PI standby and call a buddy on the San Diego force."

"Can't," he said. "The new privacy laws killed the days when a PI could call a friend of a friend for a favor. Officers who run background checks now better have good reasons. There are internal checks, as well as outsiders looking in. I don't know any San Diego cops I'd ask to risk their jobs. I went through the databases only licensed pros can access."

Helen shifted restlessly. "Fascinating history, Teach, but what did you learn?"

"I'm getting there." Phil checked the wall clock. "We're supposed to see our lawyer at seven to meet with our client. It's six thirty. I didn't expect you back so late. How big is that yacht? You toured it for hours."

"I also had to get fitted for my crew uniforms. I pick those up tomorrow," Helen said. "I want to grow old with you, but not while you're telling this story. What did you find?"

"Violet told us Blossom Mae was from San Diego," Phil said. "She didn't know her birth date, but she guessed her father's new wife was thirty-five."

"That's about right," Helen said. "Blossom has a few lines around her eyes, but her neck and her hands look young."

"I searched a ten-year window," Phil said. "No Blossom Mae was born in San Diego between 1970 and 1985. I did find a Mildred Mae Fennimore, born in 1976, which would make her thirty-six."

"That age works," Helen said.

"So does the face," Phil said. "I saw Mildred's booking photo. She looks madder than a wet cat and her hair is dirty blond. But it's definitely Blossom. That was her trick name. Blossom—born Mildred Mae—was arrested and charged with soliciting sexual acts from an undercover police officer."

"She was a prostitute?" Helen asked. "Poor Violet. She said Blossom married Arthur for his money."

"That's not illegal," Phil said, "or prisons would be packed with calculating cookies."

"Calculating cookies?" Helen said. "You sound like a shamus."

"I am one. So are you. The police raided a massage parlor called Beautiful California Girls Body Works."

"That explains Blossom's wardrobe," Helen said. "Half madam and half matron. Wonder where she learned to act like a well-bred wife? Was Blossom convicted for prostitution?"

"Dirty blond Mildred Mae skipped San Diego before her court date," Phil said, "and forfeited a thousand-dollar bail. There's a warrant for her arrest. I think that's when she became brunette Blossom Mae and got a job on a cruise ship giving massages."

"Violet suspected Blossom's magic fingers weren't just massaging Arthur's back," Helen said. "Wait till she hears this. She'll explode."

"That's what worries me," Phil said. "Our client is as unstable as a grenade with the pin pulled. That's why I wanted to make my report at the lawyer's office: so Nancie can defuse our client."

"Nancie's earning her money," Helen said.

"So are we," Phil said.

"After you give your report, I'll tell her about the club clothes I saw in Blossom's closet," Helen said. "I won't mention that Blossom asked me to give away Arthur's things—or that I kept a wedding picture and a watch for her."

"Do we still want to give Arthur's clothes away?" Phil asked. "I'd better check with Nancie."

"I'll freshen up while you make the call," Helen said. "Meet you at my car in five minutes."

Helen's PT Cruiser crawled through the rush-hour traffic toward the lawyer's office while the two private eyes discussed the case. "Nancie says you should donate Arthur's clothes, except for the keepsakes," Phil said. "She says that's Blossom's legal right and there's no evidence she killed Arthur. Also, it maintains your cover."

"Violet knew there was something wrong about her step-mother," Helen said, "but no one believed her. Now it's too late."

"For Arthur," Phil said. "But we still might stop Blossom from spending his millions."

Helen parked next to a shiny silver Saturn. "I think that's our client's car," Phil said. As they knocked on Nancie's office door, he whispered, "Battle stations."

Nancie was dressed for success—and client control. Her stern navy suit and no-nonsense attitude had tamed more than one unfriendly witness.

Violet was a dark mass hunched in the lime green client chair. Arthur's death had taken its toll on his daughter. Her silk shantung suit looked expensive and uncomfortable. Sleepless nights had etched lines into her face and sorrow had stamped dark circles under her eyes.

Helen felt a pang of sympathy. Their news would make her feel worse.

Nancie peered over the top of her horn-rimmed glasses. "Violet, as I told you, Coronado Investigations has found some new information," she said. "You may find it upsetting. Before we proceed, I'm warning that you will not act on their information without my consent. If you do, I will not keep you as my client. Do you understand?"

Violet nodded. Her face shone with hope. "What is it? What did you learn? I was right, wasn't I?"

"Phil will make his report," Nancie said. "Then Helen. I want you to hear all the facts before we decide how to proceed. Phil?"

"Your suspicion that Blossom has a shady past was correct," Phil said.

"I knew it!" Violet squealed, and hugged her fat beige purse like a stuffed toy.

"Violet!" Nancie said. "You promised to listen."

"I'm sorry," Violet said. She folded her hands like a reprimanded schoolgirl and listened until Phil finished. "That woman is nothing but a high-class hooker."

"Not even high-class," Phil said.

"Alleged hooker," Nancie corrected. "Blossom hasn't been convicted."

"I don't understand," Violet said. "How did that woman get a job with a respectable cruise line?"

"The cruise line made a mistake," Phil said. "Or didn't vet her properly. It happens."

"If that woman jumped bail, we can have her arrested," Violet said. "All we have to do is call the police. We'll see how good she looks in handcuffs."

"That's exactly what we're *not* doing," Nancie said. The fierce little lawyer glared at her client. "Blossom now has the money to fight these charges. Her lawyers will tell the court she has reformed and become a good wife. She'll get a slap on the wrist—at most. If she's hauled out to San Diego, she'll close up her house in Fort Lauderdale. That would stall our investigation. We've worked hard to get Phil an inside job."

Violet reluctantly agreed. "Have you found anything suspicious?" she asked.

"Haven't had a chance to search the house," he said. "I was too busy with the funeral reception. It's not going to be easy, Violet. We don't know what poison to look for and the house is fifteen thousand square feet."

Helen jumped in with, "I found something. I searched Blossom's closet while I was at the reception—the one she wouldn't let anyone enter. She has two sets of clothes: a prim and proper wardrobe and club clothes that leave nothing to the imagination."

"Fran's right. There's another man," Violet said, her voice hard and flat.

"Maybe she wore those wild outfits for your father," Phil said.

"No, I stopped by at four o'clock one afternoon when they first returned. Daddy was in a dressing gown with a silly look on his face and that woman was wearing a white frilly negligee. My father told me she was a *lady*." Violet smothered that word with bitter sarcasm.

"You found out what she really was, Phil—a hooker. Her kind of woman needs a man. A young man. Fran saw her dressed to meet him. Follow Blossom when she leaves the house and she'll lead you to him."

Fran also saw poisons on the kitchen counter that turned out to be harmless spices, Helen thought. Our case is based on dislike and delusion.

Nancie was giving Violet a dose of reality. "Tailing Blossom will cost extra," she said.

"I don't care what it costs," Violet said. "That woman has a lover. I know it and so does Fran. Just like I knew she was no innocent young wife. Find the man and you'll find the poison that killed my father."

CHAPTER 15

P hil barged into Helen's bedroom with three bulging plastic bags.

"Retail therapy?" she asked. "I know we had a tough interview with our client tonight, but you've never gone in for recreational shopping."

"I've been working," he said. "While you were lolling, I bought disguises to tail our suspect."

"Ordinary detectives get their disguises at Goodwill," Helen said. "And I wasn't lolling. I was packing."

"I am no ordinary detective," Phil said, and grinned. He dropped the bags on Helen's blue bedspread. Thumbs, attracted by the rustling and crinkling, jumped on the bed and cautiously circled the mound of bags. The cat sniffed one, then backed away. He prodded a red bag with his big six-toed paw. It crackled invitingly. Thumbs leaped on it and a shock of wild brown hair spilled out of the bag. The cat hissed, swatted the hair and disappeared under the bed.

"What's in there?" Helen said. "It upset Thumbs."

"Items that will render me invisible when I follow Blossom," Phil said.

Helen reached up and ruffled his thick silver hair. "With that hair?"

"I am a master of disguise," Phil said. "Watch."

He disappeared into the bathroom with the bags. Helen was packing a navy canvas carryall for her yacht cruise. She folded a pink T-shirt into the carryall while Phil slipped out of the bathroom, a vision in black dreadlocks with a red, green and yellow Rasta tam plopped on top. A neon tie-dyed shirt, red board shorts and round John Lennon sunglasses completed the ensemble.

He tapped her on the shoulder and said, "Don't worry. Be happy."

Helen put her hands over her face and moaned, "My eyes, my eyes. I may go blind."

"You have to admit this doesn't look like me."

"I recognize the smug look," Helen said. "Except for that, it's a good disguise. Where'd you get the dreads and the tam?"

Phil pulled them both off his head. The dreads were attached to the hat. "No problem, mon," he said in a bad Jamaican accent. "All in one. They sell them in souvenir shops."

"I've seen pale guys on vacation with Rasta tams and dreads," Helen said. "I didn't realize they were wearing wig hats."

"It takes many beers to look this stupid," Phil said, abandoning the accent.

"That's good for one trip," Helen said. "But what happens if you don't catch Blossom the first time?"

"Wait and see," Phil said, shutting himself back into the bathroom.

While she waited, Helen mentally inventoried the contents of her carryall: underwear, sandals, casual T-shirts and shorts, sample-sized toiletries.

"Ta-da!" Phil threw open the bathroom door. Now he sported a camo visor with a burst of wild brown hair on the crown, like a clump of dead grass. A "Guns, God and Guts" T-shirt stretched across his chest. His jeans needed a wash. Phil twirled so Helen could see the jeans' sagging seat.

"No wonder Thumbs hissed at the hair," Helen said. "If he sees the whole outfit, he may never come out from under the bed."

"You don't like Bubba?" Phil asked. "I was hoping you'd admire my new look." He waited for a reaction.

Helen laughed.

"Laugh away. You haven't seen Jimmy Ray," Phil said. "He'll be here in a moment."

Phil shut the door while Helen zipped up the navy carryall. There would be just enough room for her uniform shorts and polo shirts.

My uniforms might be crumpled, she thought, but I'll be ironing eighteen hours a day. I can press my own clothes, too.

The bathroom door opened again. Phil lounged in the doorway. "Wanna go to the dump and shoot rats?" he asked.

Now he wore a greasy Marlins cap with dirty-blond curls hanging down the back of his neck. He had the same saggy jeans and a smiley face T-shirt with a gray bar across the mouth. "Silence Is Golden, Duct Tape Is Silver," the shirt read.

"What is that hairstyle?" Helen asked. "A half mullet?"

"Something fishy, darlin'," he drawled. He gripped a tin of Skoal chewing tobacco in one hand and a Dr Pepper in the other.

"When did you start drinking Dr Pepper?" Helen asked.

"I'm recycling," Phil said. "That's where I spit my 'baccy juice."

"Ew," Helen said.

"Exactly the reaction I wanted, little lady," he said. "Glad you appreciate my accessories."

"There isn't more, is there?" she asked.

"That's how I like my women—begging for more," he said, his fake redneck accent thickening. "You-all wait here a minute. I got another surprise."

When the bathroom door shut, Thumbs slunk out from under

the bed, looked around, then raced out of the bedroom before Phil debuted his next disguise.

This time, he had his distinctive silver hair tucked under a clean blue ball cap. He wore a fresh blue coverall that said BOB on the pocket, and carried a blue toolbox.

"What's the problem with your air-conditioning, ma'am?" Phil asked politely.

"Nothing," Helen said. "I am totally cool. Bob looks reliable enough to let inside my house. But how are Bob and his buddies going to tail Blossom? She must know you drive a black Jeep. You park it at her house."

"I worked that out, too," Phil said. "I'm having a rental car delivered to the parking lot next to the entrance of Hendin Island. It's a medical office building. The rental stays there until I need it. If Blossom leaves the house, I run to the parking lot and follow her. With the traffic on Las Olas, it takes a while to turn out of Hendin Island Road. She won't get far. Rental cars are anonymous. Even a great detective like me has trouble finding my own rental unless I park it by some landmark."

"Blossom is no dummy," Helen said. "She might catch on if the same rental keeps following her."

"Also thought of that," Phil said. "Once I use the rental, I exchange it for another. I have full-sized cars from Chevy Impalas to Hyundai Sonatas waiting in the wings."

"Bob is going to drive a Chevy Impala to fix the air-conditioning?" Helen asked.

"Of course not," Phil said. "Good catch. You're thinking like a detective. I rented a white panel truck for Bob. The truck is in the parking lot, too. I slipped the building manager a little cash to park there and had magnetized signs made up at the copy shop for the van."

He ducked back into the bathroom. Helen heard more rustling, then Phil returned with two plastic signs that read PALM BEACH COOL GUYS AIR-CONDITIONING SERVICE.

"Slap these on the sides, and Bob looks like the real deal," he said. "There was an extra charge for fast service, but Violet says she doesn't mind paying. I can keep doing this for weeks."

"Do you think Violet and Fran are right and Blossom killed her husband, Arthur?" Helen asked.

"The more I find out about Blossom, the more I think she did," Phil said. "At first, I discounted a lot of what Violet said as jealousy. The housekeeper may not know curry, but she knew something was off. After you discovered those wild clothes in Blossom's dressing room, I started to think Fran did see her leaving to meet a lover. I wish I had a better idea how Blossom killed her husband."

Helen felt uneasy. Talking about Arthur triggered her worries about her dead ex-husband and the blackmailer. Just my luck he'll call when I'm out of the country, Helen thought.

"Where did you go?" Phil asked. "You zoned out on me."

"Sorry," Helen said. "Nervous about my trip. Promise me if my sister, Kathy, calls while I'm gone, you'll contact me."

"Hey, what brought that on? Kathy's fine."

"I know," Helen said, "but a lot can go wrong. She has two little kids." And I'm lying to you and I feel terrible that I can't tell you, she thought.

Phil put his arms around Helen. "Hey there, are you that worried?" he asked.

She felt like a lower life-form. "It's the yacht," she said. "That's a new world for me. I wish I knew more about emerald smuggling. Do you know any smugglers?"

"Me?" Phil said. "Would true-blue Bob the cool repairman know shady characters like that?"

"Certainly not," Helen said. "But Phil the private detective would. He'd meet them in the line of duty."

"Hm," Phil said. "Let me think. I know bikers who beat up people for cash. I could get you a bargain rate on a hit man who'd give you up if the cops looked at him sideways. I know low-level drug dealers, a clutch of shoplifters. . . . Wait a minute. I forgot about Max. Max Rupert Crutchley.

"He tends to romanticize his smuggling. But I know for a fact Max was a scuba diver and a treasure hunter. Found some Spanish treasure off the Florida coast. Shipwreck-salvage treasure hunters blow through cash like coke addicts and they always need investors. A potential investor hired me to investigate Max. He wanted to make sure Max wasn't running drugs. Max was clean and I said so. I knew he was bringing in emeralds, but I kept quiet about them."

"Why?" Helen said.

"Didn't like the twit who hired me. When I made a suggestion, he said, 'We don't pay you to think. We pay you to find out. Is he or is he not smuggling drugs?'

" 'He's not,' I said.

"The twit never asked about emeralds and I never mentioned them."

"Do you think Max would talk about emerald smuggling?" Helen asked.

"After a few beers, we may have trouble shutting him up," Phil said. "When do you have to report to the yacht?"

"Seven tomorrow night," Helen said.

"I get off work at five," Phil said. "I'll call Max and see if we can have an early dinner with him tomorrow. What time do you sail?"

"The *Belted Earl* is a motor yacht," Helen said. "We cruise at nine o'clock for Atlantis."

"A moonlight cruise," Phil said. "Romantic."

"Just me and my scrub brush," Helen said. "We'll work all night, but the yacht gets into the Bahamas about ten the next morning. That way the crew can check in with immigration, run errands in port and hit the bars while the owners go to Atlantis."

"You sound like an old salt already," Phil said. "The crew really goes drinking after working all night and most of the day?"

"That's what Mira said. They're still in their twenties," Helen said. "At forty-one, I don't party so hearty anymore."

"What are you packing?"

"I pick up my uniforms tomorrow," she said. "The rest is ready." She held up the bulging zippered bag.

"That's all?" Phil raised an eyebrow in surprise.

"There isn't room on board for lots of crew luggage," she said. "I'll bring this and carry my BlackBerry in my purse, so I can keep in touch with you. The captain said calls from the Bahamas to the U.S. are outrageous—a hundred dollars or so for a few minutes. He agreed I could put the phone charges on his bill."

"You got that in writing, I hope?" Phil asked.

"You bet." Helen tossed the fat carryall on the floor. "I'm following another rule for new crew: Never bring more than you can carry off in a hurry. If things go bad, I can abandon these T-shirts and sandals."

She pulled Phil down on the bed. His cap slid off when she ran her fingers through his long hair and she tugged on the coverall's zipper.

"Why don't you slip out of that, Bob?" Helen said. "I'm feeling hot."

CHAPTER 16

"Helen!" Phil called her on the phone, talking fast. "Blossom is on the move. I'm tailing her."

"Where? What? What's going on?" Helen had been snoozing since Phil left for the Zerling mansion this morning. Today was her last chance to relax before she started working on the yacht.

"I'm following Blossom," Phil said. "She's acting suspicious. She told me she was going shopping, but I thought, Why tell me? I'm the hired help. Did I wake you?"

"Never mind that. Where are you now?" Helen asked.

"Sitting behind her red Porsche at the stop sign. She's trying to turn out of Hendin Island onto Federal Highway. She—"

An angry horn blast and screeching brakes interrupted him. Helen winced, held her breath, then asked, "Was that an accident?"

"Almost," Phil said. "Blossom nearly got creamed trying to make a left through the traffic while talking on her cell phone. She's still at the stop sign, but at least she put down her phone."

"What if she looks in her rearview mirror and sees you?" Helen asked.

"She won't recognize me," Phil said. "I'm Jimmy Ray, driving a rented Chevy."

"Jimmy Ray with the greasy gimme cap and half mullet?" Helen asked.

"Don't dis Jimmy," Phil said. "He's doing a good job. There she goes. She made it this time. Hang on. I'm following her."

Helen heard more honks. "Phil," she shouted into the phone. "Be careful."

"Can't talk, darlin'," he said. "Jimmy Ray is chasing Blossom."

Helen waited for Phil to report back and paced the terrazzo floor. He was a good driver, but he was driving a strange car. Blossom sounded reckless. What if Phil got hurt trying to follow her?

Helen wandered into her living room, plumped a pillow on the turquoise Barcalounger and noticed a light layer of dust on her kidney-shaped coffee table. Cleaning could wait until she got home from the *Belted Earl*, she decided. She'd be dusting enough on the yacht.

Helen surveyed the midcentury antiques in her living room. She'd learned to like their colorful, playful forms. Margery had bought them when the Coronado was new. They'd aged gracefully, like the building.

She carried her empty coffee cup into the kitchen and checked the clock. Three thirty-two.

"Phil? Are you still there?" Helen said into her phone.

No answer. Phil must have left his cell phone on in the passenger seat. She heard ordinary street sounds, the soothing ocean roar of the traffic, the hiss of a bus's brakes. Those were more reassuring than furious horns and frantic screeches. He must be safely working.

She felt Thumbs rubbing his furry head against her bare legs.

"You only love me when it's dinnertime," she told the cat, as she scratched his ears. He nudged her hand and patted his food bowl with his mittenlike paw. She poured him dry food and fresh water. "Phil will take care of you while I'm gone," she said. "He'll spoil you rotten."

Thumbs, face down in his food, ignored her.

Helen went back to pacing. She checked the clock again. The hands were moving so slowly she wondered if it was broken. She checked her watch. No, it was only three thirty-eight.

"Phil?" she said into the phone. "Where are you?"

"Dixie Highway," he said. "Near a grungy convenience store."

"Doesn't sound as upscale as Blossom's Hendin Island home," Helen said.

"No mansions in sight," he said. "This strip mall has an auto-parts dealer, a thrift store and a radiator shop. Blossom just turned into the lot. I'm pulling into the pawnshop lot across the street to watch her."

"Is she going to a Seven-Eleven?" Helen asked.

"Too high-class," he said. "This is a nameless, paintless cinder block dump. Sells giant sodas, cigarettes, lottery tickets and chili dogs with a side of salmonella. It's also a pickup spot for day laborers. I've passed it early in the morning when the contractors' trucks arrive. The day laborers are a rough-looking crew. A sensible woman wouldn't walk in that store alone. Hell, I'd think twice about it. It looks like a holdup waiting to happen.

"At least this part is easy. Blossom's flashy red sports car sticks out like a sore thumb in the lot. She's parking the Porsche by the door, next to a beat-up van with its back doors wired shut. Wait! She's getting out."

"She's not going inside, is she?" Helen asked.

"She's heading toward the door. Is that woman nuts, wearing jeans that tight? Now she's sashayed past the door to the pay phone. She's gripping her purse and she's got an orange card in her hand, like a credit card. Man, that phone looks filthy. I don't know how she can hold the receiver to her face. She's punching in numbers. Looks like someone answered. Now she's talking and giggling. Blossom looks like a very merry widow."

"Can you hear her?" Helen asked.

"Not across the street," Phil said. "Jimmy Ray can't get too close. But I can take some pictures. She's still talking and laughing. That's right, Blossom, smile for the camera. Gotcha!" Helen heard the camera click.

"Oh, this is good," Phil said. "This is major."

"It is?" Helen said.

"Think about it," Phil said. "Why would Blossom use a pay phone, when she has landlines in the house and a cell phone in her purse?"

"Her cell phone battery was running low?" Helen guessed.

"Then she'd make the call from home," Phil said. "Instead, she drives to this risky place. Why?" He didn't wait for an answer. "Because she doesn't want a record of this call."

"That doesn't make sense," Helen said. "She's a rich widow. She doesn't answer to anyone."

"She doesn't have the money yet," Phil said. "Arthur's estate is still in probate and will be for months. The court likes to give creditors time to collect their debts. Anybody who watches TV knows cell phone calls are easily traced. Someone could see Blossom's phone bills and start asking questions. She knows Arthur's daughter is looking for trouble. Blossom doesn't want to give Violet an opening."

"Sounds far-fetched," Helen said.

"It's not," Phil said. "Blossom is smart. With ten million dollars at stake, she's taking no chances. She's being extra careful until she gets Arthur's fortune. Wait! She hung up the phone. She's hurrying back to her car. Blossom just turned onto Dixie Highway."

"Toward her home?" Helen asked.

"Toward downtown Lauderdale. Too early to say if she's going back to Hendin Island or somewhere else. Gotta go."

"Wait!" Helen said.

He must have tossed his phone on the car seat. Helen heard Phil's car crunch over gravel. Then it seemed to be traveling on a smooth road. At least he didn't hang up.

At last he came back on the phone. "We're at a stoplight," Phil said. "I'm two cars behind her."

"Phil, what if you're still following her when it's time for us to meet Max?" Helen asked.

"Then you'll have to handle dinner alone," Phil said.

"I'd better get dressed," Helen said.

"I'll meet you at the restaurant," Phil said. "The light's changed." Silence.

Helen hit the speaker button and carried the phone with her into the bedroom to change into her white dress uniform. Helen pulled her skort off the hanger. She hadn't worn that skirt-shorts combination since she was a teenager.

She was brushing her long brown hair when Phil came back on the line, talking in short, excited bursts. "Helen! She's not going home. She's parking! In a lot off Las Olas. Jimmy Ray is going to follow her. Wait there."

"Where am I going?" Helen said, but Phil was gone again. Judging by the muffled sounds coming from the cell phone, he'd jammed it into his (or Jimmy Ray's) pocket.

She buttoned her white jacket. The sleeves were perfectly tailored for her long arms.

Phil was on the phone again. Now his voice was a whisper. "She's gone into a boutique on a side street near Las Olas. A girlie place called Grisette's."

"Isn't *grisette* a French name for a prostitute?" Helen said.

"That's a little harsh," Phil said. "Grisettes are generous girls. They take no money for helping their fellow men."

"What's the shop look like?" Helen said.

"The clothes in the window are mostly black, but they don't look like something a new widow would wear. Blossom is pressing a buzzer. . . . Now a saleswoman is letting her inside. Jimmy Ray isn't going to try getting in there. He'll sit at the sidewalk café across the street, get himself a nice six-dollar coffee and put it on his expense account. This could take a while. Helen, I'm hanging up. I'll call you when she comes out."

"Phil, it's nearly four o'clock," Helen said. "I have to leave in half an hour to meet Max by five."

After Phil hung up she slipped on her deck shoes, then checked that her carryall was packed for tonight's yacht trip. She'd take it with her. Phil could drive her to the marina and Margery or Peggy could give him a ride back to his Jeep tomorrow.

She was looking for her purse when her landline rang. It was Phil.

"Blossom has left Grisette's," he said. "She's carrying a pink shopping bag. Now she's stashing it in her Porsche. Jimmy Ray is going to follow her."

"Is she going home?" Helen asked.

"Can't tell," Phil said. "Jimmy Ray is behind her. The late-afternoon traffic is slow. I think she's heading toward A1A. Looks like she wants to drive home along the ocean."

"Are you following her?" Helen said.

"I'm not getting stuck in that traffic with the gawking tourists. I'll stay on Federal Highway. Jimmy Ray has to hightail it back to the medical-building parking lot and disappear. I need to transform myself into an estate manager again. You go meet Max. I'll call you as soon as I'm free. Turn on your cell phone."

"Be careful, Phil," Helen said. "Don't let her catch you."

Helen grabbed her purse and the carryall and patted Thumbs good-bye. The April evening was pleasantly warm. Margery, Peggy and Pete the parrot had assembled early by the pool for the nightly sunset salute. Peggy wore a cool green sundress that matched Pete's feathers. Their landlady's purple caftan floated on the evening breeze. Her nail polish was the color of the evening sun and her cigarette was an orange beacon.

Peggy whistled when she saw Helen in her dress uniform. Margery raised her wineglass and called, "Hey, sailor, can I buy you a drink?"

"I'll take a rain check," Helen said. "I'm meeting someone for background information. Then I report to the captain. I don't want to have alcohol on my breath the first day on the job."

Margery sailed over, her silver earrings and bangle bracelets jingling. "Then I'll tell you good-bye," she said. "And be careful."

"You worry too much," Helen said. "I'm cruising on a luxury yacht."

"With people rich enough to buy their way out of trouble," Margery said. "You're going undercover as a nobody maid. You'll be alone on the ocean trying to catch a smuggler.

"Remember, the easiest way to get rid of a body is dumping it over the side of a ship."

With that warning, she blew out a ferocious cloud of Marlboro smoke.

CHAPTER 17

H elen waited for Phil outside Aruba, a beachside restaurant in Lauderdale-by-the-Sea. Aruba was in a cluster of small seaside restaurants and souvenir shops.

The ocean air was a soft caress. Helen heard the soothing *whoosh* of the waves. She looked like she belonged near the ocean in her yacht dress uniform: white skort and short white jacket with epaulets.

Phil jumped out of his black Jeep, tossed his keys to the valet and saluted Helen.

"Where do I enlist?" he said. "I love women in uniform. Do you get a gun?"

"I get a caddy loaded with spray cleaner," she said, laughing. "I can shoot to kill—germs."

He took her in his arms and said, "You've already shot me through the heart. I'll miss you. A whole week, huh?" He unbuttoned the top button on her uniform. "Do we have time to go back and—?"

"No," Helen said. "We don't. We're supposed to meet Max. What's he look like?"

"A short older guy with gray hair," Phil said.

"That isn't a good description in Florida," Helen said. "Half the men in there have gray hair."

They scanned the gray-haired men bellied up to the bar—literally.

"No Max," Phil said. He checked his watch. "It's four fifty-eight. He'll be here."

"What happened with Blossom?" Helen asked. "Did you transform yourself back into an estate manager before she got home?"

"With minutes to spare," Phil said. "Well, seconds. I also carried her new clothes to her bedroom."

"Is Blossom still sleeping alone?" Helen asked.

"So far as I can tell," Phil said. "Arthur's dressing room was still empty. I didn't see another toothbrush and the seat was down on the toilet."

"Always a giveaway," Helen said. "What did Blossom buy at Grisette's?"

"They sure weren't mourning dresses," Phil said. "They made her club clothes look like something she'd wear to tea with the queen. She bought a silky coral number with major holes—on-purpose holes."

"Cutouts, I think they're called," Helen said.

"That dress will leave all her back and most of her front bare. She bought a hot pink sequin something I guess was a dress. I've seen bigger scarves. I left the bag on her bed.

"Blossom was waiting for me downstairs in the den in a tight black top and those painted-on jeans. She'd draped herself over the rosewood bar. Her conversation was full of innuendos. She asked me to make her a manhattan. 'I'm not a good bartender,' I said.

"'I'm sure you're good at everything, Phil,' she said. Then she brushed against me. It didn't feel like an accident."

"Maybe she needs a visit from her minister," Helen said, fighting back her fury.

"No, no," Phil said. "I might learn something this way."

"Like what a slut she is?" Helen asked.

"Trust me," Phil said. "She'll let her guard down."

"As long as she keeps her clothes on," Helen said.

"She's no competition," Phil said. "I should be worried about you in that hot uniform alone on a yacht. Some millionaire might carry you off." He kissed her again.

"Hey, you two, stop that! Quit smooching out here in front of God and everybody!"

Helen and Phil saw a suntanned man in a Hawaiian shirt smiling and waving.

"Max, you old pirate," Phil said. "Since when did you confuse yourself with God? Meet my wife, Helen Hawthorne."

Max barely reached Helen's shoulder. He was barrel-chested with short, powerful arms. Helen estimated his age at sixty-something. He wore a shark's tooth on a thick gold chain and a chunky pinkie ring with a square-cut emerald.

The sun caught his ring and it glittered with green fire.

"Max Crutchley," he said, crushing Helen's hand. "Ol' Phil got himself a babe."

They followed a thin pale-haired hostess past tables filled with diners to a glass-topped table overlooking the wide, sandy beach.

"Best view in the house," Helen said.

They watched a hefty, sunburned man stumble past the window with a sloshing foam cup.

"I could do without him," Max said. "But that blonde in the bikini is easy on the eyes."

"I meant the ocean," Helen said.

"Sure you did," Max said. "That's a pretty muscular example of ocean life under the palm tree."

Phil snickered.

"I thought we could talk private-like back here," Max said. "My usual beer dives are okay for Phil, but not for a lady."

Phil winked at her. Max was definitely old-school, Helen thought.

A waiter appeared and Max and Phil ordered beer and burgers. Helen wanted a club soda and the seafood stir-fry.

"Let me get you a real drink, Helen," Max said.

"Thanks, but I have to report to the yacht right after dinner. That's why I'm in uniform."

"You make one hell of a sailor," Max said.

After the waiter left, Helen said, "Phil told me you're a diver."

"Used to be," Max said. "Bad ticker now. Can't dive anymore. Felt like they cut off my arm when the doc said no more. I loved diving, the riskier the better. Had a few close encounters with sharks, but it's beautiful down there. More honest, too. Easier to spot the sharks."

"They wear suits on land," Phil said.

"What do you want to know about emeralds, Helen?" Max asked. "Phil says you're working a smuggling case. Should you let your lady do something that dangerous, Phil?"

Helen bridled at that, but Phil put his hand over hers, a warning to let him talk. "I don't 'let' Helen do anything, Max. She does what she wants. She can handle herself. Our client needs a woman operative."

"I'm hired to find a smuggler who's part of the yacht crew," Helen said. "The captain found a box of emeralds hidden on his ship on his last trip. By the time he went back for the stones, they were gone."

"Cut or uncut emeralds?" Max asked.

"Cut stones."

"Smart." Max nodded approval. "Uncut emeralds only have potential value because they can have flaws called inclusions. I was witness to the cutting of a large emerald. Thanks to an unseen inclusion in a potential hundred-thousand-dollar gemstone, the value dropped dramatically during the procedure. Where does this yacht sail?"

"Mainly to the Bahamas and other Caribbean islands," Helen said.

"I'm guessing this is originating in the Bahamas," Max said. "Been a smugglers' haven since the old pirate days. How long has this smuggling been going on?"

"The captain doesn't know," Helen said. "As soon as he found the stones, he hired us."

"So he's a straight arrow?" Max asked.

"Absolutely," Helen said.

The waiter arrived with monster plates of food. Max covered his burger and fries with a bloodbath of ketchup. Phil poured ketchup and hot sauce on his. Helen nibbled on her stir-fry.

Max looked around to make sure there were no eavesdropping waiters and the other diners were busy with their own conversations.

"It's likely these emeralds are transported to the Bahamas by yacht," Max said. "Yacht traffic emerging from Latin America is monitored by the U.S. Coast Guard in Bahamian waters and by the United States Army in the Caribbean. I was aboard a treasure-hunting boat in Bahamian waters just north of Havana. We received a lot of attention from a Coast Guard cutter. Had machine guns aimed at us."

"Any reason the Coast Guard would be interested?" Phil asked.

"Of course not," Max said, playing with the emerald ring on his little finger. Helen thought that gave him away.

"Oh, hell, Phil, I can't bullshit you," Max said. "You knew what we were doing. I never understood why you didn't turn me in."

"Didn't like the twerp who hired me," Phil said. "The investor. He wanted to make sure you weren't running drugs. I tried to say I thought you were jewel smuggling, but he interrupted and said, 'I'm not paying you to think. Is he smuggling drugs?' I told him you weren't."

"You told the God's honest truth," Max said. "Thanks to you, he invested in our salvage operation and we found Spanish gold. He was happy and I owe you big-time. Still do."

"Forget it," Phil said, and sipped his beer.

"I have friends on both sides of the law," Max said. He turned to Helen. "You've got a tough job. Emeralds are easy to hide aboard a yacht." He took a ketchup-slathered bite of burger.

"That's what the captain said. Isn't Colombia where emeralds come from?" Helen asked. She speared a scallop in her stir-fry.

"It's a major source," Max said. "Brazil is another. So are Egypt and other parts of Africa. Cleopatra's mines in the deserts near the Red Sea produced some of the first emeralds. Egyptian stones are small and dark. They say Cleopatra loved her emeralds more than all her other jewels.

"The Romans believed that emeralds did not fatigue the eyes like other gems. Did you know the emperor Nero wore emerald sunglasses to watch the gladiators die? Wonder how red blood looked through green glasses? Blood and emeralds. They go together."

Max abandoned the wreckage of his dinner to continue his lecture. "Mel Fisher, the greatest treasure hunter of all, discovered emeralds in the shipwreck *Nuestra Señora de Atocha*. Colombian emeralds. Mel found more than half a billion dollars in treasure in that salvage operation. When that Spanish ship was wrecked in the Florida Keys, two hundred sixty-four people died. More blood and emeralds."

Helen tried not to look at her watch. They had to leave soon. How could she steer Max back to the subject? She tried to signal Phil, but he was finishing his beer.

"Does your captain know if he found Colombian emeralds?" Max asked.

Good, Helen thought. Max was back on track.

"He didn't know," Helen said. "He's not an expert. The captain thought they looked like the emeralds he saw in the jewelry shops at Atlantis. The colors ranged from blue-green to deep green."

"Could be Colombian," Max said. "An expert would know for sure. You said they were in a box. What kind?"

"A plastic tackle box. The captain said it was filled with stones."

Max whistled. "That's worth hundreds of thousands. Maybe more, depending on the quality. Your smuggler is smart, but not smart enough. He knows enough to smuggle in cut emeralds, but not how to treat them right. Loose stones should be stored in individual velvet compartments, not dumped in a box where they could get chipped or scratched."

"What happens to those emeralds once they reach the U.S.?" Helen asked.

"The smuggler may try to fly with them to a dealer," Max said. "The stones are not detectable during electronic screening procedures, so someone could have a suitcase full of gems and it would go unnoticed. Unless it was hand searched.

"The smugglers are probably connected to a sleazy but legitimate dealer in gemstones. Believe me, in my brief experience with—uh, friends—they knew a few of those in Manhattan and Miami. Found them to be very unpleasant. Smart but real pricks. Pardon my language."

"You don't have to apologize," Helen said. "If the smugglers sell to a sleazy dealer, what's their cut?"

"I suspect it's like using a fence," Max said. "The smugglers will get a fraction of the real value."

The waiter reappeared. "All finished?" he asked. "How about dessert or coffee?"

"No, thanks," Helen said.

The waiter put the check on the table and Phil reached for it. Max grabbed it first. "It's good for my reputation to be seen with such a classy lady, even if she is married to this gray-haired geezer. Good luck catching your smuggler.

"Be careful, Helen. Remember what I said about blood and emeralds. That kind of money makes people crazy."

CHAPTER 18

Helen caught a ripple of excitement aboard the *Belted Earl*.
White-uniformed staff were hurrying through their chores.
She saw the edge of a box being carried into the crew mess
and the flash of a feather duster. She heard feet pounding up the spiral
staircase to the main deck.

Finally, the cruise felt real. She was an undercover operative. This
was more exciting than standing in a shop until she ached from
boredom.

Helen followed Mira through the secret passage to the crew
quarters. The head stewardess wore her dress uniform and her hair
was caught in a twist by her two-toned silver barrette. Her fresh-
scrubbed face and bright smile made her look like a teenager.

Mira slid open the second door in the passage. "Stow your bag in
your cabin," she said. "You can unpack later. Louise has the top
bunk. She outranks you as second stewardess."

Helen followed Mira down the passage. White plastic caddies
bristling with brushes, dusters and cleaning supplies were stowed in
racks along the wall near the far entrance.

"This is yours," Mira said, pointing to the lowest caddy. She pushed open the door and they were through the looking glass into the carpeted guest quarters.

"Always use the passage," Mira said. "A stewardess is never seen while cleaning. This will be an easy trip. We have only two couples and they're staying in the two closest staterooms."

The names PARADISE and BIMINI were on carved door plaques.

"Ralph and Rosette have Bimini with the peacock blue accents," Mira said. "Pepper and Scotty will sleep in Paradise. It's azure blue." Both were paneled with that honey-colored oak.

"Gorgeous silk spread," Helen said.

"It's custom-made," Mira said. "So are the sheets and pillowcases. You're looking at about four thousand dollars' worth of bedding."

"What's the routine when the guests arrive?" she asked.

"The staff lines up when the guests come aboard," Mira said. "Louise and I will serve drinks and the chef will have a buffet ready in the dining room. The boys will carry in the luggage and you'll unpack it."

"By myself?" Helen asked. She tried to hide her panic. What if the guests complained and she was thrown off before the cruise started?

"Don't worry," Mira said. "These wives usually go down with you when you unpack. Each room has a safe. They'll put their jewelry away and you won't have to touch it."

"Good," Helen said. The panic was starting to fade.

Mira opened the closet door and they were enveloped by the sweet smell of cedar. "If the wives decide to eat while you unpack, the jewelry goes in the underwear drawer here. When you clean, if money or jewelry is left lying around, you never touch it."

"We had those same instructions when I worked at the hotel," Helen said. "Not that our guests had valuable jewelry."

"We had one incident where a girl was accused of stealing a sapphire necklace," Mira said. "Turned out the wife never brought it on board. But the captain had to search our cabins and warn us that stealing was a firing offense. The wife finally called home and her maid found it in the bedroom. The wife was mortified. She tipped the girl three hundred dollars, but it was still uncomfortable."

"Do we get tips?" Helen asked.

"It's up to the guests," Mira said. "Sometimes a guest will slip us each a hundred dollars or give the captain money for the crew. But Earl gives us a generous yearly bonus."

I won't be working here for a year, Helen thought. At least, I hope not.

"The guests on this trip have been generous in the past," Mira said. "They'll be here in less than an hour. The guests' clothes go on these hangers. Make sure the hangers face the same way. Later tonight, you'll change out the silk spread for the sleeping duvet.

"Louise and I will serve the guests and watch the on-deck head. We'll stay in touch with you by two-way radio."

Mira showed Helen how the black radio worked and helped clip it to Helen's belt. It felt awkward.

"You'll also walk Mitzi, Beth's miniature poodle."

"On which deck?" Helen asked.

"Well, we call it walking, but Mitzi has the run of the guest area. We keep a flat of grass for her on the upper aft deck and Beth puts 'puppy training pads' in her stateroom bath, but Mitzi rarely uses them. If you're lucky, she'll use the marble in Beth's bathroom. She prefers carpet. We have special cleaners for both."

"Terrific," Helen said, her heart sinking. She wasn't even a sea-going Cinderella, condemned to kitchen drudgery. She had latrine duty.

"Is Mitzi a nice dog?" she asked.

"She never bites," Mira said.

"That's not an endorsement," Helen said.

"Beth loves her," Mira said, "but the dog is spoiled and yappy. The captain banned her from the bridge and the crew areas for safety reasons. He said Mitzi might get hurt if we stepped on her.

She is underfoot when she's on board. Be careful you don't trip over her."

"What are the guests like?" Helen asked. "Do they bite?"

"Pretty undemanding," Mira said. "Ralph and Rosette are Earl's age. Ralph belongs to an old Chicago family. He doesn't have Earl's business success. Rosette and Ralph have been married thirty years. She can be snobbish but she's not rude.

"Scotty and Pepper are newly married. She's wife number four, I think. She used to be a cocktail waitress. Scotty is about seventy and gives Pepper anything she wants, as long as she does what he says. Scotty will probably get tipsy. Pepper is maybe twenty-five. She may say something ugly to you if she's had a fight with Scotty. She's pretty and Scotty is jealous. They fight a lot."

"How will I know if they've been fighting?" Helen asked.

"You'll hear them," Mira said. "We hear everything on this ship. There is no privacy."

We hear everything, Helen thought. Will I hear the rattle of smuggled emeralds? The sound of the smuggler opening a bilge or the bosun's locker late at night?

Mira glanced at her watch. "It's seven twenty-eight," she said. "You have an appointment with the captain at seven thirty. He's a stickler for time. I'll take you up to the bridge. You can meet the other staff later."

Helen followed Mira up the crew mess stairs and through the galley, where the dark-haired chef was chopping a red pepper at a counter. "Hi, Suzanne," Mira said.

Suzanne smiled a hello and waved.

Mira walked briskly along the narrow teak deck to the front of the yacht and knocked on the bridge door. "Captain?" she called. "Helen Hawthorne is here." Mira told Helen, "I'll leave you here. I have to go back to work."

Helen thought the bridge looked beautifully useful. The walls and ceiling were paneled in that same honey-colored wood. Six inward-slanting windows gave panoramic views of the muddy New River and the shining white yachts in the marina. The bridge windows had giant wipers, like car windshields. Over the windows were huge built-in monitors. Under the windows were radar screens, electronics and various controls.

Smack in the middle was the pilot's wheel in sleek steel and wood.

Captain Josiah Swingle strode through a side door in his white dress uniform with four bars on the shoulder.

"Welcome aboard," he said. Captain Swingle sat down on an upholstered bench that was taller than a regular couch. Helen stayed standing. "Mira has explained your duties?" he asked.

"Yes, sir," Helen said. "I'm hoping to catch the smuggler on this trip, but I wonder if the person has stopped."

"Why would he?" the captain asked.

"I talked with a man who used to be an emerald smuggler. At least, I think he was. He was definitely familiar with the business. He told me a tackle box full of emeralds could be worth thousands— even hundreds of thousands—of dollars. I wonder if your smuggler made enough money and quit."

"Smugglers never make enough money," the captain said. "There's no telling exactly how much he got for that box, but I doubt he made anywhere near its full value. Smugglers are fueled by greed and live for risk. This one won't stop. I read where the price of emeralds has gone up. Even so-so stones are selling for twenty-five percent more this year."

"Why the increase?" Helen asked.

"The rich are nervous," he said. "The market is unstable and they're putting their money in gold, diamonds and colored stones. If their securities tank, the stones are still worth something. If nothing else, their wives can wear them. You'll see our guests wearing fortunes.

"We aren't carrying a full complement of guests this time, so the smuggler will have more free time. He may grow bolder. If you don't discover him on this trip, you'll work the next one."

"I'll get him this cruise," Helen said. If she needed an incentive, she had it: Catch the smuggler or more hard labor on the *Belted Earl*.

"It's about time for me to pick up the owners and their guests at the airport," he said.

"Let me remind you: None of the other crew knows why you're here. This is my ship. You answer to me. If you have any suspicions about my crew, you come to me. Don't act on your own. Catching a smuggler can get you killed. Understood?"

It was the third time today Helen had heard that warning.

"Yes, sir," she said.

CHAPTER 19

Three black Lincoln Town Cars silently rolled through the marina, stopping in front of the *Belted Earl*. Dark-suited chauffeurs popped the trunk latches, then jumped out and opened the rear passenger doors on noiseless, oiled hinges.

Captain Josiah Swingle stepped out of the first car. He'd met the yacht owners and their guests when their private plane landed. With his sun-reddened skin and air of confident command, the captain was a handsome introduction to the *Belted Earl*.

The other men weren't as ornamental. Two wore silk Tommy Bahama shirts and beige pants. The third man wore a white polo shirt and navy linen pants. Helen noticed all their pants were wrinkled—proof the fabric wasn't adulterated with polyester.

Next, a tanned and toned blonde slid out of the first car. Helen guessed her age somewhere south of forty. Her long gauzy green caftan looked almost edible. She wore a savage gold necklace set with emerald nuggets. More emeralds dangled from her ears. Her outfit was outlandish and otherworldly. Helen couldn't guess the designer, but the clothes and jewelry shrieked money.

This must be Beth, the former model married to Earl Briggs.

Beth's dramatic entrance was spoiled by the yapping white fur-ball she cradled like a baby. Mitzi, the miniature poodle, Helen decided. The dog had a green bow in her curly white hair and a collar of dime-sized emeralds.

Beth took the arm of a portly fellow with a majestic belly and a noble forehead. Winged black eyebrows underpinned that great expanse of brow. Earl Briggs, the yacht owner.

Beth didn't walk in her high-heeled sandals. She strutted. The world was her runway. Earl looked proud to plod beside his exotic spouse. He wore the satisfied smile of a man who had everything.

Beth and Earl walked arm in arm up to the captain. "Evening, Captain," Earl said in a flat Midwestern accent.

"*Yap!*" said the poodle, then erupted in nonstop barks.

Earl fought to drown out the noisy dog. "I assume we're leaving at nine tonight?"

"I wanted to talk to you about that, sir," Josiah said, over Mitzi's yips and yaps. "We may want to delay our departure by a few hours."

"Why?" Earl asked. "It's a beautiful night." The eyebrows took wing and a frown flitted across his wide brow.

"*Yap!*" Mitzi said.

The frown deepened.

"*Yip! Yap!*" Mitzi barked louder. Helen saw the dog's pink tongue and tiny sharp teeth. The poodle wore enough jewels to pay the crew for a month.

"It's perfectly calm," Earl said. His own calm seemed to be receding fast.

"*Yip!*" The poodle's yaps grew shriller. They were needles in Helen's eardrums.

Earl winced slightly, then asked, "So what's the problem, Captain?" The frown dug deep furrows in his brow.

Mitzi's yaps grew into poodle pandemonium. Earl turned to his wife and said calmly, "Beth, keep that damned dog quiet before I shut it up permanently."

Beth backed away slightly and cuddled the poodle in her arms. "Sh! We must be quiet, baby," she told Mitzi. "I know you had a difficult flight, but your daddy had a hard day, too. He makes the money for you and your daddy's tired."

"I am not the father of a damned dog!" Earl howled. Beth flinched.

"I'm sorry, sweetheart," Earl said. "Can't you keep her quiet until I finish this conversation?"

Beth nodded.

"Now, Captain," Earl commanded, "explain why we can't leave at nine tonight."

"We're expecting rough seas, sir," Josiah said. "They're due to wind, not a storm system. Once we leave the coast of Florida, we'll be in four- to six-foot waves. You may want to wait until the sea is completely laid down."

"Is it safe to cruise?" Earl asked.

"It's safe, but it could be uncomfortable," Josiah said. "This trip will be similar to the last cruise back from Atlantis. If we wait five hours until the waves calm down, we'll have a smooth crossing. We'll still get into port tomorrow—about two o'clock in the afternoon."

"And if we leave at nine tonight?" Earl asked.

"We'll make it about ten in the morning," Josiah said.

"We'll lose half a day's gambling if we wait," Earl said. He turned to his guests. "What do you think?"

"Hell, I'm no coward." Thin and dry as beef jerky, this man had thick unnaturally white hair and a gin-burned face.

"Nor I," said the older woman next to him. She was a match for her mate: so thin she looked freeze-dried. Her wrinkles and iron gray hair were proudly untouched. Her deck shoes and navy-striped Lilly Pulitzer pants and shirt seemed practical after Beth's unearthly outfit. Helen guessed they were Ralph and Rosette, Earl's society friends.

"I'm no wuss. I want to start gambling." The third man's dome was aggressively bare and wreathed in cigar smoke, like clouds around a mountaintop. "As long as the scotch holds out, we'll be fine."

That must be Scotty, Helen thought. The fluffy blonde clutching his arm was his young wife, Pepper. She whimpered and her pink ruffles trembled. "I don't like being seasick," she said. Her face was hidden in waves of golden hair. "Can't we wait a little?" Pepper kissed Scotty's large, hairy ear. "Please?"

"Now, kitten, be good," Scotty said, "and I'll buy you something pretty at Atlantis."

"Emeralds?" Her eyes glittered with greed. "I like Beth's emeralds. Even her dog has bigger emeralds than me."

"Then we'll get you the biggest emeralds we can find," Scotty said, as if he were promising a child ice cream. "Once we get to the Bahamas, you can have lots of nice shopping. The captain and I won't let anything bad happen."

Helen expected him to pat Pepper on her head.

"Well, it's unanimous, Captain," Earl said. "Everyone wants to leave at nine tonight. If it's safe to cross, we don't care about a little discomfort."

The men didn't, anyway.

"Yes, sir," the captain said, his face expressionless. Helen suspected Josiah was a crafty poker player.

Matt, the bosun, and Sam, the deckhand, stood ready to carry the guests' luggage into the yacht. Matt was generically handsome, a catalog model with neat brown hair and regular features.

Sam was eye candy. His white uniform didn't hide his ripped chest and bulging calves, and it definitely set off his bronze tan. He had a roguish smile and sun-bleached hair.

Helen couldn't take her eyes off Sam. Neither could Pepper. Helen saw the fluffy blonde eye him like a starving woman staring at a steak. Her hips had a little extra swing when she pattered past Sam in her pink stilettos.

The rest of the crew lined up like a nautical receiving line, starting with Carl, the first mate. Andrei, the Bulgarian first engineer, had dark hair and swarthy, pitted skin. Dick, the second engineer, was a stair step down in rank and height. Chef Suzanne Schoomer, looking lost outside her galley, towered above him. Helen stood beside the chef.

The chief stewardess, Mira, had put on a new smile to greet the guests. This one looked forced. She balanced a tray of Baccarat champagne flutes. Louise, the second stewardess, was so small Helen wondered how she could support the heavy tray of salmon mousse appetizers.

The owner Earl nodded at the crew and lumbered inside. Beth stopped in front of Helen and said, "You're the new stewardess. Here. Mitzi needs a walk." She plopped the squirming poodle in Helen's arms. The dog yapped and scratched Helen's arm, trying to escape.

Helen hung on. If she lost that dog, she'd lose her job. "But—" She started to say she was supposed to unpack the guests' luggage, then stopped. The owner outranked Mira.

The chief stewardess intervened. "Helen has to unpack the guests' luggage," she reminded the owner's wife.

"Oh, the girls can unpack," Beth said. "They have to put away their jewelry, anyway. I'll take them downstairs. Helen can help them after she walks Mitzi." She pulled an emerald-studded leash out of her purse and hooked it to the dog's collar. Mitzi whimpered.

"Go on," she said, shooing Helen down the gangplank. "Walk Mitzi before we cruise. Then give her a bowl of bottled water." The dog whined and circled Helen's legs, tangling her in the leash.

"We've laid in Evian for her," Mira said.

"She doesn't drink Evian now," Beth said. "It upsets her tummy. She prefers Fiji water. I hope you have some on hand."

"We have six kinds of bottled water," Mira said, "including Veen, 10 Thousand BC and Bling H2O. Paris Hilton gives Tinkerbell Bling."

"That little tart would," Beth said. "Probably got a free case. Send someone out to buy Fiji. Send him. He's just standing there." She pointed at Andrei. His olive skin went a shade darker. The mighty engineer was not supposed to be an errand boy, but he started obediently toward the parking lot.

"Suzanne, did you fix Mitzi's food?" Beth asked.

"I baked the organic peanut butter treats she likes," the chef said, "and made her organic chicken and rice."

If I hate cleaning up after a dog, Helen thought, I wonder how our chef feels about fixing canine cuisine.

"Here, doggy," Helen said. She wasn't a dog lover and Mitzi knew it. The poodle stayed rooted to the teak deck. Helen gave up coaxing Mitzi, picked her up and carried her off the boat.

On the dock, Mitzi anointed the pilings while Helen said, "Good dog." When she got home, she'd give Thumbs an extra treat for being an uncomplicated cat.

She wished she'd brought along her BlackBerry. She was worried her sister would get a call from the blackmailer and panic.

"Hey!" a man said. "Should you be walking alone with thirty thousand dollars' worth of emeralds?"

Helen jumped and turned around. Andrei, the first engineer and Fiji fetcher, swaggered up to her as if he were the hottest man on the yacht. He had a cheesy seventies handsomeness. What did he use on his hair? Engine oil?

Andrei's small brown eyes looked shifty, but Helen wondered if she was influenced by the captain's suspicion that he might be the smuggler.

He held out a calloused hand. "Andrei," he said. "I was busy when Mira showed you around. Now I have to be an errand boy for this mutt. I should wring her neck and take the collar and leash. She's wearing round-cut emeralds. That's an uncommon cut."

"It is?" Helen asked. "Why?"

"The classic emerald cut yields a bigger stone with fewer inclusions."

Inclusions. Helen had heard that word before—from Max the smuggler. She decided to see how much Andrei knew. "What are inclusions?"

"Flaws," Andrei said. "Emeralds aren't as hard as diamonds. Too many inclusions can destroy the value." He crouched down to examine Mitzi's collar. The dog growled at him.

"Mitzi has ten round-cut emeralds on her collar and six more on the leash. The colors are fantastic and the polish is excellent. I'd say they're worth about two thousand dollars a carat."

"You know a lot about emeralds," Helen said. No wonder the captain was suspicious.

"I get around." Andrei flashed his white teeth. "What about you?"

"I live in Fort Lauderdale," Helen said, ignoring his double entendre.

"I mean, wanna hook up? She doesn't know how long it takes me to buy Fiji water, and it's going to be a long, hard night. I could give you something long and hard before we cruise."

What a sleaze, Helen thought. "Not interested. I have someone."

"Bet he's not as good as me." He thrust his hips forward.

Ew, Helen thought. "I'm busy," she said.

"Watching a dog pee?" he asked.

"Better than hanging with a hound," Helen said. She picked up Mitzi and carried her back toward the yacht. Why did Andrei have to look and sound like a classic villain?

It made this job tougher.

CHAPTER 20

Helen's two-way radio crackled as she was smoothing the duvet in the Paradise stateroom.

"Main salon head needs attention," Mira said.

"Roger that," Helen said.

Again? The yacht hadn't even left port and this was the third time Helen had cleaned that head. Pepper had used it again. Helen recognized her candy pink lipstick on the discarded tissues. The flossy blonde was not a good sailor. She would earn those emeralds.

Helen grabbed her cleaning caddy, slipped on another pair of disposable gloves, bolted through the secret passage and sprinted up the crew mess steps to the on-deck head.

She was greeted by chaos. Pepper must have showered in the marble sink. Water was splashed on the floor, the mirror, even the hand-carved wall sconces. Helen brushed the toilet bowl, wiped the sink and carefully blotted the droplets off the hand-painted wallpaper. Both hand towels were streaked with mascara and lipstick. She replaced them. That made six towels in an hour—for one head. No wonder the crew did laundry eighteen hours a day.

She emptied the wastebasket and wiped the fingerprints off the light switch. Pepper had washed her hands with the Bvlgari soap bar, so Helen opened a fresh one—the third bar so far—and pocketed the damp bar, used once. It smelled heavenly. She hoped she got to use it in the bath she shared with Louise.

She surveyed the room and mentally went through her checklist. She'd missed something. Toilet paper! She folded the tissue into a neat point. Done.

The yacht hummed and rocked slightly. Helen wondered how long before it hit the six-foot waves. On the way back downstairs, Helen caught a glimpse of the port at night. The lights sparkled like jewels and the stars were diamonds on black velvet. The water was smooth and black as obsidian.

She wished Phil were here with her to enjoy the view. Her wistful longing was interrupted by the padded sound of shoes on the thick carpet. Guests! She mustn't be seen. Helen picked up her caddy and disappeared down the stairs to finish the turndown service for the Paradise stateroom.

Scotty had unpacked his own luggage, and Helen wished he'd let her do it. He'd scattered cigar ashes over the carpet and desk and used a porcelain vase for an ashtray. She hoped the vanilla air freshener would disguise the cigar odor and it wouldn't seep into the other rooms.

Bimini was next. Scrawny little Ralph Randolph was a big slob. He'd spilled champagne on the built-in dresser. Helen gave Mira a frantic radio call and the head stewardess told her how to fix the damage to the oak finish.

Ralph's bathroom habits would shame a pig. Helen guessed she should be grateful Mrs. R. seemed neat. Her husband made enough mess for two people.

She wondered if she could get a minute to call her sister. She was worried the blackmailer would call Kathy again and demand more money. Her sister panicked every time he called. Last time she'd insisted Helen fly to St. Louis because Kathy was scared to leave the cash on the Dumpster.

Why shouldn't she be? Helen told herself. The creep was threatening Kathy's son—and your nephew. Your sister has every right to be afraid. You got her into this mess.

When Coronado Investigations started, Helen knew the day would come when she'd be stuck on a case when the blackmailer called. That's why, on her last visit, she'd put Kathy's name on Helen's local bank accounts. Now her sister could withdraw money without Helen. But she worried that Kathy would be too afraid to go to the bank if he called.

Helen thought the blackmailer enjoyed Kathy's fear almost as much as the money. She'll be crazed when she discovers I'm out of the country. I'll have to get her through this crisis long-distance.

But maybe the blackmailer hasn't called. Maybe I'm just borrowing trouble. If I could get two minutes with my phone, I'd know for sure.

She was halfway down the passage to her cabin when her radio sputtered. "Mrs. Crowne has left the on-deck head," Mira said.

Helen quietly cursed Pepper and her overbearing husband and went up the stairs with her cleaning caddy. Again.

About an hour out of Fort Lauderdale, the rough seas started. Helen kept running through the secret passage and up and down the steps, cleaning, scrubbing, folding toilet paper into points. The guests used so many towels she'd had to replenish the supply in the cabinet. She could feel the yacht bouncing a bit, but she wasn't sick.

I'm an old sea dog, she thought.

In a weird way, she was grateful for the ceaseless work. She didn't have time to worry about Kathy.

At eleven o'clock, the men retreated to the sky lounge for scotch and poker. Now Helen had two guest heads to clean and another flight of stairs to climb.

"I'm not feeling so good," Helen heard Pepper tell Beth and Rosette in the main salon. "I think I'll go to bed."

"You do that, dear," Beth said. "We'll stay here and talk."

The salon's sofas and end tables were securely bolted to the floor. Beth and Rosette, the society woman, seemed unfazed by the rough seas. Beth held Mitzi in her arms while the poodle whimpered. The two women sipped champagne, nibbled on snacks and delicately knifed reputations. Helen rested for a moment at the top of the crew mess stairs and listened.

Rosette waited until Pepper's footsteps faded down the main staircase, then said, "Really, I don't know why Scotty bothered marrying her."

"You don't?" Beth said, archly. "Her attractions are obvious."

"We can all see them," Rosette said. That "all" was etched in acid.

"I think she's rather sweet," Beth said. "She's better than that horror he had before Pepper. What was her name? Belinda? Blanche?"

"Blossom," Rosette said.

Helen nearly dropped her cleaning caddy. She leaned forward to hear more.

"I think Scotty paid that one by the hour," Rosette said. "What street corner did he find her on?"

"She was from somewhere in California," Beth said. "He flew her back on his plane and bragged she'd made him a member of the Mile High Club. Scotty has always had a taste for the demimonde."

"You don't have to be so delicate, darling," Rosette said. "He likes hookers. He told my husband he doesn't have to romance them—they're paid to worry about how he feels. He was feeling a bit battered after his last divorce. I don't care who he sleeps with, but he dragged that one to dinner with us. That was the limit. I pleaded a sick headache."

"If you'd seen the sleazy rag she wore, you really would have been sick," Beth said. "I couldn't escape. You stuck me with her. That was very naughty of you."

Did Scotty date Arthur's future wife? Helen wondered. Blossom was her trick name. Maybe lots of hookers used it. She did have outrageous outfits in her closet and an arrest for prostitution. Her clothes and behavior around Helen were impeccable, but Fran the housekeeper insisted Blossom had dressed to meet a man.

"Thank gawd Scotty came to his senses," Rosette said. "She mentioned getting married on the beach once too often and he finally put her on a plane back to whatever whorehouse she came from."

"Not before she stole his watch and who knows how much cash," Beth said. "Scotty was too embarrassed to report it."

"I think he got off cheap," Rosette said.

Helen jumped when she heard Mira clattering through the crew mess. "Helen!" the head stew said. "Why are you lounging on the stairs? Go see if Mrs. Crowne needs anything."

Helen shot through the secret passage to the Paradise stateroom, where she heard Pepper being violently sick. Then the bed creaked and there were alarming moans.

Helen tapped on the Paradise door. "Mrs. Crowne?"

"What?" Pepper gasped.

"Do you need anything, Mrs. Crowne?" Helen asked. "May I bring you some hot tea? Ginger ale? Dramamine?"

"Nothing works," Pepper said. "I've tried it all."

"Would you like your bathroom cleaned?"

"No, let me die in peace," Pepper said, and groaned like something from a newly opened grave. "Wait! Come in. You can get me something."

Pepper was shivering under the duvet, curled into the fetal position. Her creamy skin had a green tinge and her golden hair was plastered to her damp forehead. "I want a bucket," she said.

"Like a plastic scrub bucket. I don't want to keep getting up to

barf. I wish I'd never seen that salmon mousse. Oh, God, not again."
Pepper jumped up and streaked toward the stateroom's head.

Helen gently closed the door, then radioed Mira. "Give her one
of the small plastic buckets in the passage," the head stewardess said.
"You're lucky. Some guests use the wastebaskets."

By eleven thirty, the wind was stronger. On her trips upstairs,
Helen saw whitecaps on the black water. The boat was rocking like
the devil's cradle. Occasionally, she heard a crash as something slid
off a shelf. The chef, Suzanne, had packed the galley cabinets with
Bubble Wrap and was taping the doors and drawers shut. Mira and
Louise were securing dishes and ornaments. The deckhand and sec-
ond engineer had zipped the canvas covers on the deck furniture.
Now they were lashing it to the rails.

Helen felt queasy. She couldn't walk through the shifting secret
passage without barking her shins or hitting her elbow. Slowly, her
body got used to the yacht's movement. First the ship would plunge
down—taking her stomach with it—then rock back and forth until
the next big wave hit it hard and the process started over.

The wooden blinds swung and banged against the windows,
and the waves slapped the boat so loud Helen heard them when she
cleaned the sky lounge head on the third deck. The stink of Scotty's cigar hung in the sky lounge. Her queasy stomach did a backflip
and Helen raced downstairs to her cabin. If she was going to get
sick, she'd use her cabin head. It didn't have to be cleaned every
time.

Yeah, I'm a real old salt, Helen thought as she worshipped the
porcelain. She sat briefly on her bucking bunk. The room spun.

Her radio crackled into life. "Helen, where are you?" Mira asked.

"Sick," Helen said.

"You're not allowed to be sick," Mira said.

"Nobody told my stomach," Helen said.

"I mean it," Mira said. "You have to take hot tea, a soft-boiled
egg and saltines to Mrs. Crowne. Louise is taking care of Mrs. Ran-

dolph. I'm delivering an egg and toast to the missus. Come up to the galley now."

Helen ran into Louise in the secret passage, almost literally. She plastered herself against the wall while Louise tried to ease by with a tray loaded with gold-rimmed china and Baccarat crystal.

"A soft-boiled egg and ginger ale for Mrs. R.," the stew said. She was so tiny, she barely came to Helen's shoulder.

Carrying that tray must be a chore for her, Helen thought.

The ship made a sudden lurch and Helen reached out and caught the Baccarat glass before it tumbled over the side of the tray.

"Thanks," Louise said. "I can't afford to lose one hundred fifty bucks if that breaks. I wish I was off this damn yacht. I'm sick of waiting on rich idiots. Oops!" The yacht leaped again and Louise staggered down the passage and through the looking glass.

Later, Helen would remember that conversation.

It was the last time she ever spoke to Louise.

CHAPTER 21

Helen dragged her aching body up the stairs again, pulling herself up by the rail. She tried not to think about carrying a tray of food back down it. She had a job to do. She had a smuggler to catch. Nobody died of seasickness, did they?

At last, she was upstairs. Chef Suzanne presided over a shifting galley, where water sloshed out of steaming pots and sizzled on the Thermador stove top. Helen caught glimpses of other top-of-the-line brand names, including Sub-Zero.

Suzanne, a thin woman with straight dark hair and serious brown eyes, pointed to a napkin-covered tray on the center island. The chef had used thin, gold-rimmed china for the soft-boiled egg, saltines and tea.

"That goes to Mrs. Crowne," Suzanne said. "The men are asleep—or passed out—in the sky lounge. Mira covered them with blankets and they're snoring."

The boat took another downward plunge and Helen grabbed the railing along the counter to stay upright.

"How do I get this downstairs?" Helen asked.

"Walk with your feet wide apart for balance," Suzanne said.

"Keep them spread as wide as your shoulders. Hold on to the tray with one hand and the wall with the other. And be careful. That's Rosenthal china. Any breakage comes out of your pay. You'll have to check on your charge every fifteen minutes."

"She told me to go away once I delivered the bucket," Helen said.

"You still have to stay awake in case she calls you. Mira left a thermos of coffee in the crew mess. That should keep you awake."

Helen waited until the yacht was out of the deep swing and into the smaller rocking motions. As she started out of the galley, the yacht took another steep plunge. The china rattled and the gold-rimmed cup slid off the tray and smashed on the floor.

"It's only a cup," Suzanne said. "We have lots of those."

"Where's a broom?" Helen asked.

"I'll sweep it up. You get that food to the guest," Suzanne said.

"How much is it?" Helen asked.

"Eighty dollars," Suzanne said.

Helen hoped she could put the cost of the broken china on her expense account. She picked up the tray again. After what seemed like hours, she made it down the stairs and through the passage to Pepper's door. Her muscles ached from the effort to keep her balance.

She knocked, and found Pepper still huddled under the duvet.

"Put it on the nightstand," Pepper said as she tried to sit up. She was still wearing her pink ruffled outfit, now hopelessly wrinkled.

A small rail around the stand's edge kept the tray from sliding off. Helen poured Pepper a cup of oolong. She was shocked by the woman's pasty face. As Pepper sipped the sloshing tea, her color returned.

Helen had braced her legs to keep from falling as the yacht was slammed by another wave. She felt like she was riding a surfboard. The sea seemed to be getting wilder.

"Don't you get seasick?" Pepper asked.

"A little," Helen said.

"But you still have to work? That's awful," Pepper said. "I wouldn't do it."

I wouldn't marry a rich old man like Scotty, Helen thought, but said nothing.

"Sit down," Pepper said. "Talk to me. Those ladies upstairs are old and Rosette is mean. When I came out of the john I heard her tell Beth that I dressed like a cocktail waitress. Well, what's wrong with that? That's how I met Scotty. I always look nice. Rosette doesn't bother. She's just jealous. Don't you think?"

Pepper didn't want an answer, just a sympathetic ear. She prattled away as she sipped her tea. About ten minutes into the monologue Pepper said, "I guess my husband is still playing poker, huh?"

"He was. I think he fell asleep in the sky lounge," Helen said.

"Good," Pepper said. "I can be up and dressed pretty by the time he's awake. I wanted to fly to Atlantis and meet him at noon tomorrow. That's what everyone does. But he insisted on going with his buddies on the *Earl* and dragged me along. Well, he's going to pay. I'm getting emeralds and diamonds both."

Helen hoped Pepper planned to stash that jewelry. She suspected Scotty would dump her when she was no longer ornamental.

"You look like you're feeling better," Helen said.

"I am," Pepper said. "The tea helped. Do you know how I met Scotty?"

Helen sat in the stateroom, listening to Pepper drone on. Her radio didn't erupt into more commands. The boat's rocking gradually grew more gentle.

She sat up suddenly, wondering where she was. Then she heard Pepper snoring softly. Helen was sitting in Pepper's stateroom. She'd fallen asleep while Pepper had been talking.

The teacup and the saltine dish were both empty. The teapot was cold. So was the untouched egg. What time was it?

She checked her watch: five forty-three. She wished she could call Phil and tell him what she'd learned about Scotty and his hooker girlfriend. It might be connected to the Zerling case. But she had to report to work at six a.m.

Helen tiptoed out, carefully shutting the door, and opened her cabin. She hoped she could shower without waking Louise.

But Louise's bunk wasn't slept in and there was no light on in the bathroom. Poor Louise, Helen thought. She must have had to work all night, too. And she hates this job even more than I do.

Helen showered quickly and changed into her work uniform of shorts and a polo shirt, then climbed the stairs again. In the galley, the lights were blazing. The air was scented with coffee and cinnamon rolls were baking in the oven. Suzanne was slicing a pineapple on a cutting board. The tall woman had her dark hair tied back. This morning, she seemed worried.

"Morning, Helen," Suzanne said. "Have you seen Louise? She was supposed to help set up and serve breakfast."

"Not since last night about three o'clock," Helen said. "She was carrying a tray to Mrs. Randolph and I met her in the passage. Her bunk wasn't slept in. I thought she was working all night."

"Odd," Suzanne said. "She's so reliable. I've tried to radio Mira, but I can't reach her, either. She must have turned off her radio by mistake. The captain wants to go through Bimini customs at eight."

"Bimini? Aren't we cruising to Atlantis?" Helen said.

"Change of plans," she said. "A waterspout was reported to the south of us. The National Weather Service issued a warning."

"That's like a tornado, right?" Helen said.

"Right. It wasn't safe for us to continue the voyage. The captain found shelter in Alice Town and anchored. We'll clear customs this morning, then sail on. Expect the guests to be grumpy about this change in plans."

Helen looked out the galley window. The morning sky was dark and velvety, but she saw a narrow silver line on the horizon, the first sign of dawn. In the distance Helen could make out a white cabin cruiser. Two sailboats bobbed close to the yacht.

"There are some battered-looking boats down by the swim platform," Helen said.

"Oh, good," Suzanne said. "Hope they're fishermen. Maybe I can get fresh lobster or fish."

"You can buy fish from boats you don't know?" Helen said.

"That's how a chef gets the catch of the day," Suzanne said. "Local fishing boats bring it straight to the yacht. They tend to overcharge, but it's always fresh. Stay here and I'll be right back."

Suzanne ran out the galley door. Helen saw the fishing boats were moving away from the *Earl*. Now Helen heard a woman's voice—it was the missing Mira. She was talking too loud and too fast.

"I told her she shouldn't go," Mira said. "But she said last night was the last straw. Now she's gone."

"She can't be," Suzanne said. Her voice was lower and calmer.

"She took off in that cabin cruiser," Mira said.

Louise jumped ship? Helen had to know the details. She deserted her post and ran down the circular stairs to the swim platform on the lower aft deck. Suzanne, Sam and Carl were listening intently to Mira. Suzanne didn't notice that Helen had joined the group.

"Louise kept a stash of a thousand dollars' cash for emergencies," Mira said. "She said this was an emergency—she had to save her sanity. She paid that charter boat a thousand dollars to take her away. That white one there."

She pointed toward the horizon where the cabin cruiser was disappearing fast.

"I tried to stop her, but she pushed me away," Mira said. "Louise said she was desperate. I tried to hang on, but I couldn't. I hurt my knee and hit my head. Look."

Mira showed them a nasty scrape on her right knee and a dime-sized bloody spot on her scalp. "She pulled out my barrette," she said.

"I think we'd better report to the captain right now," Carl said.

CHAPTER 22

J osiah Swingle was dangerously angry. He did not shout when
Mira told him that Louise left the ship. If anything, his voice
was lower and calmer. But Helen saw his jaw muscles bunch as
he clenched his teeth. That was the only signal to beware.

The captain called an emergency meeting in the mess while the
crew ate breakfast. He looked tired this morning, though his uniform was fresh and he'd taken time to shave.

The crew was quiet. Their usual chatter had dried up. Suzanne
had set out breakfast for the staff. Helen grabbed a tortilla stuffed
with cheese, eggs and potatoes, and poured a cup of coffee. She sat
down at the table next to Sam. Even after a rough night the young
deckhand looked ridiculously handsome. He gave her a tentative
smile and scooted over in the booth.

Andrei sat on the other side, glowering at his coffee. Carl, the
first mate, had stayed on the bridge. Suzanne perched on the stairs,
ready to sprint up to the galley if she heard anyone come into the
dining room.

The captain stood in the center of the room.

Mira sat at the edge of the U-shaped booth and recited her story again. "Everyone knows that Louise was ready to quit," she said, looking around the room for confirmation. "She told all of us she was sick of working on the boat, didn't she? Well?"

After an awkward silence, Matt the bosun said, "That's true."

"I heard her say it," Andrei said.

"Me, too," Sam said.

"I bet she even told you, Helen," Mira said.

"She said she was sick of waiting on rich idiots," Helen said.

"Sh! Keep your voice down," Mira cautioned. "What if a guest heard you?"

"You asked," Helen said, trying to keep her voice mild.

"Louise may have complained," Suzanne said, "but we all do that. She's always been reliable. I don't believe she left. She might quit when we got to Atlantis—like the stew Helen replaced—but I can't see Louise leaving us in the lurch."

"You didn't work with her the way I did," Mira said. "Louise said the storm was the last straw. She knew we had at least ten hours of sailing today. She said she couldn't stand this yacht another minute. She was afraid she might hurt herself—or a guest."

Josiah Swingle was a judge listening to the arguments. Now he spoke for the first time since he asked Mira to give her account. "Why would a lone woman with a lot of cash go off on a strange boat in a foreign country?" he asked. "It's dangerous."

"It wasn't risky," Mira said. "She left on a fishing charter boat that operates out of Miami. The captain was anchored in the same cove as us. He was heading home and happy to have the extra money."

"What was the name of this boat?" Josiah asked.

"*Aces High*," Mira said. "It docks at the Miami Beach Marina with the other fishing charters."

"Describe it," the captain said.

"Typical charter fishing boat," she said. "Hatteras cabin cruiser, white with a tuna tower. Maybe thirty feet long. Well cared for. I don't know the size of the crew, but the captain said he had a party of four fishermen aboard. I think Louise saw the boat, flagged them down and offered the captain cash to take her home. I heard voices and came down to the swim platform. Louise was boarding the boat. She'd already handed her duffel to a crew member. I tried to stop her and that's when she fought me. Suzanne heard the commotion upstairs. By the time she came down, the boat was gone. Carl was there, too."

"I'll tell the Bahamian custom agents," the captain said.

"Will this make trouble for us?" asked Andrei, the first engineer.

"I don't think so," Josiah said. "I haven't cleared her into the country.

"Back to work, everyone. We're all behind schedule. The owners are going to customs at eight o'clock. I'll go with them. We have to present ourselves in person. You'll leave here at eight fifteen so I can clear in the crew."

The captain stalked off toward the bridge and the crew got their orders from their immediate supervisors.

"Helen, we have to do Louise's work as well as ours," Mira said. "Start the laundry, then go to the galley and help serve breakfast. The men are awake and out of the sky lounge, so I'll start cleaning it."

Mira was taking on a tough job, Helen thought. Scotty and his cigars left more ash than a volcanic eruption. She put her breakfast plate and cup in the crew galley dishwasher, threw two loads of towels in the washer and ran upstairs to the coffee- and cinnamon-scented galley. The chef seemed content in her kingdom.

"Finish setting up for breakfast," Suzanne said. "The guests could show up any moment—at least I hope so. They have to go through customs early if we're going to make Atlantis today."

Suzanne had prepared a buffet with colorful fruit salad in melon bowls, baskets of fresh-baked bread and muffins, bowls of Greek yogurt, granola, steel-cut oatmeal, crisp bacon, plump sausages and fried potatoes.

"All you need is an ice sculpture and you'll have a buffet big enough for a cruise ship," Helen said.

The chef peeled the tape off the cabinets and removed the Bubble Wrap that kept the china from shifting during the storm. Helen saw at least four sets of china.

"What service should I use?" she asked.

"The Spode Stafford Flowers on that lower shelf." Suzanne handed her a plate with delicate flowers and a scrolled gold rim.

"Pretty," Helen said.

"I'll say. It's eight hundred a place setting," she said. "We only bring it out when the sea is calm."

"My hands tremble at the thought of carrying it," Helen said.

"Just be glad you don't have to serve a formal dinner. Missus likes to use her Royal Copenhagen Flora Danica. That's seven thousand a place setting."

"I could trip and wipe out a year's wages," Helen said.

The footsteps on the guest staircase silenced their conversation. A rumpled, red-eyed Scotty staggered into the galley, trailing wisps of cigar smoke. He'd changed into fresh clothes, but still smelled like stale stogies.

"Got any coffee?" he asked. Exhausted by those three words, he sat in the dining room. Earl and Ralph followed a little later. Earl managed one word: "Coffee." Ralph grunted. Helen wasn't sure if that was a command or a greeting.

After a coffee infusion, the men ordered hearty meat-and-cheese-stuffed omelets with sausage, bacon and fried potatoes. Helen delivered the food without a mishap.

"Got any hot sauce, Chef?" Earl asked.

"Six kinds," Suzanne said. "Louisiana Hot Sauce, Tabasco sauce, Scorned Woman—"

"Stop! I'll take Scorned Woman," Earl said. "Don't bother with a sissy bowl. Serve it straight from the bottle."

Helen watched Earl drown his omelet in the fiery brownish sauce.

"Jeez, Earl, is your mouth lined with asbestos?" Scotty said.

"Best cure for a hangover I know," Earl said as the sweat broke out on his forehead.

"The best cure I know is to keep drinking," Scotty said.

All three men abandoned their breakfasts after a few bites. After two cups of coffee, Scotty was alert enough to ask, "Why are we anchored? This isn't Atlantis."

"Change of plans," Earl said. "Captain got a warning about a waterspout last night and dropped anchor off Bimini. We have to go through customs at Alice Town when they open at eight. If we're lucky, we'll get to Atlantis this evening."

"Think we better wake up the girls?" Scotty asked.

"Yap!" Mitzi said, and all three men winced.

"Beth is here," Earl said.

Beth was a vision in an indigo linen pantsuit and a heavy Native American squash-blossom necklace. Languidly beautiful, she rolled Mitzi in an aqua stroller and parked it beside her chair. The poodle wore a silver squash-blossom collar studded with dark blue lapis.

Mitzi yapped again and Beth saw her husband frown. She cooed at the little poodle and fed her organic chicken and rice from a Spode bowl.

Rosette, thin and dried as a strip of leather, showed up about seven fifteen in a nautical striped top and linen pants. She played with her oatmeal. Beth squeezed lime juice on a mango and tortured it while she stuffed Mitzi with food to keep her quiet.

Everyone drank gallons of coffee, but nobody was hungry, except Pepper. She arrived at seven thirty, looking outrageously fresh in a white off-the-shoulder top and tight emerald green pants.

Pepper cheerfully attacked three fried eggs, bacon and half a loaf of toast. "I feel really good this morning after barfing my guts out all night," she said.

Beth and Rosette glared at her but said nothing.

Scotty smiled his approval. "Good, you're up early," he said.

"I'm wearing my green outfit so we can go emerald shopping this morning," Pepper said.

"We're not shopping this morning," Scotty said.

Pepper's face fell and her candy pink lower lip trembled.

"We'll get your emeralds," Scotty said, gnawing on his cigar, "but the captain had to anchor in Bimini last night because the storm was so bad. We'll go through customs here at Alice Town. Because you've been a good girl, I'll buy you a bracelet *and* a necklace."

Pepper squealed and hugged Scotty. He patted her round bottom. Rosette looked as disgusted as Helen felt. How could a woman stand being treated like a child? she wondered. Maybe the little-girl act was worth a lot of grown-up jewelry.

At seven forty-five, the captain appeared. Earl stood up. "Customs opens at eight. Let's get moving," he said. "When do we get to Atlantis, Captain?"

"If we get back to the boat by nine," Josiah said, "it will take about half an hour to pull up the anchor and start the engines. If we're lucky, we'll be in Atlantis by seven thirty tonight."

"So we can shop for emeralds today!" Pepper said.

"And have dinner at ten at Atlantis," Beth said. "Mira, will you make reservations at Nobu for us?"

"What the hell's Nobu?" Scotty asked.

"Nobu Matsuhisa has like the hottest Japanese restaurants in the world," Pepper said. "We're lucky Atlantis has one."

"I don't want Japanese hash," he said. "I want real food."

"You can still get your boring old steak," Pepper said. "But, please, can't we go? I was so sick during that awful storm."

"And you can have steak for lunch, Scotty," Beth said.

"Time's a-wasting, people," Earl said. When he herded his guests down the gangplank, the crew breathed a collective sigh of relief. Fifteen minutes later, Carl led the crew through customs.

On the short walk, Helen straggled behind the others, puzzling over Louise's behavior and the captain's question: Why would a lone woman get on a strange charter boat with a purse full of cash? She didn't believe in blaming the victim, but that seemed like an invitation to rape and murder.

The soft Bahamian air, the warm April sunshine and Alice Town's tiny yellow, red and aqua buildings were a pleasant distraction. Helen loved the Bahamian voices—light, soft and musical with a hint of clipped British vowels.

At the customs shed, a Bahamian agent gave an official smile. "Welcome to Alice Town, Captain Swingle," he said.

"Glad to be here," he said. "I heard the waterspout advisory and found a safe harbor here last night. One of my crew was so shaken by the rough seas she went back on another ship."

Now the customs agent's smile vanished. "What is this woman's name?" he asked.

"Louise Renee Minette, of Fort Lauderdale," the captain said. "She's traveling back on a fishing charter operating out of Miami Beach, *Aces High*."

"I do not remember any woman passenger aboard a charter boat by that name this morning," the official said. "I will check the records. The charter can legally pick her up and take her back, but that captain has to clear her out of our country. If he did not, we will send customs agents after him."

Good, Helen thought. We'll know when Louise gets back to the USA—or if she doesn't.

"No worries, Captain," the official said. "She is not your responsibility anymore."

Josiah Swingle smiled, but it did not reach his eyes.

CHAPTER 23

"It's so big," Pepper squealed. "I forgot how big it is. Especially from this angle."

Mira was right, Helen thought. You could hear everything on the yacht—whether you wanted to or not. She eavesdropped while she collected empty Baccarat flutes as the yacht cruised into Atlantis.

Sunset stained the channel's wide pearly water a luscious pink. Helen and Mira had been serving drinks and appetizers for nearly three hours. Beth and Rosette took well-bred sips and nibbles. Pepper attacked the puff pastries and chicken skewers as if she'd been marooned on a Bahamian island.

Scotty had spent the afternoon playing poker and pounding scotch. He was a genial drunk. He called Pepper "my lucky lady" and sat her on his knee. Pepper's top was smudged with cigar ash, but she didn't seem to mind.

"As soon as we dock, we'll go shopping, just the two of us," he told her. "Aren't you glad you listened to me and went on the yacht?"

"No. I hurled all night," Pepper said, and treated him to a delectable pout. "But this is awesome."

Helen heard Rosette snort. "Awesome," she muttered to her husband. "Only that brainless nitwit would say 'awesome.'"

But Atlantis was awesome against the seashell pink sky. The monumental marina with its soaring granite walls and bronze dolphin sculptures could have been built by a god.

The Atlantis resort and casino is on Paradise Island, once called Hog Island. That name wouldn't do when Huntington Hartford, the A&P heir, bought the property: Pigs and groceries were a bad combination. He rechristened it Paradise and the name stayed even after he was gone. This earthly Paradise provided the fabulous sugar-sand beaches and clear aqua water for such movies as *Thunderball* and the Beatles' *Help!*

Only the rich were allowed into Hog heaven. The marina handled yachts up to 240 feet long and banned boats under 40 feet. In this company, the *Belted Earl* was only a midsized yacht. Helen thought the *Earl*, with its elegant curved hull, was handsomer than the tubby mega-yachts.

As the ship grew closer, they were hailed by a muscular dark-skinned man in a yellow speedboat.

"It's Action Jackson!" Mira cried. "He's the Bahamas' unofficial greeter."

Jackson was a bullet-headed man in a bright red cap who'd crowned himself the Limbo King of the Bahamas. He offered to take everyone on a tour.

"What fun!" Pepper said. "Let's go. We can meet the natives!"

"Don't encourage that revolting man," Rosette said. "Can't you do something about him, Earl? He's dirty and so is his boat. Look. He's attracting more vermin."

Now the yacht was surrounded by a flotilla of little boats offering pink conch, yellow bananas and hairy brown coconuts.

Helen didn't think Jackson was dirty. She liked his Bahamian lilt. Mira called Carl, the yacht's second-in-command, on the radio.

The white-uniformed Carl was nearly six feet tall, with a round, open face, shrewd eyes and no-color hair. He looked like the Western hero's best friend. He was under thirty and already developing sailor's sun wrinkles.

He climbed down to the swim platform. Action and the swarm of small boats followed him. Carl seemed to be talking more to another boat captain in ragged shorts and a faded T-shirt. Helen caught a few phrases: "not a good time"..."come back"..."you need to hide."

Hide? she wondered. Hide what? Did Carl tell someone on a little red boat, "See you ashore"? That couldn't be right.

Action left with a flash of his wide, white smile and a wave of his thick brown arm, and the smaller boats followed. Carl climbed back up to the guests.

"They're gone, Mrs. Randolph," he said.

"Thank goodness," she said. "With the crime rate in Nassau, I don't know why those people are allowed to approach yachts in the harbor."

"It would have been fun to limbo," Pepper said.

Scotty wrapped her in a bear hug. "But not as much fun as buying emeralds. Are you ready? We go as soon as the ship docks."

When the pink castle towers of Atlantis came into view, Pepper jumped up and said, "I want to see us dock." She dragged Scotty to the rail.

"Let's go, too, dear," Ralph said. "The view is magnificent."

Rosette rolled her eyes, but joined her stringy spouse on deck. Beth and Earl followed hand in hand, leaving Mitzi behind. The poodle ran inside and squatted on the salon carpet.

"Better walk that dog before they come back," Mira said. "Walk the dog" was the cleanup code. Helen got down on hands and knees to wipe up the dog pee, vowing to treat Thumbs to the finest catnip in Lauderdale and herself to a stiff drink when she was home.

"Come on out," Mira said. "When the yacht docks, two stews have to be on deck to stand by the fenders and make sure they're in place, in case something goes wrong."

Helen was amazed how quickly and smoothly the *Belted Earl* was docked. She'd had a harder time parallel parking in downtown Lauderdale.

"I'll meet you in the crew mess," Mira said, "and help with the laundry."

Mira was loading wet clothes into a dryer when Helen got there. The head stew looked annoyed. "Helen, why did you throw Pepper's clothes in the laundry?"

"Just the jeans," Helen said.

"Guests' jeans are dry-cleaned," Mira said, "unless they tell us otherwise."

She held up Pepper's jeans. They looked small. Helen hoped they hadn't shrunk in the wash.

"Now I'll have to take these to the Atlantis dry cleaner and hope they can be rescued," Mira said. "You haven't started any of the guests' ironing."

"I'll fold laundry and iron now," Helen said.

Helen's radio squawked. "Missus wants to see you in the galley," Suzanne said.

"Probably wants to talk about the dog," Mira said. "When you get back, work on the laundry. Don't forget to iron the guests' underwear."

Helen picked up Ralph's stained, ragged tightie whities. "Even the holey underwear?"

"Guest underwear is always perfect, no matter what the condition," Mira said, crisp as new cotton sheets. "Now run upstairs to the missus."

Helen had lost count how many times she'd sprinted up and down those steps. Mitzi greeted her with a welcoming yap in the galley, while her mistress continued with Suzanne's instructions.

"Scotty and Pepper are shopping," Beth said. "The rest of us are going to stretch our legs. We'll be back about eight thirty to dress for dinner at Nobu. You don't have to worry about making dinner tonight, Suzanne. We'll probably want something light when we return later this evening—actually, it will be more like tomorrow morning. The boys like to play poker until three or four."

"How about lobster salad?" the chef asked.

"That will do for the girls, but the boys will want more meat."

"I have enough Niman Ranch steaks."

"Good. They never get tired of T-bones."

"I'll make fries," Suzanne said.

"And onion rings," Beth said. "They love your onion rings. Make enough for all the boys and Pepper. That little girl has a big appetite. Oh, and maybe a light dessert. That's it. You don't have to do anything else."

Beth seemed oblivious that she'd given Suzanne orders for dinner for six people at three in the morning.

She turned to Helen. "Mitzi needs a walk. She had that little accident in the salon, but it's all gone now, thanks to Auntie Helen."

Great, Helen thought. I'm now a poodle's relative.

"Our little Mitzi girl was so excited, she just couldn't wait, could you, sweetie? Now it's time to tinkle again."

"*Yap!*" Mitzi said.

Beth handed the dog to Helen, as if presenting her a gift. Mitzi cuddled in Helen's arms. "She likes you!" Beth said. "I can't take Mitzi into Atlantis. They don't allow dogs, not even sweet doggywoggies like you, Mitzi. But Auntie Helen will take good care of you. Here's her leash."

Beth attached a work of art trimmed in Native American silver to the dog's lapis and squash-blossom collar.

"Enjoy your walk, baby girl," Beth said.

Mitzi yapped once, then licked Helen's nose.

"You're growing on me, fur face," Helen said as she carried the little white dog off the yacht. On the dock, Mitzi stopped at every post and piling while Helen praised her. "Good dog," she said. "The more you do here, the less work you make for me on the boat."

Helen enjoyed watching the marina, swarming with white-uniformed crews. Deckhands with bulging calves and thighs carried cases of beer and booze aboard the yachts. A female crew member in khaki shorts trundled a cart piled with pineapples, lemons and bananas. Near the entrance, Helen saw a tall brown-haired man in white shorts and a polo shirt. He looked a lot like Carl, the *Earl*'s second-in-command. A slender woman gripped his arm.

"Come on, Mitzi," Helen said, coaxing the poodle along the dock toward the pair. As she got closer, Helen saw that the man had the same lanky body as Carl. Ten feet closer and Helen stopped dead, Mitzi's leash wrapped around her feet.

She knew that round, open face. She recognized those squint lines. It was Carl. But it couldn't be. The first mate was on board with the captain and the Bulgarian engineer, wasn't he?

No, that was definitely Carl, talking to a dark-skinned woman with cropped hair and clean-cut features. Her navy Ralph Lauren shirt and shorts were no crew uniform. She was somewhere in her twenties, but she wasn't flirting. She handed Carl a black Prada backpack so heavy she nearly stumbled under its weight.

"Do what you can to get rid of them and don't forget my share," she said. "Be careful. This thing weighs a ton."

"Not to me," Carl said, buckling it onto his broad back. But he couldn't manage his usual easygoing amble. Carl struggled to walk under this burden, and stopped in surprise when he saw Helen.

His greeting sounded like an accusation. "Escaped your yacht chores, I see," he said.

"Nope. Got more work," Helen said, holding up the leash. "I'm in charge of Mitzi this evening. We're heading back now. Handsome backpack. Looks heavy. Do you need help with it?"

"Do I look so weak I can't carry a little backpack?" Carl asked.

But it's not a little backpack, Helen thought. It's huge. And I want to know what makes it so heavy.

Carl wasn't going to tell her. She changed the subject. "Are you surprised Louise jumped ship?"

"That's what Mira claims," he said. "The captain believes her, but I have my doubts. That fishing charter was too far away to have just left our boat. Besides, I know Louise. She's not a quitter. Even if she was sick of being a stew, she'd want a good reference."

"So where is she?" Helen said.

"I hope to God I'm wrong and she took that fishing charter," Carl said. "Otherwise, she fell overboard."

"Would she go out on deck during the storm?"

"Unlikely," Carl said. "The wind was so bad I could hardly open the bridge hatch."

"What are the chances of Louise surviving if she fell into the water?" Helen asked.

"None," Carl said. "Zero. Nada."

CHAPTER 24

Helen was the most popular crew member on the *Belted Earl* that night. She'd volunteered to take the twelve-hour watch that started at eight o'clock.

One crew member always had to be on board the *Earl*. Thanks to Helen, the rest could party after the owners and guests left for dinner. The crew needed that free time. They'd been tumbled around like clothes in a dryer last night, then spent the day cleaning, cooking and catering to the guests.

The crew cheered Helen and made extravagant promises.

"Can I bring you back a rum punch?" Sam asked.

"One lousy drink?" Matt the bosun asked. "That's all for a night of freedom? I'll bring you a whole six-pack of cold Kalik and a conch salad."

Helen laughed and shook her head.

"You can have three bars of Bvlgari soap," Mira said. "Only used once."

"Now, that bribe I'll take," Helen said.

"I'll make your favorite dessert for the crew dinner," Suzanne said. "Just name it."

"I like all your food," Helen said. "I don't have favorites. Well, maybe chocolate."

"Piece of cake," the chef said. "A double chocolate mocha cake."

"Sold!" Helen said, laughing.

"Seriously, Helen, I have to start working at midnight," the chef said. "I can come back at eleven if you need to get away."

"No, thanks," Helen said. "As soon as the guests leave, I'll finish the stateroom turndowns and the laundry. Then I want to rest."

Helen did want to rest. She also wanted to talk to Phil with no eavesdroppers. And search the cabin for clues to Louise's disappearance. The captain might believe she'd left the ship, but Helen had her doubts. She'd heard her gripe like everyone. But why would a hard worker like Louise abandon a good job—and a good paycheck— without notice? Why go home on a strange charter? Just because the unknown captain and crew were American didn't mean it was safe to travel with them.

She was shaken by her conversation with Carl. It had never dawned on her that Louise might have been lost overboard.

While the crew waited for the owners and guests to return from Atlantis, Helen and Mira prepared the party area on the upper aft deck for predinner cocktails.

"This is my favorite place on the yacht," Mira said, leaning against the rail. "It's perfect for a party: open to the island breeze with a canopy of stars."

"I'd love to stretch out in this chaise," Helen said, plumping the azure cushions. "And have someone bring me champagne."

She knew there was no chance of that. After they finished, Helen ran downstairs and threw in another load of laundry, then started the stateroom turndowns. Like all the crew, she watched the clock. It was now eight thirty-six. The owners and guests were late.

Earl, Beth, Rosette and Ralph straggled back at eight fifty-two, then settled into the teak lounges and rattan settees, laughing and lingering over drinks. Mitzi curled up at her mistress's sandaled feet.

Scotty and Pepper arrived at two minutes after nine. "I can't wait to show off Scotty's presents!" she said.

Soft music, flower-scented breezes and the slap-slap of waves on the hull lulled the yachters into a pleasant daze.

The chef, Mira and Helen pasted on smiles and prayed they'd leave for dinner soon. The clock hands were racing now, killing the crew's precious free time.

In between serving cocktails, Helen slipped on disposable gloves and cleaned the guest heads six times and answered yet another carefully coded call to "walk the dog." How big were the kidneys on a six-pound poodle? she wondered as she scrubbed the carpet.

At nine seventeen, Earl finally said the words the crew waited for: "What time are our dinner reservations?"

"Ten o'clock," Beth said.

Scotty checked his watch. "Then we'd better get in gear," he said.

"I can't wait to try the food," Pepper said.

"At Nobu's prices, she'll bankrupt him by dessert," Rosette whispered to Ralph. Her stringy spouse snorted.

Earl gently shooed his guests to their staterooms.

Helen and Mira hurried to clean up again. Helen came downstairs in time to see the guests leaving. Well-tailored black dinner jackets slimmed the tubbier men. Pepper looked like a Hollywood queen in a long white sheath and a glittering diamond-and-emerald choker and bracelet. She'd gotten her wish—her emeralds were bigger than Beth's. Helen thought the choker was an oddly symbolic choice.

Beth could still command a catwalk in her sleek black strapless column set off by vivid floral bands. Helen recognized the gown from Armani Privé's "homage to Japan" collection. Beth had arranged her blond hair geisha-style.

Rosette wore an aquamarine necklace and a prosaically pricey evening gown striped in Caribbean colors that bared her scrawny arms.

Helen could feel the group's almost theatrical excitement. They were looking forward to dinner—and to their own grand entrance.

Once they were gone, Mira rushed off to clean the master stateroom. Helen ran downstairs to take more towels out of the dryer and throw in a load of crew laundry. Mitzi trotted behind her. Helen poured the poodle some Fiji water, scratched her soft ears and carefully shut her in the crew mess. Its tile floors were easier to clean than the carpet. Mitzi happily chewed on a peanut butter treat.

The Paradise stateroom wasn't too bad, but Bimini was a wreck, thanks to Ralph. He flung his clothes about like confetti. The bathroom was unspeakable. The man wasn't as housebroken as Mitzi.

She was scrubbing the gold fixtures when she heard Mira scream: "Helen, what have you done?" She hurried into the crew mess.

"Why did you wash a red T-shirt with the white polos?" Mira asked. She held up a wet red shirt. "This is Matt's new T-shirt. You threw it in with the crew polos and dyed them pink."

"I'm sorry," Helen said. "What do I do now?"

"The rest of the crew laundry," Mira said, "so they have enough *white* shirts for tomorrow. And this time, separate the colors."

"Is there any way I can make up for this?" Helen said.

"You already did," Mira said. "You took tonight's watch. Everyone makes mistakes. Just don't do it again, okay?" She smiled. "It's ten thirty. I'm leaving."

"I'll throw in another load of guest towels after I ruin the rest of the crew's laundry," Helen said. Mira laughed.

Helen yawned. "I need to rest while the owners and guests are at dinner."

At last, Mira was gone and Helen was alone. Time to search the cabin she never got to share with Louise. Both bunks were made, their covers drawn tight. Louise's three drawers were empty. None of her things were in the closet. Nothing was under Helen's bunk.

She found traces of sticky tape on the wall over Louise's bunk. Did the stew take a family photo or boyfriend's picture?

Louise's toothpaste and toiletries weren't in the bathroom cabinet. Helen opened a bottle of aspirin and shook out two tablets—not worth packing. Neither was the small box of tampons. But it rattled oddly when Helen moved it. Inside was a prescription bottle for Louise Minette, filled with half-orange, half-white capsules. "Dilantin," the label read. What was that?

Helen fished her BlackBerry out of her purse and Googled "Dilantin." It was an antiseizure drug. Could Louise work on a yacht if she took that? Maybe that was why she'd hidden it. Would she leave it behind? If Louise had a seizure on the trip home, she could die. Unless she never made that trip. In that case, where were her luggage and her purse?

Helen would have to tell the captain what she'd discovered. In the meantime, she left the tampon box there.

I've found something, Helen thought. She punched in Phil's number. She felt like she'd been away for a month instead of a day.

"Helen!" he said. "I've missed you. I had a break in the case."

"Tell me," she said.

"I can't use names on a cell phone. Too risky. I followed the lady this afternoon—or rather Bob the Cool Guy did. He drove north to Deer in the Headlights, a bar in Deerfield Beach. Cool Bob got out his toolbox and followed her into the bar. Let me tell you, she was one hot widow in a red strapless top, skintight black pants and red heels."

"You're quite the fashion expert," Helen said.

"Bob is a trained observer," Phil said. "He observed the subject throwing herself into the arms of a shaggy-haired surfer dude. He must have been in mourning, too. He wore a tight black T-shirt and jeans.

"Bob told the waitress he was there to check the air-conditioning vents. He went around the corner from the lady and Surfer Dude's booth, opened his stepladder and unscrewed the vent cover. Bob heard everything the lady and the dude said."

"Very cool," Helen said. "What was it?"

"I'll tell you as soon as you get back," he said.

"Can't you give me a hint?" Helen begged.

"All I can say is our client was right. The lady has a boyfriend."

"Anything else?" Helen asked.

"Oh, yes," Phil said. "Your sister's called four times so far tonight. She won't say why, but she wants to talk to you, no matter how late."

"I'll call as soon as I hang up," Helen said, hoping her voice didn't shake. She had a good idea why Kathy had called.

"How about you?" Phil asked. "How was your trip?"

"Rough," Helen said. "A waterspout was sighted and we had to find a safe harbor in Bimini. Then Louise the second stewardess disappeared—or quit; I can't tell which. She supposedly hitched a ride home on a Miami fishing charter. The Bahamian officials are looking for her. But Louise left behind some seizure medicine. I think that points to a disappearance."

"Why would she quit like that?" Phil asked.

"She's sick of her job and wants to be with her boyfriend in Fort Lauderdale. I heard her say that myself. But if she didn't take that charter boat, she must have fallen overboard. That means she's dead, Phil. It makes me sick to think about it.

"Oh, and a guest used to date a hooker with the same name as our client's stepmother. Can you e-mail me the photo you took of her? I want to show it to the captain."

"And the other staff, too," Phil said.

"No, I'm supposed to be undercover," Helen said. "There's a lot going on here. I think the first mate is smuggling something. The creepy first engineer, Andrei, met some guy at the Lauderdale marina and he may have made plans to meet up with someone tonight. Everybody is off the yacht now except me. Wait a minute! Phil!"

"What? Helen, talk to me."

"There's a little boat approaching the yacht," Helen said. "It doesn't have any running lights. Stay on the phone with me until I know who it is."

Helen peered out the window on the main deck. "It's the Bulgarian engineer. He's staggering drunk and carrying something in his backpack. How did he get so smashed in two hours? He's coming in by the swim platform. I'd better watch him in case he falls."

"Helen! Don't do anything stupid."

"He's so drunk he's in more danger of hurting himself than me," Helen said.

"Don't hang up," Phil said.

"Sh!" she said. "He's aboard now, crashing around the lower aft deck. I'll stay up on the main deck."

Helen heard knocks, thunks and a curse as the Bulgarian engineer made his way to the crew mess. Then she heard a tremendous crash and a yip. What if that brute kicked the poodle?

"I think he hurt Mitzi," Helen said. "I'm going downstairs to check. I'll keep the phone on."

"Helen! What do I do if anything's wrong?"

"Call the captain's cell phone. You have his number."

Helen slipped her phone into her pocket and cautiously made her way down to the crew mess. Mitzi was cowering behind a laundry basket. The Bulgarian engineer was gobbling cold leftover pasta out of a plastic bowl. Next to him was a backpack with a square bulge.

"Helen!" His smile revealed yellow teeth. His accent was thicker when he was drunk. "Have surprise for you. You like chocolate, no?"

"Yes," Helen said.

"Good. I bought big box of chocolate liqueur. Gourmet chocolate bottles filled with Jack Daniel's, Grand Marnier, Cointreau, Baileys Irish Cream." He patted the backpack. "You have some with me?"

"Sure," Helen said. She wanted to see what was in that backpack.

"All ladies like chocolate," he said, and exposed more teeth. Andrei would have to drink his women into bed, Helen thought.

Andrei stood up. "I take piss first. Then we open chocolate and be friends."

Classy as ever, Helen thought.

Andrei opened the hatch to the crew cabins and stumbled down the passage.

Helen could hear Phil sputtering and shouting, even though the phone was in her pocket. She took it out.

"What the hell are you doing?" Phil shouted. "He's drunk and you're on that boat alone with him."

"I have my cleaning caddy with me. I can shoot him in the face and blind him. I have to hang up now and see if Mitzi is okay. I'll call you as soon as I can."

She hung up over Phil's furious protests.

CHAPTER 25

∙ ∙ ∙ ∙ ∙ ∙ ∙ ∙ ∙ ∙ ∙ ∙ ∙

Helen heard hoggish grunts and swinish snorts coming from a crew cabin in the passage. Andrei, she decided. She slid open the door. The Bulgarian engineer was sprawled motionless on the lower bunk, mouth open, left arm flung out. His chest wasn't moving. Maybe he was in a coma. Or dead. She'd read about death from alcohol poisoning and Andrei had drunk a lot in a hurry.

Helen moved closer to check. She wasn't losing a crew member on her watch. The engineer erupted in a loud snort and an explosion of alcohol fumes. She leaped back and softly shut the door.

Andrei was dead drunk, not dead.

Time to open that backpack he'd abandoned in the crew mess. The boxy bulge inside tantalized her. It was the right size for a haul of emeralds. Helen wanted Andrei to be the smuggler. He was the most dislikable crew member. Once she caught the smuggler, this case was closed. She'd stay as a stew until the boat docked in Fort Lauderdale, but then she'd be free.

A whimpering Mitzi met Helen at the crew mess hatch. She was limping slightly. Helen picked her up. The poodle was warm, soft and light as a powder puff. As she petted her, Helen gently felt the tiny body for bruises or breaks. Mitzi didn't yelp when she touched her.

"Good girl," Helen said, gently setting the little dog back on the floor. "What meanie would kick you?"

She fetched Mitzi another peanut butter treat. Mitzi sat up and danced.

"I think you're okay, girl," she said. "I didn't see Andrei kick you, but I'll let the captain know he has a possible puppy abuser on board."

"*Yap!*" Mitzi said.

"Sh! Don't wake him. I'm trying to get him arrested for smuggling."

The bright-eyed poodle wagged her tail. Helen quickly unzipped the backpack. She saw green. Lots of green.

A huge dark green box marked "Fine Chocolate Liqueurs."

No! That couldn't be. There must be some mistake. There had to be. The box was shrink-wrapped with plastic, so she couldn't open it. Helen rattled it.

That was not the sound of loose gemstones. Helen's heart sank. Andrei was no smuggler.

She took out her phone and checked her messages. She had one from Phil with an attachment and twenty-six from her sister, Kathy. She listened to Kathy's first message. Her little sister was crying with fright. "Helen, it happened. I knew it would. You have to call me *now*! Please. I don't care if it's two in the morning."

Helen didn't bother listening to Kathy's other messages. She could almost see her sister anxiously pacing in her homey kitchen. I did this to you, Helen thought. You had a perfect life in the burbs until I married Rob and put you on the road to worry. No wonder your hair is getting grayer.

Kathy must have been sitting next to the phone. She answered on the first ring in a heartrending whisper. "Helen! What took you so long? Never mind, Phil told me. You're in the Bahamas. You have to come home now, Helen. He's alive and he wants thirty thousand dollars."

"Who's alive?" Helen asked.

"Rob!" Kathy's voice was a stifled shriek, the sound of a mouse caught by a bird of prey.

"How do you know?" Helen asked.

"Because he talked like Rob. He used that voice-changer thingy again, but only Rob says those things."

"Kathy," Helen said. "Slow down and tell me exactly what was said."

"Okay, okay. He called right before Tommy came home from school. He said, 'Tell Sunshine if she wants to keep her nephew out of the newspapers, I need sixty thousand.' Rob always called you Sunshine."

"It's a common nickname, Kathy." But Helen felt the panic clawing her insides. Rob couldn't be alive.

"He also said a good Catholic like Mom would be happy that her favorite son-in-law was buried in the church. It's him. I know it's him."

"Kathy, that proves nothing," Helen said. "The blackmailer saw us bury Rob in the church basement. The whole neighborhood knows Mom was super devout." Inside, the panic broke loose and scrabbled up her rib cage, trying to crawl out. Helen had kept this secret too long.

"He said you owed him thousands and he was going to collect every nickel," Kathy said. "It's Rob."

It sure sounds like my greedy ex, Helen thought. But Kathy and I tried every test we knew to make sure Rob was dead. There was no movement, no detectable heartbeat, no breath. How did he survive?

Because he's Rob. If the nation was nuked, only Rob and the roaches would crawl out from the ashes. Her mind was racing. He was alive.

"Helen, are you there?" Kathy asked.

"Kathy, this is good news," Helen said. "If Rob is the black-mailer, he can't call the police. Ever. He'd have to admit he was blackmailing us. If he made it out of that basement alive, he should have told the police right away. Instead, he acted like Rob and started demanding money from me. Don't you see, Kathy? This is good news. Tommy is off the hook."

"Unless I'm wrong and it's not Rob," Kathy said. "Then we're in trouble. Can't you come to St. Louis?"

"No, honey," Helen said. "I'm out of the country. I won't be back for at least four days."

"What should I do? He wants the money tomorrow."

"Pay him," Helen said. "We knew this might happen. That's why I set up the joint accounts. That's my share of the money from the sale of the house Rob and I had. I've lived without it so far. It will buy us a little peace of mind. Get thirty thousand in cash and give it to him."

"And then what?" Kathy's voice trembled. "He'll call again and he'll want sixty thousand dollars. He doubles his demands each time. You don't have that kind of money."

"We'll catch him next time," Helen said. "I promise. Just pray it really is Rob. Then Tommy will be free—we'll all be. I have to hang up, Sis. You'll be okay."

"Promise?" Kathy sounded younger than her four-year-old, Allison.

"Absolutely. I love you," Helen said. "I have to call Phil."

Boy, did she have to call Phil. He'd left ten messages while she'd talked to her sister. She opened the attachment first. It was a good shot of Blossom, with silky black hair, red lipstick and skintight jeans.

Helen tried to head off Phil's anger by a rapid-fire announce-ment: "It's me, I'm fine. Kathy's fine. Andrei is not the smuggler."

"But—" Phil said.

Helen didn't allow him an opening. "Cut the lecture," she said. "You don't need to protect me. If I'm your partner, you have to trust me."

"Trust you!" Phil yelled. "Partners keep each other informed. What you did was—"

Helen heard a clunk and checked the security camera. A short young woman was coming up the gangplank, carrying a huge load of something. Blankets? Clothes? Helen could see only her blond hair and muscular legs. Mira.

"The head stew is back," Helen said. "Love you." She hung up.

Mira seemed to be hauling a bale of sequins, chiffon and ruffles. Her small, pretty face looked more doll-like than ever surrounded by taffeta and satin.

"Can you help me carry this?" She didn't wait for an answer. Mira plopped half the pile into Helen's arms.

Evening dresses, Helen thought. With grimy hems, grubby trim and a slight scent of sweat and mildew.

"Where did you get the fancy clothes?" Helen asked.

"Little secondhand shop in Nassau," she said. "I can't wait to show my boyfriend."

She held up a formfitting red evening dress that looked too long for her. Then she pulled out a shopworn rainbow—green, gold and blue—sparkling with sequins, jewels and bugle beads. There were filmy formal skirts and a passel of ruffled petticoats. Some of the dresses were bedraggled. Others had split seams and missing beading.

Helen searched for some tactful words. "Where will you wear them?"

"Oh, they're not for me," Mira said. "I bought them for my boyfriend."

"And he's a—?" Cross-dresser? Helen wondered.

"Actor in a Fort Lauderdale theater company," Mira said. "They're doing a production of *Rain*. The real production, not the watered-down version like that movie where Sadie Thompson was a nightclub singer. In Kevin's production, she's a whore with flashy clothes. I got this whole lot for twenty bucks. The clothes need a little work, but the company has a seamstress who can fix anything. They'd cost a fortune in Fort Lauderdale, even in this state. Good, the crew mess table is cleared. I can sort them there."

Helen's stomach turned at the thought of eating off a table that had held those dirty clothes. "Can we put down something first?" she asked.

"Good idea. Use the drop cloth in the cabinet."

Helen put her pile on the floor, then spread out the drop cloth. Mira dumped her mound of gaudy dresses on the table. Helen heaped hers next to them. A worn red velvet gown with fake rubies at the neck slid off the table. Mira caught it, folded it neatly and started another pile.

"It must be fun to date an actor," Helen said.

"It is," Mira said, folding a clingy black dress. "I like Kevin's job and his friends. Even though they're actors, they're more real than the people on this yacht. The owners and their friends, I mean."

"Sounds like you're tired of your job," Helen said.

"I am. It's no secret. I've been a stew for five years," Mira said. "I'm nearly thirty. It's time for a change. The money is good and I've managed to save some. I'm going to invest in Kevin's theater company. They're short of money, like most companies, and if they don't get a cash infusion soon, they'll close. Kevin would be lost without his theater. I want him to be happy."

"Is this your last trip on the *Earl*?" Helen asked.

"No, I have one more and then my contract is up. I can't wait to collect that last paycheck. Then I'm outta here. What about you? You have a boyfriend, right?"

"Phil," Helen said, and smiled. "I can't wait to see him when we get back."

"I can tell by the way you smiled this dude is the one," Mira said, folding a pale blue gown with sparkles on the full skirt.

"He is," Helen said.

"Good," Mira said. "Then I don't have to deliver the lecture about island men I give the new stews."

"Tell me anyway," Helen said.

"A lot of island men are good-looking. They have pretty accents and lovin' ways. The girls think what happens in the islands doesn't count. So they have an island boyfriend or two and think the dude back home won't ever know. But some of those handsome men give our young stews souvenirs—the kind that are hard to cure."

"Got it," Helen said.

"It's not just the stews," Mira said. "I've known a wife or two who told her husband she was spending the afternoon at a spa. It wasn't a facial that gave her that glowing complexion."

Mira folded the last dress, a grimy white formal with a rhinestone bodice. Now she had a stack nearly as tall as she was. "These are too bulky to keep in my cabin," she said. "I share with Suzanne and we can barely move around."

"Want to keep them in my cabin?" Helen said. "You can put them on Louise's side of the closet."

"That's very generous," Mira said. "But I'd better not, in case they have fleas or roaches. Lots of critters in the tropics, and some of them hitchhike home. Suzanne nearly dropped a plate when a big spider crawled out of some bananas she brought on board."

"Ick." Helen shuddered.

"I'll pack these in a waterproof duffel and store it in the bosun's locker."

"Aren't you afraid someone will take them?" Helen asked.

Mira laughed. "If the boys unzip this bag and see ruffles and sequins, they'll drop it like it's hot."

CHAPTER 26

· · · · · · · · · · · · · · · · ·

S am was drunk as a sailor.

At three in the morning, the deckhand staggered up the gangplank with a bottle of rum, stumbled through the aft deck and tumbled down the steps into the crew mess. He stayed flat on his back, not moving. His sun-streaked blond hair hung in his eyes. His mouth hung open.

Helen, who'd been nodding off over a mug of coffee at the table, was instantly awake. "Sam, are you hurt?" she asked. "Say something."

"Oops!" he said, and waved the half-empty rum bottle in the air.

Okay, his right arm isn't broken, Helen thought.

"Can you sit up?" she asked.

"Don't wanna. Room keeps spinnin'," he said.

Then he sat up and cradled the bottle. "Saved the rum. Save the baby rums. They're en-endangererer—in trouble!"

"Right," Helen said. "Let's get you to bed. You have to get up at six."

"Cap'n back yet?" he asked.

"Everybody's here except the owners and guests," Helen said, taking his arm. "We don't want them to see you. Come on. Time to go to your cabin."

Sam grabbed the crew mess table and pulled himself upright, swaying as if the yacht were plowing through heavy seas. Helen put her arm around his waist and guided Sam down the crew passage.

The deckhand was at that stage of intoxication where he loved the world. "You're nice," he said. "You got a boyfriend?"

"Yes," Helen said.

"Thought so. Nice girls all got boyfriends. The good ones are taken. That leaves the bad ones for me." Sam gave Helen a lopsided grin. "Lots of those. Mira's a nice girl, too." He hiccuped. "An' she has a boyfriend. We're friends. Just friends. Me and Mira. 'Cause Mira's a nice girl. She'd do anything for Kevin. She said she'd steal for him, even kill for him. She loves him that much. She tole me."

"Good for her," Helen said, sliding open the door to the cabin Sam shared with Matt. The bosun was curled up asleep.

"Sh!" Helen said, and pulled back the blanket on the lower bunk. Sam fell on it, fully dressed. Helen pulled off his deck shoes. By the time she'd covered up the deckhand, he was asleep, his arms wrapped about the rum bottle like it was a teddy bear.

Helen's radio crackled at her belt and she hurried out before she woke up Matt and Sam.

"I need you to help set up," the chef said. "Mira will serve and you'll clean."

Helen was groggy after nearly two days without sleep, but she didn't break any gold-rimmed china.

Mira reported to the galley puffy-eyed, her face scrubbed clean, her blond hair drooping. She struggled to hide a yawn.

Suzanne seemed surprisingly alert, as if working in her galley invigorated her. The chef's white uniform was fresh and her long dark hair was neatly tied back. The galley was far cleaner than Helen's kitchen.

The late-night feast was ready for the final preparation: The onion rings were battered, the fries were cut and the grease was bubbling in the deep fryer. Thick, marbled steaks rubbed with garlic waited for the grill. The lobster and avocado salads chilling in the fridge looked like pink and green abstract art.

Helen's stomach growled when she saw them. "They're gorgeous," she said, shutting the fridge door.

Suzanne was whisking something in a saucepan with sure, swift strokes.

"Do I smell chocolate?" Helen asked.

"Sure do. That's a chocolate lime rum cake on the counter," Suzanne said. "I'm finishing the sauce—it's caramelized sugar, dark rum and lime juice."

"That cake looks moist," Helen said, hoping Suzanne would get the hint.

"It is," the chef said. "It's also for the owners and guests."

It was nearly four o'clock when Beth, Earl and their guests returned. The men's tuxes looked rumpled and Scotty's jacket was sprinkled with cigar ashes.

"I'm starved," Earl said. "When's dinner?" He'd untied his bow tie and the ends dangled on his pleated shirt.

"I want a T-bone," Scotty said. "Auto-accident rare."

"I could eat a horse," Pepper said.

"Told you that Japanese hash wouldn't be enough," Scotty said.

"But it was amazing," Pepper said. "And I can tell everyone I was there." Pepper hadn't lost her sparkle, even at four a.m. Neither had her jewelry.

Beth was glamorous, but a little worn. Rosette looked like a plucked chicken in a designer dress.

"I could do with a nibble," Beth said. "We'll have our lobster salads as soon as the steaks are grilled, Mira."

"The chef says the steaks, fries and onion rings will be ready shortly," the head stew said. "She's starting them now."

"Let's have a drink while we wait," Earl said.

The first round of scotches and champagne disappeared faster than water in the desert. The second went almost as fast. Suzanne was plating the steaks, fries and onions when Beth told Mira, "It's four thirty. We're tired. We're going to bed."

"No food, then?" Mira asked.

"No," Beth said. "Good night."

The party rose, yawning and stretching, and strolled off to their staterooms without another look back. Helen saw Pepper heading for the guest head and knew she'd be looking at more cleaning. She stayed out of sight, found her caddy and slipped on another pair of disposable gloves. Sure enough, Pepper had splashed water around like a sparrow in a birdbath.

I've either cleaned the last head of the night, or the first of the morning, Helen thought, as she stripped off her gloves and carried the towels down to the crew mess. She'd start the laundry in an hour and a half.

Her radio crackled again. "Help me clear, Helen," Mira said.

The two stews had the dining room dusted and sparkling in twenty minutes.

"Nobody ate anything?" Helen asked, as she polished the dining room table.

"Not a crumb," Mira said. "They had too much to drink. Scotty, for all his talk about wanting a T-bone, was snoring in his chair after his second scotch. Pepper had to wake him up to go to sleep."

"They didn't even apologize," Helen said.

"Don't have to," Mira said. "They're guests."

"What happens to the food?" Helen asked Suzanne.

"Would you like a lobster salad or a T-bone?" the chef asked.

"Can I have both?" Helen asked. She'd nuked leftovers for her dinner. They were delicious leftovers, but that was hours ago. She was hungry.

"Fries and onion rings, too, if you want," the chef said.

"And a slice of cake?"

"No," Suzanne said. "I haven't put the sauce on the cake yet. It will be good tomorrow. I guess that's today. Either way, the cake will still be fresh in a few hours."

She fixed Helen a plate heaped with steak, onion rings and fries, and handed her a lobster salad. "Go eat in the crew mess," she said. "I have to bake bread and muffins for breakfast."

"Aren't you angry that they didn't eat your meal after all your work?" Helen asked.

"It's part of the job," she said, and shrugged. "That's why they pay me so well. Like I said, it's their money and their food. If they eat it or throw it out, it's all the same to me.

"Now, shoo. You have to start work in a little over an hour."

Helen wondered about Suzanne's unnaturally calm acceptance. Was it real? Or was she hiding her anger?

CHAPTER 27

"Why were you staring at him?"

Helen heard a man's voice—raging, demanding, drunk. Scotty? It couldn't be. He was such a good-natured guest, playing poker, pounding down scotch and patting Pepper's bottom. Mira had said that he was jealous, but Helen had never seen his surly side.

Now she heard his snarl clear back in her cabin.

"I didn't do anything. He was our waiter. Of course I looked at him." Pepper. She sounded frightened.

"You weren't looking at his face," Scotty roared. "You were watching his ass."

"No, I wouldn't do that." She was pleading. "You know I love you. Let me show you how much. Let—"

Scotty cut her off. "I don't want to hear it. I know what I saw."

Helen stepped into her shower, eager to avoid Pepper's groveling. It hurt to hear the woman humiliate herself. Helen would hide behind a curtain of water until it was over.

After she and Mira had cleared up the dining room this morning and Helen ate her lobster salad and T-bone, she had only forty minutes before she had to report to work. There was no chance to sleep. A brisk shower would have to revive her.

Helen stepped out of her box-sized bathroom in a cloud of steam and heard, "I said I was sorry. But I didn't look at him, except as a waiter. Please believe me." Pepper was crying and begging.

"You're lying." Scotty's voice was a dangerous rumble.

"I swear. Ask Beth. Ask Earl. And Ralph and Rosette. They were at our table. They didn't see anything."

"I'm not asking," Scotty said, his voice a whipcrack. "If our hosts and friends didn't notice your outrageous behavior, I'd rather they didn't find out what a slut you are."

"I'm not a slut," Pepper wailed. More weeping. Then silence. Helen hoped Pepper would pack her jewelry and leave, but she knew the little blonde wouldn't abandon her steak-eating sugar daddy.

Helen dressed quickly and brushed her hair, trying to ignore the murmurs and sighs drifting her way. Pepper's voice was light and teasing. "You know I love you. Let me do it the way you like. Come on. Don't be a stubborn old silly."

The silence changed to low moans and grunts. Makeup sex, Helen thought. She shut her cabin door and ran into the mess, where she was greeted by the crew eating breakfast. Sam winced when they shouted hello, and gulped more coffee. His face was pale under the tan.

"Helen! It's steak and eggs for breakfast," Matt said. "T-bones, the breakfast of champions. Join us."

"Thanks. I ate an hour ago," Helen said. She threw in two loads of towels, relieved that her chattering colleagues and the roaring washers drowned out the sounds of Pepper and Scotty in bed.

Helen heard Scotty whistling when he strolled out to the aft deck for breakfast an hour later. She was glad Mira served him. Helen didn't think she could look at the man. She'd liked him before she'd heard him arguing. Helen bet Pepper wasn't whistling this morning.

Her radio erupted. "Mrs. Crowne requested a cleanup in her stateroom," Mira said.

Helen grabbed her caddy and rushed through the passage, wondering what kind of damage the couple had done during their fight.

"Come in," Pepper said, when Helen knocked on the door to Paradise.

Pepper saw a bare-backed Pepper sitting at her dressing table, combing her bouncy curls. At first, Helen thought she was naked. Then she realized that Pepper was wearing a pink halter top cut low in the back—and probably the front. Her tight pants gripped her bottom. Pepper will do anything to keep that rich old man, Helen thought, and felt sorry for her.

The stateroom was neat, except for the clothes on the floor and the rumpled bed. She tried to block the picture of Pepper placating Scotty on those sheets. A half-empty glass of red wine was abandoned on the nightstand.

"How may I help?" Helen asked.

Pepper turned to face Helen, her eyes glittering with malice. "I had a little accident in bed," she said. She walked over, picked up the red wine and poured it on the sheets.

Helen stared. She couldn't believe Pepper had deliberately poured wine on the bed.

"Fix it," Pepper said. "That's your job, isn't it? I'm going to breakfast." She slammed the door to Paradise.

Helen stripped the bed while she muttered to herself. "I can't believe I felt sorry for you, bimbo," she said, pulling off the duvet.

"I hope he screws you blind." She ripped the pillows out of their cases.

"You deserve to live with Blubber Bucks until you're so old you have to pay young men to get in your bed." Helen yanked off the sheets.

"You had an accident in bed, all right. You crawled between the sheets with that cigar-smoking snake." Helen had stripped the bed. There was no wine on the mattress.

By the time she'd carried the mountain of laundry into the crew mess, Helen decided that living with Scotty was punishment enough for Pepper. When I'm in bed with Phil, I'll think of you with your flabby old coot. No, I won't. I'll think of Phil. My man's good in bed. You made your bed, Pepper. Now lie in it and grovel.

Helen treated the red wine stains. Mira had said the sheets were custom-made and cost about twelve hundred dollars a set. If she couldn't get the wine out, would she have to pay for the sheets, too? She'd wind up owing the yacht owners before she finished this job.

Helen still hadn't a clue who was the smuggler. When Andrei was passed out, she'd missed her chance to search the cabin he shared with Carl. She should have checked the first mate's bulging back-pack. She'd been so sure Andrei was the smuggler. Then she'd talked to Phil and her terrified sister, and her night was consumed by other worries. She was too—

Frantic barks came from the aft deck, followed by a curse, then a crash of glass and china. Apologies poured from Beth. "I'm so sorry. Do you need to see a doctor? Do you need stitches? Can you work?"

Work? Beth was apologizing to a crew member?

Mira radioed Helen. "Come out to the aft deck," she said. "Help me clean up."

The outdoor breakfast was chaos. Earl was blotting spilled coffee with a napkin. Scotty was yelling and waving his cigar. Rosette and Ralph had backed away from the table. Pepper had stopped stuffing her face with a blueberry muffin.

Beth, in mustard-colored cotton, gripped Mitzi, who struggled to get free. The poodle wore a topaz collar and had blood on her muzzle. Beth tried to hush her little dog, but Mitzi would not stop yapping at Andrei. She must have bitten the engineer on the ankle. Helen saw blood seeping through his white sock.

A coffee cup and Baccarat glasses were overturned. Mira was carrying away a platter of bacon swimming in orange juice.

"For chrissakes, shut that damned dog up," Earl said, his voice tight with fury.

"I don't know what got into Mitzi," Beth babbled. "She's never bitten anyone. Ever. She's such a good dog."

She still is, Helen thought. And a brave one. Mitzi had attacked the man who'd kicked her. The blood spot on Andrei's sock was the size of a quarter, but he acted as if he'd been savaged by a pit bull.

"Perhaps I should see a doctor," he said. "For stitches. Or a shot. Sam or Matt can take me."

"They have to clean the boat, Andrei." Carl, the first mate, had been called to the crisis. "I can put a Band-Aid on it. Doesn't look like such a little dog could do much damage."

"She did," Andrei said. "She has powerful jaws."

Mira, who was clearing more plates, snorted and tried to turn it into a cough.

"I can't spare anyone to take you to a clinic," Carl said.

Beth put her hand over Mitzi's mouth to silence her barks and growls. Was she worried Earl would banish the dog from the yacht?

"Atlantis has a hotel doctor," Beth said. "They can take care of you. Mira, call the hotel and have them send a cart to fetch Andrei. You can ride in a golf cart, can't you?"

"Oh, yes," Andrei said, a little too cheerfully. He turned his face back into a mask of pain. "I'll manage."

Helen gathered up the coffee cups and carried them into the galley.

"May I bring you any more food?" Mira asked the guests. "Would you like fresh coffee? Juice?"

"I want to head to the casino," Scotty said. "What about you, boys?"

"I'll take the girls to the spa as soon as I speak to Suzanne," Beth said. "Helen, are you afraid to watch Mitzi?"

"No, she's a good dog," Helen said. She carried the poodle into the galley and fed her a peanut butter treat, while Beth relayed her instructions to the chef. "We'd like lunch at three o'clock. Make something local, Suzanne."

The guests and owners never returned for Suzanne's lunch of Caribbean lobster curry. But they did turn up at eight that night with four friends from another yacht, expecting dinner for ten.

Somehow, Suzanne made the food appear. The crew ate the lobster curry for dinner, and Earl and Beth's guests raved over the chef's spiced pork and pigeon peas and rice.

The day passed in a blur of work for Helen. While she cleaned staterooms and heads and folded laundry, she tried to make her sluggish brain run through the list of possible smugglers.

Andrei was out. Helen had watched Mira unpack the costumes, so it wasn't the head stew. Sam didn't seem to think about anything but rum and girls.

Dick the second engineer kept to himself. He was worth watching. So was Matt the bosun. And Suzanne. The chef brought boxes and bags aboard every day they were in port. It would be easy to hide the emeralds in those packages. She had five days to accumulate a stash.

As the day dragged on, Helen got her second wind—and an inspiration. Mira said that Louise had jumped ship carrying a bag.

Helen thought it was risky to board a strange fishing charter. But what if Louise already knew the captain? That was the easiest way to get those emeralds into the States. Especially if Louise knew Captain Swingle was on to her.

The missing second stew would be easy to find. Bahamian officials were pursuing her. Captain Swingle had her Fort Lauderdale address.

Once Louise arrived, Helen and Phil could track her down.

CHAPTER 28

"The girls are tired of champagne," Beth said. "What else can we serve for cocktails, Suzanne?"

Helen nearly dropped her duster when she heard that request. She was cleaning the plantation shutters in the main salon while Beth planned tonight's dinner with the chef. *Bored with champagne*: That seemed to sum up life on a yacht.

Beth looked like a tall, cool flute of champagne with her golden hair, pale gold silk caftan and glowing topaz jewelry. Mitzi wore a matching jewel-studded collar.

"Something island-y," Beth prompted the chef.

"I could make planter's punch," Suzanne said, "or strawberry rum sliders."

"Sliders look pretty," Beth said. "Let's do those. I want a special dinner, a real taste of the Caribbean."

"We could start with salmon tartare, made with fresh Atlantic salmon," the chef said.

"No, Scotty complained about the sushi at Nobu. Better go with a cooked appetizer."

"How about seared scallops with fingerling potatoes and then callaloo soup?" Suzanne asked. "We'd need meat for the main course. Niman beef tenderloin with mushrooms."

"Very festive," Beth said. "The boys will like the beef, but the girls will want chocolate for dessert."

"A bittersweet chocolate soufflé with cinnamon and caramel sauce," Suzanne said.

"Perfect," Beth said. "Have Mira call the dockmaster's office for flowers. Don't let the florist make the table arrangements too tall. I want my guests to see one another when they talk. Use the candles and my best china, the Royal Copenhagen. Dinner at eight, then."

Mitzi yapped a greeting when she saw Helen, and Beth smiled at the lowly stew. "Oh, Helen, watch Mitzi while we shop," she said. "Look how she runs straight to you. No, no! Mitzi, that's the carpet, not your puppy pad. Oh, well, looks like you don't have to walk her after all. See you at eight."

She sailed out, oblivious that her dog had whizzed once more on a custom-made carpet and that Helen would have to clean it on her hands and knees. Mitzi rubbed her nose against Helen's forehead while she attacked the spot with an enzyme cleaner.

"It's a good thing I like you, pooch," she told the dog. "Otherwise, I'd drop-kick you over the side."

Mitzi wagged her tail.

The last few days had passed in a blur of work. Helen had cleaned the heads and staterooms and done laundry. She'd checked the bilges and talked to her coworkers, hoping to find out something, anything, that would help her find the emerald smuggler.

Helen was grateful she'd have turndown service and head cleaning tonight, instead of serving Beth's grand dinner on seven-thousand-dollar-a-setting china. She was so tired, she was sure she'd break something. She felt like she was sleepwalking as she mopped the floor in the Bimini stateroom head. Mira popped in and screamed, "What are you doing?"

Helen was instantly awake. She knew she was using the right cleaner for marble. She'd checked. "Mopping the floor," she said.

"You never put a bucket of soapy water on a marble floor," Mira said. "Never. It leaves a ring." She snatched up Helen's bucket and moved it to the commode lid.

"There," she said, and managed a smile. "No harm done. I caught it in time. I stopped by to give you our good news. The yacht owners and their friends will spend all day tomorrow at Atlantis. They're letting the crew take the tender and the toys—the Jet Skis and the WaveRunners—to a cove where we can swim and play."

"Wonderful," Helen said.

"We need to have all our work finished before noon tomorrow."

"Sounds like fun, but I'll stay on the boat," Helen said. And call Phil and search for those emeralds, she thought.

Mira looked disappointed. "Oh, Helen, you need your fun or you'll burn out," she said. "The only way we stand these brutal hours is if we get to play."

"You go ahead," Helen said. "I need my rest, too." She faked a yawn.

"How much rest?" Mira asked. "Do you want to sleep the whole afternoon or would you like to make a little extra money? Andrei and Carl always pay a stew to clean their cabin. Louise did it, but she's gone. You'd be doing me a favor if you took the job."

"I'd be delighted," Helen said. She was, too. She'd wanted to search that cabin since she'd seen Carl board with his mysterious backpack.

"You won't thank me when you clean the boys' shower," Mira said.

"They can't be any worse than Ralph," Helen said.

"I'll throw in a load of laundry for you as a thank-you present," Mira said.

The day passed quickly. Helen caught a glimpse of the splendid table before the glittering guests sat down to dinner at eight. The soft candlelight warmed the honey oak table and made the crystal sparkle like fine jewels. The centerpiece was delicate seashells and small, exquisite flowers.

"It's lovely," Helen said as she hurried off to clean the guest head. Scotty had turned the bathroom into an ashtray. How did he get ashes on the sconces? And did he have to stub out his cigar in the marble basin?

The harder she scrubbed, the more the cigar residue turned into a streaky paste. I'm not cut out for this job, she thought resentfully. Phil's working for a hot, horny widow and I'm swabbing toilets like a drudge. I'm sure my husband isn't interested in a woman like Blossom. Well, pretty sure. But I'd feel a lot better if I could go home and make sure. And I can't do that until I solve this wretched emerald case.

Helen gave the basin one last swipe. There. The cigar ash was gone. She sprayed the head with vanilla air freshener to get rid of the cigar stink and slipped downstairs to fold more laundry and finish the guest turndown service.

After dinner, Ralph, Scotty and Earl knocked back the last of the thirty-year-old cognac. At three in the morning they stumbled off to bed.

Helen helped Mira clean the upper aft deck. All the men had been smoking cigars, and Helen was dusting away the ash.

"Did I tell you my good news?" Mira asked, gathering up the cognac bottle and glasses. "I got a text from my boyfriend. We're going to New York as soon as we get back to Fort Lauderdale. The yacht gets in about eleven and the crew should be finished by noon. Kevin and I are booked for a three o'clock flight to LaGuardia that afternoon. Four days in Manhattan."

"Bet you can't wait to see the Broadway shows," Helen said.

"I can't," Mira said. "But Kevin has a chance to try out for an off-Broadway show. Well, off-off-Broadway. But it's still a New York theater credit."

"Congratulations," Helen said. "That's—"

Crash!

"Was that coming from the galley?" Helen asked.

"Sounds like it," Mira said. "I hope Suzanne didn't drop any Baccarat."

The crash was a disaster. Suzanne had broken a Baccarat snifter and an entire place setting of the rare Royal Copenhagen. More than seven thousand dollars would be docked from her pay.

The chef was picking up the pieces from the galley floor. Long strands of dark hair had escaped their clip and her face sagged with fatigue. Her fingers trembled as she cleaned up the broken pieces. Helen thought she saw tears in Suzanne's sad brown eyes.

"I'm sorry about that," Helen told her.

Suzanne shrugged. "Those are the breaks, no pun intended," she said. "I'll roll with it."

Helen wasn't sure she believed her.

CHAPTER 29

· · · · · · · · · · · · · · ·

At eight the next morning, Helen saw the chef stumble through the galley door, loaded with cloth bags and cardboard boxes of fish and produce. A coconut teetered atop a bag of lettuce, limes and lemons. It tumbled off as the chef crossed the threshold.

Helen abandoned her cleaning caddy and caught the coconut before it hit the floor. Suzanne didn't acknowledge her timely catch.

"Here, let me help you," Helen said, taking a bag overflowing with oranges. "Where are the boys?"

"Working," Suzanne said. She sounded impatient. "We're all working so we can swim this afternoon. They have to wash the boat before we can go."

The chef unwrapped a fat silvery fish, so fresh it smelled like the sea. In another bag, Helen caught a flash of glittering green. "What's that?"

"Nothing," the chef said. "I have work to do. So do you."

Dismissed.

As she left with her caddy, Helen saw the chef stow the bag with the tantalizing glimmer in a cabinet. Helen would investigate later.

The guests were up shockingly early this morning, eager to go to Atlantis. The crew would be gone in a few hours. Helen couldn't wait. She even looked forward to cleaning Andrei and Carl's cabin. The first mate had acted oddly with that backpack. Helen had to know why.

Shortly after eleven o'clock, the crew was at the swim platform in their suits, bodies shiny with sunscreen, beach towels slung over their shoulders. Mira climbed aboard the tender and issued a half-hearted invitation. "You're sure you won't come with us?"

"Go!" Helen waved them away. "You're wasting party time."

"Listen to the lady," Sam called, popping a beer and toasting her.

Helen ran back into the yacht. She was alone, except for the captain. She found her cell phone, then ran up to the bridge and tapped on his door.

The captain was frowning at paperwork. "You've found the smuggler," he said.

"Not yet," she said. "I need your help with another case. Do you recognize this woman?"

The captain studied the photo on her cell phone, then said, "Her name is Blossom. She was a guest about a year ago. Scotty brought her."

"Is she a hooker?" Helen asked.

Josiah hesitated.

"Our conversation is confidential," Helen said. "This woman may have murdered a man in Florida. She has an outstanding warrant for prostitution in California. We're trying to trace her movements before she met the victim."

"I believe she's a prostitute," Josiah said. "She dressed like one and her behavior upset the women. Scotty shipped her back to California after the cruise."

Helen noticed that "shipped" made it sound as if Blossom were defective merchandise. "Did she steal from him?" she asked. "You're not breaking any confidences. I heard Beth say so."

"Yes," Josiah said. "She ran off with about fifty thousand dollars in cash and jewelry. Scotty refused to report it."

Helen nodded. "She surfaced in Lauderdale about a month ago, newly married to another rich older man. His family believes she killed him. But Blossom has completely changed her appearance."

"Not completely," Josiah said. "I recognize her."

"You know the rich better than I do," Helen said. "Let me run a theory by you: Blossom wanted to marry a rich man. She latched onto Scotty, but made major mistakes. Scotty wanted rid of her. She stole from Scotty and used his money to land another prospect."

Josiah nodded. "That could happen."

Yes! Now ideas zinged through Helen's brain, sparking thoughts and creating connections.

"With Scotty's fifty thousand, Blossom could buy a new identity and the right wardrobe," Helen said. "She was aboard the *Earl* long enough to know how women in this world dress. She could have hired a personal shopper. Does that make sense?"

"It does," Josiah said. "It's possible she learned from her mistakes and caught another wealthy man. But I'm paying you to catch my smuggler."

"I should have something for you by tomorrow," Helen said. In fact, I'm on my way to catch the smuggler now, she thought.

Helen headed straight for the galley where Suzanne had stashed the bag with the fascinating flash of green. Please let it be emeralds, she thought. Smuggling would explain why Suzanne had laughed off the abandoned late-night dinner and shrugged away seven thousand dollars' worth of broken china.

The chef had the ideal setup for smuggling. She had to go into town every day to buy fresh food. She talked to strangers in the marketplace and fishermen in port. She and the deckhand carried boxes and bags back to the yacht daily. Cute, ditzy Sam would never search them unless they were loaded with free beer.

Helen went straight to the cabinet and opened it. The chef was bold. She hadn't bothered hiding the bag. Helen's heart leaped when she saw the green sparkle in the strong Bahamian sunlight. She reached for that green glimmer.

And pulled out a T-shirt trimmed with fake green jewels and the slogan IT'S BETTER IN THE BAHAMAS.

Emeralds, indeed! Helen threw it down in disappointment. Then she got a grip on herself, folded the shirt, put it back in the bag and slammed the cabinet shut. The chef hadn't been hiding anything. She was simply in a sour mood this morning.

So am I, Helen thought. I need to work off this anger. Time to clean the boys' cabin. She threw in two more loads of laundry, then grabbed her caddy, prepared to face Andrei and Carl's mess. She snapped on a fresh pair of disposable gloves.

When she opened the cabin door, the fug was a slap in her face. The room smelled like old socks and stinky feet. She couldn't see the floor for the dirty uniforms and mildewed towels. At least the two had made their bunks. Helen threw their soiled laundry into the passage and tossed their empty beer cans. Removing the sticky drink rings on the oak chest took real elbow grease.

The boys had managed to beat Ralph in the competition for filthiest onboard head.

Helen scrubbed furiously at the fixtures, the mirror, the furniture and finally the floor.

She would not search for Carl's black Prada backpack until this cabin was clean. The backpack would be her reward for hard work.

An hour later, the cabin smelled of lemon polish and Scrubbing Bubbles.

Helen was ready to claim her prize. It had to be in the closet, but the door was jammed. She struggled to wrench it open, felt it give, then ducked. Out tumbled smelly shoes and a landslide of girlie magazines. She wondered if the Bulgarian engineer was the one excited by *Big Booty Women.*

Carl's backpack was wedged in the far corner, a black Prada

boulder. Helen pulled it free. Please, be what I'm looking for, she prayed, as she shoved aside the debris, then sat on the floor to unzip the backpack. It was so overloaded, the zipper kept sticking. She eased it open, inch by inch.

At last, she could see what was inside: gold and white cardboard boxes, like the ones for jewelry. Yes!

Helen opened the first box and saw dull black. A women's Gucci leather wallet, still in the box.

What?

She opened another box. A slim Fendi wallet. Then a red Miu Miu cosmetics case. Helen counted some thirty wallets, cosmetic cases and clutch purses. They weren't fakes. These were designer labels.

From her time in retail, Helen estimated the first mate had about twelve thousand dollars in designer wallets stashed in that backpack.

The captain had a smuggler on board, but not the one she was hired to find. She'd tell Josiah, but she'd have to keep searching.

Wrong again, Helen thought, as she refilled the backpack and shoved it in the corner.

I'm useless on this trip. She dumped smelly shoes back into the closet and heaped the magazines after them. I'll have to clean my way to the Bahamas and back again, if I don't find the emeralds—and fast. We leave for Lauderdale tomorrow evening.

I may be a partner in Coronado Investigations, but I'm not Phil's equal. Being a private eye had sounded so romantic. At worst, I expected to be bored on a long stakeout. Hah. I'll be the only PI with dishpan hands and housemaid's knee.

She checked her watch. Two o'clock. The crew wouldn't be back for three hours. Time to face another failure, Helen thought. I have to call my sister, Kathy, and find out if the blackmailer took the cash. That was my fault twice: first for marrying Rob, then for trying to catch the blackmailer alone. The last time he made a demand,

I staked out the money drop—and fell asleep. I'm a real Samantha Spade.

Helen braced herself and speed-dialed her sister. Kathy answered on the first ring, jumping into the conversation without a hello. "Rob took the money," she said. "I left thirty thousand dollars in a grocery sack on the same Dumpster—the one in the abandoned strip mall. Then I went to Target and when I got back, the cash was gone."

"Either the blackmailer got it," Helen said, "or a homeless person hit the jackpot."

"It had to be Rob," Kathy said. "He hasn't called since. But he'll want more. What are we going to do when he doubles the money again? You can't pay him sixty thousand next time."

"I'm not going to," Helen said. "I'll bring Phil with me. We'll do a stakeout and catch him."

"But you can't! You promised." Kathy's voice was shrill with panic.

"I promised I wouldn't ruin my nephew's future," Helen said. "But if the blackmailer really is Rob—and you're convinced he is—then it's time to call in Phil and end this charade. I'm not lying to my husband anymore, Kathy. It will ruin my marriage. You can do what you like about your Tom, but I'm bringing in a professional detective. We can trust Phil to protect your boy. He'll be angry at me, but he'll help. I just hope I don't lose the only man I've ever loved."

A chasm seemed to open before Helen. Life without Phil would be unbearable.

Kathy's frantic plea interrupted Helen's vision of her lonely, loveless future. "What do I do the next time he calls?" she asked.

"The blackmailer only calls your landline," Helen said. "I'll send you a telephone jack and a pocket digital recorder. Hide them near the phone. When he calls, stick the suction cup on the receiver and record his call. When Phil catches the blackmailer, we'll have a recording for the police. Rob will be trapped. Tommy will be saved."

"I'm not good with mechanical things," Kathy said.

"Then you'd better learn," Helen said. "I'll send you the recording equipment. Set it up and call the time and temperature recording every day. Do it until you can slap on the jack's suction cup automatically."

"I'll try," Kathy said.

"No," Helen said. "You will practice until you don't have to think about it. It's the only way to save your son. Promise?"

"I promise," Kathy said. "Are you sure this will work?"

"You know I'd do anything for Tommy," Helen said. "I love you, baby sis."

After Helen hung up, she realized she hadn't answered Kathy's question.

She still had time to call Phil before the crew returned. She hoped he could answer his cell phone at work. She didn't exhale until he said, "Helen! I can talk for a minute. I'm outside checking the pool."

"I have news," Helen said. "The captain confirmed the shady lady dated a yacht guest." She repeated their conversation, minus any names.

"Good work," he said. "Have you found the smuggler?"

"No," Helen said. "The boat doesn't get back until the day after tomorrow. We'll finish our chores about noon."

"Plenty of time to catch a crook," Phil said. "You'll find him. I'm always right."

"I won't waste time discussing that. What's happening with our other case?"

"Lots," he said. "I can't say more on a cell phone. I found out what killed our man. But I can't connect it to the lady yet."

"Has she been meeting with Surfer Dude?" Helen asked.

"Yes and no," he said. "They met once and I followed them. The second time Surfer Dude had a fatal accident."

"He's dead? She killed him?" Helen asked.

"The police aren't sure, but I am. He died in West Hills. Our friend Detective McNamara Dorsey is on the case."

"She's good," Helen said. "She'll figure it out."

"If she doesn't, I'll give her a little help."

"Did the lady kill him the same way?" Helen asked.

"No. I'll keep looking for the method."

"Be careful, Phil. I love you and I don't want to lose you."

Helen heard a thunk and laughter. The crew was back. She sleepwalked through her work for the rest of the day. The owners and guests returned at two a.m. and went straight to bed. The staff was free.

Helen showered and dried off in her narrow bath. She banged her elbow on the wall and noticed she was nearly out of toilet paper. Helen found a spare roll and took the cardboard core off the holder. The spindle sprung apart. Inside was a tightly wound wad of bills.

Hundred-dollar bills.

Helen counted them. One. Two. Three . . . on up to ten. One thousand dollars.

She stared at the money while the thought formed in her buzzing brain. Louise didn't buy a trip home on the charter boat. The thousand-dollar stash was still in her cabin.

CHAPTER 30

Mira had lied. Louise hadn't left the yacht on a Miami-based fishing charter.

Helen staggered out of her steaming bathroom with the thousand dollars still clutched in her hand. She sat on her bunk, stunned.

Why did Mira lie? What did it mean?

Was Louise washed overboard? What was she doing out on deck? And why didn't Mira report her missing?

A wave of sickness flooded through Helen. Louise was dead. There was no way she could have survived that violent sea. And Mira had kept silent. Louise's death must have been Mira's fault somehow. Either Louise fell overboard—or she was pushed.

The head stew didn't want to admit her responsibility.

It was two forty-eight in the morning. Helen didn't want to wake the captain at this hour. He couldn't save Louise now. This news could wait another three hours.

Louise is dead. She's dead. Dead.

Helen couldn't stop thinking about it. She'd seen the wild water from the safety of the yacht. She'd felt it slam the ship. Poor little

Louise, lost in the ferocious waves. She could see her hopeless struggle as the ship sailed away.

The second stew's death added to Helen's sense of failure. Louise was dead and Helen had failed to find the smuggler. Now she'd have to work another week on the yacht. Life aboard the *Earl* had lost its charm. It was dreary and deadly.

Helen needed sleep. She put a pillow over her head, but couldn't smother the pictures flashing through her mind. She saw Louise disappearing in the crashing waves. She felt the stew's hopeless struggle. Despair seemed to seep into the cabin like damp.

Helen must have dozed off sometime after four in the morning. When she checked her alarm clock again, it was four thirty-two. She'd have to get up in less than an hour. The clock's digital numbers gave the room a faint green glow. She couldn't escape emeralds even in her bunk.

Her restless dreams were lit by the dull green glint of fake emeralds and the green fire of Max's ring. The smuggler's pinkie ring was real. She'd seen that same green sparkle since the dinner with Max.

Beth? The boat owner had worn a savage emerald necklace and her poodle had an extravagant emerald collar and leash. Pepper wore an emerald-and-diamond choker with her film-goddess dress. All those stones had had that authentic blaze, like spring leaves igniting.

But those emeralds didn't nag at Helen. There were other jewels. She could see them in her mind. They were just as sparkling, but the gowns weren't as glamorous.

Gowns! That was it!

The rubbishy gowns that Mira brought on board, covered with jewels. Helen had thought they were fake. Now she wasn't sure. Mira had stowed them in the smuggler's hiding spot, the bosun's locker.

Helen leaped out of bed, threw on her uniform, grabbed the emergency flashlight and slipped it in her pocket. She tiptoed out of her cabin. In the passage she heard a symphony of snores: The crew was still asleep. Helen climbed the ladder to the bosun's locker and turned the hatch wheel.

She was in. It was still dark outside and the space was a metal cave. She shone the flashlight around the locker, picking out shammy mops, yacht brushes and buffing tools. Mira's waterproof duffel melted into the shadows behind the plastic buckets.

Helen dragged the bag out, plopped it down on a gray plastic storage bin and unzipped it. Out tumbled grimy satin, worn velvet and tired chiffon studded with glass rubies, plastic sapphires and cheap rhinestones. Except—what was that?

The belt on a sea green gown flashed in the light. This was different from the dull glitter on Suzanne's green T-shirt. Emerald-cut stones blazed like green bonfires. Each stone was nearly an inch long. There were twenty.

Helen had found the emeralds.

Mira was smuggling jewels. Helen pieced together their conversations and indicted the head stew in her mind:

Mira said she was investing in her boyfriend's theater company. Helen knew Mira wasn't using her savings as a stew. Those wouldn't finance a high school play. Mira wanted to be a real angel and shower the theater with the proceeds from smuggled emeralds.

Mira said she and her boyfriend were flying to New York the day the *Earl* docked in Lauderdale. So Kevin could try out for a New York production? Maybe. To sell smuggled stones? Helen thought that might be the real reason. Max said smugglers took the stones to brokers in Miami or Manhattan. The stew was smart to choose New York. That put more than a thousand miles between Mira and her fence.

Helen started shoving the dresses back in the duffel, then stopped. She remembered Mira folding the dresses neatly in the crew mess. Helen pulled them back out and forced herself to slow down and carefully pack the bulky dresses. She put the gown with the emerald belt on the bottom.

Helen saw only one reason for Mira's silence about the missing Louise: She knew Mira was the smuggler. That emerald belt and the tackle box full of cut stones would give Mira at least a million dollars. Once she had the money, Helen bet, she'd never come back to the yacht.

Louise's death would be one more mystery at sea.

Helen wanted to shout in triumph. She'd found the smuggler. Once she told the captain, she was free. Wait till Phil found out. She wouldn't even mind his "I told you so" brag. She was an equal partner in Coronado Investigations.

She zipped the duffel closed and dropped it back behind the buckets. She didn't need the flashlight now. Daylight poured into the bosun's locker. The sky was a glorious pink, like the inside of a conch shell.

As she climbed back down the ladder, Helen heard the crew preparing for the day—showers, soft conversations, doors sliding shut. She was relieved she'd reached her cabin without seeing anyone.

She checked the clock. Helen had twenty minutes to dress. She could see the captain if she skipped breakfast. She was so amped on adrenaline she didn't need coffee. She washed, brushed her hair, then ran upstairs.

Captain Josiah Swingle and Carl the wallet smuggler were on the bridge. Now the lanky first mate with the no-color hair didn't look shrewd to Helen. She thought he seemed shifty.

Josiah was annoyingly alert early in the morning. Helen wondered what made some people natural commanders. Josiah wasn't the tallest man on the yacht—Carl topped him by several inches. He wasn't the strongest. Young Sam would win that title.

But he had enough authority to put them all in their place.

Helen burst through the door and said, "Captain, I need to talk to you about my contract." That was their prearranged signal that Helen had found something.

"Would you excuse us, Carl?" the captain said.

The first mate nodded and stepped outside on the deck.

Josiah checked to make sure Carl wasn't listening at the door, then said, "You found the smuggler?"

"Two smugglers," Helen said. "And I have bad news about Louise."

"Start with the emerald smuggler," Josiah said.

"It's Mira," Helen said. "She's got twenty big stones on board hidden in a duffel bag in the bosun's locker."

Helen watched the captain's face. Josiah showed no surprise. He showed no emotion at all.

"Mira," he repeated.

"She was one of your three suspects," Helen said.

"Right," the captain said.

"I think she's smuggling to help her boyfriend's theater company."

"I don't care why she's doing it," Josiah said. At last, his anger ignited. "If the Coast Guard finds those emeralds, my reputation is ruined and my boat is padlocked to the dock. It will take years to sort out the mess. I'm confiscating those emeralds and turning her in."

"You could do that, Captain," Helen said. "But if I may make a suggestion, Mira is planning to fly to New York at three o'clock, after we dock at the marina. How many times have you been boarded by the Coast Guard?"

"None," he said.

"Then why not risk one more trip and let her leave the yacht with the emeralds? When we get back to Lauderdale, Phil will make an anonymous tip and her suitcase will be searched before she boards the plane to New York. That way the *Earl* won't be directly involved in her takedown."

"I like that," Josiah said. He smiled and Helen almost felt sorry for Mira.

"Now, tell me about Louise," he said.

"I'm afraid she's dead," Helen said. "I found this—a thousand dollars' cash—hidden in the toilet paper holder in our cabin." She handed the tightly folded bills to the captain.

"I also found her seizure medicine in a tampon box in the medicine cabinet. I left it there."

"Why do you think she's dead?" Josiah asked.

"Louise left her medicine behind," Helen said.

"She could have enough pills in her purse to get home," Josiah said.

"She didn't take her thousand dollars," Helen said. "She couldn't have paid for her passage back in cash, like Mira said."

"Helen, there are other ways a pretty young woman can pay for her passage," Josiah said.

Now Helen felt naive and foolish. "You know Louise, Captain. Do you really think she'd get on a boat full of men she didn't know and hook her way back to Miami?"

"No," Josiah said. "But maybe they weren't strangers. Crews party together when they're in port. Louise or her boyfriend could know the charter captain or a crew member. She could have agreed to pay them when she got back to Florida. She could have come back for this money—or asked one of our crew to get it for her."

Helen wasn't convinced. "I still think Mira is a liar as well as a smuggler," she said.

"Why would Mira lie?" Josiah said.

"Because Louise discovered she was smuggling emeralds," Helen said. "Mira threw the second stew overboard in those high waves. Louise is dead and Mira killed her."

"Mira isn't violent," Josiah said. "I know that."

"Really? You didn't know she was a smuggler," Helen said.

Josiah didn't react. Helen wondered if he was angry.

"If Louise suspected the head stew was smuggling, she would have come to me," he said.

"Would she?" Helen said. "Louise is what—twenty-one?"

"Twenty-three," Josiah said.

"You think a twenty-three-year-old toilet scrubber would have the nerve to approach you and accuse her superior of smuggling?" Helen asked. "I'm eighteen years older than Louise, and I'd think twice about accusing Mira, except I've seen the proof."

"Proof, Helen," Josiah said. "That's what you're missing. You have no proof Mira killed Louise. We don't even know that Louise is dead. She could be drinking in a bar with her boyfriend right now."

"If she is, I'll take it all back," Helen said. "But I'm worried about her. I know she isn't your problem anymore. The Bahamian official said so."

"No, she is," Josiah said. "My ship, my crew, my responsibility. I need to know she's safely back in the States. I'll check with the Bahamian authorities and see if they've located the *Aces High*. I promise I'll tell you, one way or the other."

"A deal," Helen said.

He was the captain. On this ship his word was law. But Helen knew Louise was dead.

CHAPTER 31

Silence followed the captain's promise to find Louise. The waves playfully slapped the yacht's side and the showy tropical pink sky mocked Helen's fears.

It seemed impossible that this postcard-pretty sea had been a crazed killer a few nights ago, raising up waterspouts and six-foot waves.

But Helen knew better. The storm had been so rough she couldn't walk the short secret passage without being thrown against a wall. Even an experienced stew like Louise couldn't carry a tray without nearly dropping a glass.

Louise was small and wiry. Mira was a sturdy woman. Helen thought she was stronger and more muscular than the second stew.

How had she killed Louise? Knocked her out, then dragged her out on deck and thrown her overboard? Lured her out on deck by asking for help with an unsecured hatch? Told her a piece of deck furniture had come loose from its lashings and she couldn't reach the boys to put it back?

Any of those excuses would work. And Mira could quickly wipe up the seawater after she opened a door.

Helen hoped Mira had knocked Louise unconscious first. It would be unbelievably cruel to throw her overboard alive. No one would hear Louise's shouts for help on board the ship. She would see life—and hope—sailing away.

Helen was grateful the captain interrupted her thoughts with another question. "You said there was another emerald smuggler?" Josiah asked.

"There's another smuggler, but he's not bringing in emeralds," Helen said. "Carl is smuggling wallets."

"Wallets. What's in them?"

"Nothing," Helen said. "These are designer wallets, cosmetic cases and small purses. The real deal. He has about twelve thousand dollars' worth of smuggled merchandise in a black Prada backpack in his closet."

"Huh," the captain said.

"Are you going to fire him when you see the wallets?" Helen asked.

"He's a good first mate. I'd like to keep him. I will confiscate those wallets."

"Could you wait a bit first?" Helen said. "Otherwise, he'll know I saw you early this morning and ratted him out."

She didn't want to disappear over the side like Louise.

"I'll wait till we're back at the marina," Josiah said.

"And then you'll drop the smuggled wallets over the side?" Helen asked.

"We don't pollute," Josiah said. "But I could give them to charity."

"One more thing," Helen said. "I know why Mitzi attacked the engineer. I think Andrei kicked her when he came back here drunk."

"You think? You didn't see him?"

"No, I was upstairs. But I heard the dog yelp."

"I wish you had seen him," Josiah said. "I can't fire him for something you *thought* you saw." Josiah looked at the clock on the wall. "It's six fifteen. We need to go back to work. Good job, Helen."

Interesting, Helen thought, as she ran back to the crew mess. The captain was willing to overlook the first mate's wallet smuggling, but talked about how he couldn't fire the engineer unless I saw him kick the dog. I bet he'd like to get rid of Andrei. Maybe now he'll see a way to do that.

"You're fifteen minutes late!" Mira greeted Helen as she opened the crew door. Helen heard both washing machines churning.

"I had to see the captain about my contract," Helen said. "I wanted to talk to him before his day started."

She studied Mira's face, but the head stew seemed to accept her explanation.

"Suzanne made breakfast burritos," she said. "You can eat one now. I've started the laundry for you. I'm going upstairs to set up breakfast."

The morning light made her hair shine like dull gold, but Helen caught a glimpse of the healing wound on her scalp. Did Louise fight to leave the yacht—or fight for her life?

It didn't make any difference, Helen thought. The scab would disappear in a day or two. Even if it didn't, the wound was proof of nothing. Mira would probably get away with murder.

"I need you to finish the guests' ironing today," Mira said. "It's our last day in port and we have to hustle. Remember, we're short-handed."

"I won't forget that," Helen said as she unfolded the ironing board.

Ugh. Ironing. Her least favorite chore. This would be the last time she ironed anything, especially sheets and underwear. This morning, it didn't matter that Helen had only a few hours' sleep. She felt energized. She sang as she folded laundry and hummed while she ironed Ralph's wretched briefs. She cheerfully cleaned staterooms and scrubbed guest heads. Her real work was done.

Helen heard Beth breeze into the galley. "We'll be at Atlantis all day, Suzanne," she said. "Make something easy for dinner tonight.

Grill steaks for the boys again. They never get tired of meat. The girls will like seafood. Maybe grilled lobster?"

"How about warm lobster potato salad?" Suzanne asked.

"Good. Caesar salads for the boys, maybe twice-baked potatoes for them, and we need a dessert."

"Key lime tarts?" Suzanne said.

"Perfect," Beth said. "That was easy. Where's Helen? I want her to take Mitzi."

Helen ran up from the crew mess. Beth looked cool in white linen with a white and silver necklace. Mitzi looked like the perfect fluffy accessory, right down to her matching collar and silver-trimmed leash.

The little dog yapped a greeting when Beth handed her over. "Pretty collar," Helen said. "Is that white jade?"

"No, white turquoise," Beth said.

Helen carried Mitzi downstairs to the crew mess, where she slept in a basket of dirty laundry. When Andrei showed up for lunch, Mitzi growled at him. Helen picked up Mitzi, held her and scratched her ears while Andrei shoveled in his lunch.

"What's wrong with that crazy dog?" he asked.

"Nothing," Helen said. "Nothing at all." Mitzi quit growling when the engineer left. Helen put the drop cloth in the laundry basket and the poodle snoozed on it while Helen worked all afternoon.

When the owners and guests returned at sunset, Helen restored Mitzi to Beth, then served cocktails with a smile. All day long, she'd been counting the hours until she was home with Phil.

Dinner was casual. No one changed into evening dress. Beth and Pepper wore fresh makeup and cruise wear. Pepper's diamond-and-emerald choker looked outrageously out of place with her slinky silk tank top, but she didn't care and neither did Scotty.

"She's lit up like cheap neon," Rosette whispered to her smirking spouse. Helen noticed Ralph's narrow eyes were glued to Pepper's curvy figure.

When the *Belted Earl* sailed out of the Atlantis marina at nine that night, Helen and Mira were still serving the guests cocktails by starlight. Dinner didn't start until after eleven. The guests watched the moonlight on the silky water until nearly two in the morning.

Helen could hardly look at the satiny black sea, knowing it had swallowed poor Louise. She wasn't queasy on the trip home, though her stomach churned a bit when the ship crossed the Gulf Stream.

After the last poker hand folded at three thirty in the morning, Helen and Mira cleaned the sky lounge. At four, Helen finally fell into bed. She dragged herself out of her bunk ninety minutes later.

A quick shower revived her. So did the knowledge that this was her last day. As a special treat, Suzanne made her fabulous coconut bread for both the crew and the owners.

At breakfast on the upper aft deck, Beth looked dramatic in a red and gold silk caftan and a collar of rubies set in gold. Mitzi looked downright silly in a matching ruby collar and red bow. Rosette was drab as a sparrow in brown linen. Pepper nearly blinded the other guests when she wore her emerald-and-diamond choker with a green halter top and miniskirt. The sun danced off the diamonds and shot sparks around the table.

"I can't believe she's wearing diamonds in daytime," Rosette said, with a sneer. "She's got on more jewelry than clothes."

Pepper turned to her. "What did you say?" she asked, her voice soft.

"Nothing. I was talking to my husband." Rosette seemed to shrivel in her chair.

"I saw you laughing," Pepper said. "Let's all share in the joke."

"It wasn't funny," Rosette said. "I mentioned to Ralph that it's unusual to wear diamonds in the daytime."

"You're right," Pepper said. "It wasn't funny. But if you've got it, flaunt it. And you don't. Stewardess, I'd like more coconut bread, please."

The *Belted Earl* docked at the marina at eleven that morning.

The staff lined up in their dress uniforms to bid the owners and guests farewell. Pepper and Scotty had given big tips. Mira had gotten a hundred dollars. Helen's tip was two hundred. She wondered if Pepper was atoning for the wine incident.

You can buy forgiveness, she told herself, as she pocketed the two crisp bills.

Matt and Sam carried the luggage to the waiting limousines.

As Beth wafted past Andrei carrying Mitzi, the poodle suddenly squirmed and struggled out of her mistress's arms. Beth lost the battle to hold on to her pet.

"Mitzi! What's wrong with you?" Beth asked.

The poodle ran straight for Andrei and chomped his ankle in the same spot she'd bitten him before.

"Worthless mutt!" the engineer said. He grabbed the poodle by her throat and shook her until her jeweled collar rattled. Mitzi fought to bite him again.

"I ought to break your pointless neck," Andrei said. The little dog squealed and sank her sharp teeth into his hand.

"Don't hurt Mitzi!" Beth screamed.

"Drop that dog," Earl shouted.

Andrei kept shaking the poodle.

Josiah waded into the shrieking, screaming cluster and pulled Mitzi off Andrei's hand. Her teeth left deep bloody scrapes in the engineer's skin.

"Andrei, you're fired," the captain said.

CHAPTER 32

The caravan of black Lincoln Town Cars was rumbling out of the marina parking lot when the yacht cleanup began. The crew moved so rapidly, Helen thought someone hit a fast-forward button.

By the time the third Lincoln left the lot, the deckhand and bosun had zipped all the canvas covers on the deck furniture. Mira had stripped the master stateroom bed and was scrubbing the shower.

"Hurry!" she said. "I have to get to the airport."

Helen stripped the guest stateroom beds, dusted away Scotty's ash for the last time and vacuumed the carpets.

As she rushed through the secret passage, arms piled with damp towels and soiled sheets, she saw Carl leaning in the doorway of the cabin he shared with Andrei. Helen slowed slightly to hear their conversation.

"That's all you got?" the first mate drawled. "Those three bags?"

"Yes. And I do not think it is fair—" Andrei said, his voice a surly whine.

"Not my decision," Carl said, cutting him off. "Where are your uniforms?"

"In the closet," Andrei said. "The captain, he does this because I am foreigner." Helen noticed Andrei's accent thickened not only when he was drunk, but also when he was upset. She could feel his rage. The cramped cabin was too small to contain it.

"You've got a green card," Carl said. "You're taking a job away from a real American. Bet you bought yourself a green card marriage on the Internet."

"My green card is legal," Andrei said. "That is why I have job on American-registered boat."

Carl's drawl stretched like taffy. "Don't see your dress uniform there, Andrei. Where is it?"

"Don't know," Andrei said, his voice higher.

"I think you do," Carl said, slowly. "You still have to go through U.S. Customs. What would happen if they got an anonymous tip about your marriage? You got any wedding pictures? Still living with your wife? I bet you don't even know where she is anymore. You can get shipped back to Bulgaria if your marriage is a fraud."

Silence. Then Andrei said, "I might have accidentally packed it." He sounded like a surly child.

"Well, accidentally unpack it," Carl said.

Helen heard a zipping sound. Then Carl said, "Thank you. Soon as the captain gets back from escorting the owners and guests to their plane, he'll hightail it to immigration at Port Everglades with you and the new stew."

Customs! Helen had forgotten about that. She hurried past Carl to the crew mess, where Mira was loading both washers.

"Once we finish this laundry and clean the heads, we're done," she said. "You and Andrei have to ride with the captain to immigration. Andrei has a green card and you don't have a boat card."

"What's a boat card?" Helen asked.

"You get it from the feds if you travel by private boat a lot. They're called NEXUS cards. All the crew have them. We don't need to go through customs. The captain just calls in our card numbers when we get into port.

"We always party at the end of a cruise, but I'm skipping this one. Kevin is taking me straight to the airport. Get ready to rock, Helen. You need to party after that crossing. You like wine or margaritas?"

"Both," Helen said, "but I'm skipping out, too. I'm meeting Phil. I have to tell him to pick me up at Port Everglades."

The head stew checked her watch. "The Homeland Security office is at the other end of the port by Griffin Road. There's no gate security there. He can wait for you in the parking lot. We should be free about twelve thirty. I'll miss you, but I won't miss Andrei. I can't believe he tried to hurt poor little Mitzi."

"It wasn't the first time," Helen said. "I heard her yelp when he was alone with her in the crew mess one night. He may have kicked her."

"Well, he's gone now," Mira said. "Finish the main salon head, will you?"

Helen cleaned the head and folded the toilet paper into a neat point.

"Done," she told herself. Next she folded towels, still warm from the dryer, while Mira ironed the sheets.

Then she hurried to her cabin to call Phil. Just hearing his voice made her feel warm. No, not warm. Hot. Honeymoon hot. She wanted to be alone with her man.

"Helen!" he said. "I miss you. I need you. Our local case is breaking."

"Did you catch her?" Helen asked, careful not to use Blossom's name. "Do you know what she used?"

"Can't say on a cell phone," he said. "When do I pick you up?"

"I should be finished about twelve thirty," she said, "but don't come to the marina. I have to go through customs at Port Everglades." She told him where.

"I'll be waiting in my Jeep," he said. "I love you."

"I love you, too," Helen said. "I have good news about our other case."

"You found the . . . uh, person?" Phil asked.

"Can't wait to tell you about it," she said, and hit the END button. Two could play the "I can't say anything on a cell phone" game.

Helen stashed her cleaning caddy for the last time, tidied her cabin and packed her small bag. When she opened her cabin door, the yacht was perfumed with a delicious aroma. It didn't take much detective skill to track it to the galley, where the tall, thin chef was washing down the countertops.

"What smells so good?" Helen asked.

"I'm making pizza for the crew," Suzanne said. "What's your favorite topping?"

"I have to miss this party," Helen said. "I'm meeting Phil right after I go through customs. I enjoyed working with you."

"My pleasure," Suzanne said. "I'm guessing this is your first and last cruise as a stewardess."

Helen said nothing. Suzanne opened the oven door and took out two pizzas, oozing cheese. Red rounds of pepperoni and brown sausage were embedded in the top like greasy jewels.

"I thought so," she said. "Will you do one last chore and carry these to the crew mess?"

Matt, Sam and Dick, the second engineer, attacked the pizzas as soon as Helen set them on the table. She heard the *spoit!* of beer tops popping. Carl didn't join the hungry crew. He stayed with Andrei in their cabin. Was the captain worried his fired engineer would damage the yacht?

Helen ran down the passage and asked Carl, "Would you like some pizza?"

"No, thanks," he said. "I'm staying on board after the captain dismisses the crew and takes you and Andrei to Port Everglades. I can eat then."

Andrei was slumped on his bunk, sulking. His black polo shirt seemed to accent the dark pits in his skin. Helen didn't offer him pizza. The poodle abuser could starve.

No one mentioned Andrei during the party, but Helen thought the crew was relieved he stayed in his cabin. She wondered if Dick, the quiet second engineer, would be promoted to Andrei's job.

While the boys ate, drank beer and cracked jokes, Mira rolled a pink suitcase out to the crew mess. The fat duffel sat on top of it. She was dressed for a colder climate in jeans, a long-sleeved white shirt and a pink hoodie. "New York, here I come," she said.

"It's chilly there in April," Helen said. "Do you have the right clothes for your trip?"

"Nope, but I can buy them in Manhattan," Mira said. "I can't wait to leave."

Helen couldn't, either. By the time she and Mira had said their good-byes to the crew, the captain had returned.

A sullen Andrei dragged his dark backpack with the square bulge down the gangplank. Helen thought the fired engineer would have a harder time attracting gullible young women without his dashing dress uniform.

The three women rolled their suitcases down the gangplank. Mira ran to a dramatically handsome man of about thirty. His black clothes, thick dark hair and carefully calculated beard stubble screamed "actor."

"Kevin!" Mira cried, her pink suitcase bumping over the marina's blacktop, the duffel nearly falling off.

Suzanne drove off alone in a dented red Honda.

Helen and Andrei climbed into the captain's black Chevy for a short, silent ride to Port Everglades. Helen cleared customs quickly, then shook the captain's hand, but not Andrei's. She wanted nothing to do with him.

Outside she spotted Phil's black Jeep in the lot and ran to him. He was wearing her favorite soft blue shirt, the one that matched his eyes. His long silver hair was tied back in a ponytail.

Helen wrapped her arms around him. "Um, muscles!" she said, rubbing his back. She inhaled his scent of coffee and sandalwood and kissed him hard.

"I missed you," she said. "I'm so glad you're here."

After more kisses she said, "We still have work to do on this case. You need to tip off the feds."

Helen told him about Mira and the emeralds, then asked, "Who are you going to call? ICE?"

"The agency isn't called Immigration and Customs Enforcement anymore," Phil said. "They've changed their name to Homeland Security Investigations. I'll call an HSI agent in Fort Lauderdale. He'll know if the airport has an HSI special agent on duty. If not, TSA will do the takedown. We need to give him as many details as possible, including where Mira was coming from, how the emeralds were smuggled and a description of her luggage. They'll love a chance to seize smuggled emeralds."

"I can even give them the color of her suitcase," Helen said. "I'm no jewelry expert, but I'd say the cut stones have a retail value of several million. We'd better hurry. Mira and her boyfriend are boarding a three o'clock flight for New York."

The HSI agent was definitely interested in Phil's information. Helen heard him reciting the details:

"That's right. Her name is Mira—short for Vladimira—Fedorova, age twenty-nine, about five foot six, long blond hair, wearing jeans, a white shirt and a pink hoodie. Name sounds Russian, but she's a U.S. citizen living in Fort Lauderdale. She has a pink rolling suitcase and may also have a large navy duffel. That one's too big for carry-on. She's traveling with a dark-haired thirty-something male, first name Kevin. They're taking the three o'clock flight to LaGuardia. I don't know if he's involved. She's a stewardess on a yacht. That's how she's been bringing in the jewels. The captain got suspicious and our agency had an operative aboard. She found the emeralds on a belt in a bag of old evening dresses."

That's me, Helen thought. I'm an operative. A successful operative.

Phil repeated the information several times, then hung up. "They're going after her," he said. "I hope your hunch is right."

"It is," Helen said, with more confidence than she felt. "We should call our favorite TV reporter, Valerie Cannata. We can promise her the story, if she agrees not to use the captain's name or the ship's name. Think she'll go along with it?"

"Hell, yes," Phil said. "But she can't do the story unless she can get a camera crew to the airport on short notice. Let's hope for a slow news day. Coronado Investigations will have to stay out of this story. But we'll get plenty of publicity when we give her the scoop on the murder of a prominent Fort Lauderdale businessman."

"You're that close to a solution?" Helen asked.

"I am," Phil said. "But I need you."

Helen kissed him again. "And I need you," she said. "Could your case wait until tomorrow morning?"

"I think it's time for some undercover work," Phil said. "Let's go home."

CHAPTER 33
. . . .

P hil's phone rang at nine thirty that night. Helen sat up in bed, flipped on the light and found the receiver.

"Helen! It's Valerie."

Helen hastily pulled the sheet up over her breasts, as if the investigative reporter could see her naked.

"I wanted to thank you and Phil for the amazing tip," Valerie said. "The smuggling story runs at ten tonight."

"The feds caught Mira?" Helen was still groggy.

"Did they ever," Valerie said. "Carrying a suitcase jammed with emeralds. HSI says they have a street value of five million dollars. The feds always exaggerate, but I think she had at least three million in smuggled stones. We're the only station with the story. Thank you, thank you, sweetie. Gotta run."

"Phil, wake up!" Helen said, shaking her sleeping spouse. "Valerie called. The feds caught Mira. Her story runs at ten. We should call the captain so he can watch it."

"You make the call and I'll make a snack," Phil said. "Scrambled eggs okay?"

"You're going to wait on me?" Helen said. "What luxury."

Phil gave her a long kiss. "Scrambled eggs aren't my idea of luxury," he said. "I'd buy you a yacht if I could."

"Wouldn't want it," Helen said. "The *Earl* was gorgeous, but there was no privacy. I could hear the guests fighting—and their makeup sex afterward. I knew too much about them."

Phil slipped on his white robe. A loud meow stopped his march to the kitchen. Thumbs planted himself in Phil's path. The six-tocd cat's yellow-green eyes glowed in the low light.

"It's also time for someone else's dinner," Helen said. "Come here, big boy, and say hello."

"I already did," Phil said. "Several times."

"I meant the cat," Helen said.

Thumbs turned his back on Helen and padded after Phil to the tiny kitchen.

"You still aren't forgiven for abandoning him," Phil said.

Captain Josiah Swingle wasn't happy with Helen, either. "I thought we agreed to avoid publicity," he said.

Helen felt ice forming on her phone. "We made a deal with Valerie," she said. "If she kept you and the *Earl* out of this story, we promised her another scoop."

"I'll watch tonight to make sure she keeps her word," Josiah said. "I don't trust reporters. I'll stop by tomorrow morning to settle my bill. Seven thirty?"

Helen looked at Phil's deliciously rumpled sheets. She'd love to sleep in, but Phil had to work at Blossom's tomorrow and Coronado Investigations couldn't refuse a customer begging to pay.

"See you then," she said.

Helen stumbled into the living room, still half asleep. Phil carried two plates heaped with fluffy scrambled eggs to the coffee table. His plate was buried under ketchup and hot sauce.

"White wine?" he asked.

"I must be in server heaven," Helen said.

They sat side by side on Phil's black leather couch. "It feels so good to sit here and enjoy my food," Helen said, "without worrying that I'll have to scrub heads and serve dinner at three a.m. Now, tell me what's going on with Blossom and her boyfriend."

"This will be show-and-tell," Phil said. "I want to take you to the restaurant where she poisoned Surfer Dude."

"Can't wait to eat that food," Helen said.

"We'll eat somewhere else," Phil said. "How about a midnight Mexican dinner?"

"But we're eating now," Helen said.

"This is a snack," Phil said. "We missed lunch. We'll leave right after we watch Valerie. It's way up in Palm Beach County. You don't want to miss the world's best guacamole."

Phil switched on channel seventy-seven. Donna, the blond late-night anchor, was as bland as baby food. "And now investigative reporter Valerie Cannata has the scoop on a Fort Lauderdale resident caught smuggling a fortune in jewels," Donna said.

There was Valerie. Nothing bland about her. Valerie had the eerily youthful look of top TV pros. A red suit hugged her gym-enhanced curves, and crimson lipstick highlighted her full lips. Phil had kissed those lips, Helen thought, then reminded herself that their romance was over long before she knew her husband.

Valerie did her report with the Fort Lauderdale airport as her backdrop. Curious passengers stared as they rolled their suitcases behind the sophisticated reporter.

"Special agents for Homeland Security Investigations arrested a Fort Lauderdale woman, Mira Fedorova, as she boarded a flight for New York's LaGuardia Airport this afternoon," Valerie said. "Ms. Fedorova's suitcase contained more than five million dollars in emeralds, officials said."

The camera panned across the glittering hoard of jewels, photogenically displayed in the unzipped pink suitcase.

"Never saw a pink pirate's chest before," Helen said.

"Sh!" Phil said.

Mira's mug shot flashed on the screen as Valerie continued: "Ms. Fedorova, a twenty-nine-year-old yacht stewardess, was charged with multiple counts of smuggling. She is being held without bail as a flight risk. Federal agents are still questioning her companion. We'll have more updates on this breaking story."

"Thank you, Valerie," Donna the anchor said. "Remember, this story is on just one station—channel seventy-seven."

"I knew we could trust Valerie," Helen said. "But I still held my breath during her report."

"Josiah will be relieved his yacht wasn't mentioned. Now, on to our other case. What do I wear to this restaurant?"

"Nothing fancy," Phil said. "It's a taco truck in a parking lot."

"Very cool. Just like L.A.," Helen said.

It was a fine night for a drive on I-95. Palm trees rustled in the light breeze. The air was soft and warm. Cars whizzed past, some weaving in and out of the traffic, others poking along in the slow lane.

"Now, where did I leave off telling you the adventures of Blossom?" Phil asked.

"In the last installment," Helen said, "you were disguised as Bob the Cool Guy air-conditioner repairman. You followed Blossom to a Deerfield Beach bar and pretended to check the air-conditioning vents."

"Hey, I wasn't playing make-believe," Phil said. "I risked my neck climbing a stepladder and heroically resisted a beer and burger while I listened to Blossom argue with Surfer Dude. His name is Zack."

"Anything to this Zack besides his blond good looks?" Helen asked.

"Not that I could tell," Phil said. "The man was greedy and stupid. I was around the corner from their booth, listening as hard as I could. I'd unscrewed the vent cover and heard Zack say, 'I told you to get rid of it.'"

"Blossom started arguing. 'No. I might need it,' she said. 'Don't worry. I have a good hiding place. It's in plain sight.'

" 'What is this?' Zack said. 'Some freaking TV detective show? Why keep it?'

" 'Arthur's daughter hates me,' Blossom said. 'She's been to that lawyer, Nancie Hays. Hays is trouble.'

" 'So?' Zack said. 'You can afford good lawyers, too. If anything happens to Violet so soon after Daddy bit the dust, it will look suspicious.'

"Zack gulped his beer and ordered another," Phil said. "He told her, 'I don't know why you offed the old guy, anyway. You could have slipped out any time to see me.'

" 'No, I couldn't,' she said. 'He was around the house all the time. He couldn't keep his hands off me. It was horrible. He'd go to his office sometimes, but I never knew when. The one time I went to see you, that housekeeper caught me. Couldn't wait to tell me the next day.

" 'I wanted his money and I got it. Now the daughter's after me. She'll fight me every step of the way unless I do something. That's why I kept it. They didn't find it in him and they won't find it in her. Most medical examiners don't know to look for it and he didn't have an autopsy. She won't, either. Her death will look like a heart attack. Runs in the family.'

"Then she laughed," Phil said.

"She wants to kill Violet, too," Helen said. "That gives me chills."

"It made Zack hot under the collar," Phil said. "His voice got low and threatening. 'Don't do it, Blossom,' he said. 'Be patient a little longer. Once his estate makes it through probate, we can get married.' "

"What did Blossom say to that?" Helen asked.

"Nothing," Phil said. "The silence was so loud even a lunkhead like Zack realized she didn't want to tie the knot. He was so upset he abandoned his beer and started whining. 'What's wrong?' he said. 'I thought you wanted to marry me.'

"Blossom got real cagey. 'I'm not sure I want to tie myself down again so soon, Zack.'

"He got mad. He gripped his beer bottle so hard I thought it would crack. 'It's that new handyman, isn't it?' he said."

"Zack was jealous," Helen said.

"Of me," Phil said, and grinned. "I realize I'm serious competition—"

"Can we go back to the story?" Helen asked. "They were arguing and Zack was jealous."

"Right. Blossom said, 'Keep your voice down. He's not a handyman. He's an estate manager.'

"Zack started whining again. 'It's not fair,' he said. 'I do the dirty work—'

"'Dirty work?' Blossom said. 'You picked two off the ground.'

"'That's two more than you picked up,' Zack said. 'You thought that was a mango tree. I'm the one who found out why you couldn't eat those mangoes. I bothered to talk to the girl at the hotel.'

"'You must have been talking in braille,' Blossom said, 'the way you had your hands all over her.'

"'Well, if it wasn't for me, you wouldn't have had them,' Zack said. 'I gave you a wedding present—the way to end your marriage. A secret way. Of course it doesn't have to stay a secret. I could tell the police what really killed Arthur.'

"'You'd go to prison, too,' she said.

"'Not if I cut a deal,' he said. 'I didn't make that curry. I just gave you some pretty seeds. I had no idea they were poison. There's no proof I had anything to do with Arthur's death. No one ever saw me at his house, not even that nosy housekeeper. Don't forget, Arthur wasn't cremated. They can still dig him up and find it.'

"'I couldn't cremate him,' Blossom said. 'He had a prepaid burial plan.'

"That's when Blossom seemed to realize her hunk had his own plan. She hugged him and kissed his cheek. 'Zack, honey, I'm grateful,' she said, 'but I'm not ready to get married so soon after Arthur. It wouldn't look right. What if I gave you a gift instead?'

" 'How big a gift?' Zack asked. Suddenly he was sober.

" 'Two million dollars,' she said.

" 'Pocket change,' Zack said. 'I'm not interested in a going-away present. If I marry you, I'm entitled to five million. Actually, I'm entitled to more. But I'm not greedy. Marry me and we'll have a nice arrangement. You'll go your way and I'll go mine. We'll both have enough to do whatever we want.'

" 'I'll think about it,' Blossom said. Her voice could have frosted beer mugs, but Zack didn't notice."

Phil turned off the highway in Lake Worth, a town near Palm Beach. Soon they were in a neighborhood of Latino working people.

"Then what happened?" Helen asked.

"The bar owner came by and asked me—or rather Cool Bob—if I'd look at the filters in the main unit. I looked, but it could have been run by gerbils for all I knew. I said I had new filters in the truck, ducked out the door, jumped in the truck and didn't look back."

"That's it?" Helen didn't hide her disappointment. "You never learned the name of the poison?"

"Yes, I did," he said. "Later. I Googled 'poison,' 'mango' and 'Maldives'—that's the islands where she married Arthur. That's how I found out about the suicide tree, *Cerbera odollam*. Grows in India and southern Asia. Has pretty white flowers and fruit like small mangoes. The seeds are highly poisonous. Blossom could easily mix them in spicy food—like curry—and the old man would never know what he ate. It's a common poison in southern Asia, but not well-known here."

"Blossom got away with murder," Helen said.

"Not yet," Phil said.

The Jeep cruised down Military Trail, a wide street dotted with car repair shops, pawnshops and Latino supermarkets. Tucked between them were small cinder block restaurants, painted bright turquoise, yellow or red.

"See that Mexican restaurant there?" Phil said.

"The one with the big Closed sign?" Helen asked.

"That's where Blossom killed her boyfriend," Phil said. "Right now the docs think Zack died of food poisoning after a Mexican dinner. I know Blossom poisoned him. I saw her. I just didn't realize it. The restaurant was unfairly shut down. I'll give you the details over dinner. You're going to help me prove she's a killer."

"Do I get dessert?" Helen asked.

CHAPTER 34

Tacos al Carbon looked like a late-night fiesta. A square of asphalt behind the Jiffy Lube on Military Trail was strung with lights and packed with people. Young women in vivid clothes looked like they were finishing—or starting—a night at the clubs. They chatted and flirted with young dark-haired men. Older men and women in uniforms and scrubs had the weary look of workers heading home. Some placed orders in rapid Spanish. Others spoke slow "gringo Spanish" or English.

All were there with one purpose—to celebrate real Mexican food.

Helen saw yellow taco trucks with red awnings on one side of the lot and a yellow brick building on the other. A sign promised ROASTED CORN.

Diners picked their drinks out of white plastic coolers and bellied up to the trucks to put in their orders and pay. Phil parked the Jeep in the back of the crowded lot and said, "I know what I want. What can I get you?"

"A chicken burrito," Helen said. "And guacamole."

"You want a beer?" he asked, poking through a cooler.

"Water," Helen said. "We have to meet the captain at seven thirty tomorrow morning."

"Quick! That couple is leaving the picnic table at the end of the lot," Phil said. "Snag it."

The young Latino couple was still gathering their trash when Helen claimed the table. She watched Phil juggle two brimming paper plates, a bottle of water, a beer and an aluminum container with a white paper bag on top. Once the food was safely on the table, Phil pulled a wad of paper napkins from his pocket.

"You're good enough to serve on the high seas," Helen said.

Her chicken burrito was as big as a rolled hand towel and crammed with white meat. Phil's was the same size, but oozing brown gravy. He happily bit into it.

"What did you get?" she asked.

"*Lengua,*" he said. "That's a tongue burrito."

She shuddered.

"It's seriously good," he said, taking a swig of beer. "Tastes like delicately flavored, slightly chewy beef."

"I'll take your word for it," Helen said.

He took the lid off the aluminum container. Thick chunks of ripe avocado were covered with drifts of *queso blanco*—white cheese. He dug into it with a tortilla chip from the grease-spattered bag. "Try this guacamole," he said. "It's like avocado fudge."

"It's like avocado cream with cilantro," Helen said. "Tell me how Blossom killed Zack before I fall into a Mexican-food stupor."

"Zack's last meal wasn't nearly as good as this one," Phil said. "This time, I was disguised as Rasta Man. The couple drove to the restaurant I showed you. I followed Blossom in my rental car. Zack got there first and took a table outside. They ordered tacos, salsa and chips. Blossom fussed over Zack, dipping tortilla chips into the salsa and feeding him. He loved it. He drank beer and she had margaritas.

"He excused himself to use the men's room. While he was gone, Blossom asked for more chips and salsa. When the salsa came, she sprinkled something on it from a little bottle. I thought it was extra hot sauce. The table had a rack of hot sauce bottles. I watched her put the bottle in her purse and figured she was stealing it.

"When Zack came back, she kept kissing him and feeding him chips and salsa. He'd eaten most of the salsa and she was snuggled up to him."

"Quite a change from the furious woman in the Deerfield Beach bar," Helen said.

"She seemed in love with Zack," Phil said. "That's where I made my mistake.

"Zack was pretty drunk by now. He put his arms around her and said, 'Baby, I know it's too soon, but I love you. I can't live without you. I don't want to rush you, but I want to marry you. I've known you since San Diego. You're smart and ambitious. I'll do anything for you. I already have. I helped you get your new identity. I followed you here and then I stayed away because you asked me, though it nearly killed me. I love you. I need you. You can pick the date, but please say yes.'

"She hesitated a bit, then batted her eyelashes and said, 'Yes, but on one condition.'

"'Name it,'" he said.

"'I'll marry you after a year's mourning for Arthur,' she said. 'Will you wait for me?'

"Zack was all over her then, kissing and saying she'd made him the happiest man in Florida. He ordered more drinks. They kissed and toasted and talked about where they'd hold the ceremony. Blossom said she wanted to get married on the beach."

"Again?" Helen said. "Her beach marriage to Arthur didn't work out so well for the groom."

"I doubt if Zack was thinking of Arthur," Phil said. "He was sloshed. Blossom asked if he could make it home alone. Zack said he was fine. He knew which roads to take to avoid the cops.

"Blossom paid the bill and walked Zack to his car. He kissed her good night so hard he practically dented the car. She waved good-bye. I followed her back home.

"Two days later, I read a brief item in the *Sun-Sentinel* about a Zachary Crinlund of West Hills who was taken to the hospital at two a.m. with seizures and vomiting. He'd called 911 from his apartment. Zack lapsed into a coma and did not regain consciousness. The news said Zack's death was probably food poisoning. I think she poisoned him. That wasn't hot sauce Blossom sprinkled in his salsa. I watched her kill him."

"With the help of the suicide tree?" Helen asked.

"Different symptoms," Phil said. "I'm going to keep looking for that poison, too."

"In a fifteen-thousand-square-foot house?" Helen said. "That's impossible. You're also searching for the seed of the suicide tree, and you haven't found that, either."

"It's there," he said. "Both those poisons are. I know it. Whatever she's using, she won't throw them away."

"I don't understand why she'd keep them. That's stupid," Helen said.

"Murder has been easy for her," Phil said, "and she's gotten away with it twice—at least that's what she thinks. Killing anyone who gets in her way is becoming a habit. She murdered poor old Arthur for his money. She killed Zack when he tried to pressure her into marriage. Now I bet she's setting her sights on Violet, who hired a tough lawyer. She's going to try to make friends with Violet."

"It won't work," Helen said. "Arthur's daughter can't stand her. Violet can't even say her stepmother's name."

"Blossom is a convincing actress," Phil said. "When I watched her, I thought she was in love with Zack. We need to be careful. If she makes any overtures to our client about burying the hatchet, we can't let Violet become her friend."

"That should be easy," Helen said. "We'll clue in Nancie, her lawyer. Do you want to meet with both of them?"

"Not yet," Phil said. "Zack lived in West Hills. That's Detective McNamara Dorsey's territory. Right now Zack's death isn't officially a murder. I'm hoping to give Detective Mac those poisons. I'm searching the Zerling house a few rooms at a time. I've done the pool house, two guest rooms and three baths. Tomorrow, I search the breakfast room and the kitchen."

"Be careful, Phil," Helen said. "Don't eat anything Blossom gives you."

"I don't," he said. "I bring my lunch. But she keeps asking me to have a manhattan with her. I keep telling her I'm a beer drinker." He emptied his bottle.

"Maybe she needs a condolence visit from her spiritual adviser," Helen said.

"Just what I was thinking," Phil said. "But it's not quite time to call in Reverend Hawthorne."

"It is time to take her home," Helen said. "And we won't get back to the Coronado before one in the morning. Don't forget our early appointment with the captain."

The drive home seemed faster and the other drivers crazier—or drunker. Phil let a pushy Mustang pass him and kept well out of the way of a speeding BMW.

"We're going seventy and that Beemer passed us like we're standing still," Helen said.

"He can have the road," Phil said, and put his arm around her. "I've got you."

Helen felt safe, despite the drunken drivers. "What does 'Tacos al Carbon' mean in Spanish?" she asked.

"I think it means the meat is grilled over hot coals," Phil said. "A few years ago, Mexican-Americans got a chuckle over a big chain that sold 'tacos del carbon.' That translated as 'tacos made of carbon.' Another disaster was when Chevy advertised their Novas in Mexico and South America and the cars didn't sell. Detroit didn't realize that *no va* meant 'doesn't go' in Spanish."

Phil suddenly swung the Jeep into the slow lane.

"Yeow!" Helen said. "That red Chevy Corvette is sure going— way over the speed limit."

Phil eased up on the gas and the Chevy streaked past them. Helen was relieved when they reached the Coronado.

In the moonlight, the apartment complex was a pale monument to Florida's midcentury past. All the lights were out, and they tiptoed past Margery's apartment. Helen stifled a shriek when she saw a tall figure step out from behind a palm tree.

It was their landlady in a purple silk robe and a small cloud of cigarette smoke.

"I'm enjoying the night," Margery said. "I see you two finally got out of bed. Where did you go? The taco truck in Palm Beach?"

"So much for privacy," Phil said.

CHAPTER 35

· · · · · · · · · · · · · · · ·

H elen heard Captain Josiah Swingle knock on the door of Coronado Investigations at precisely seven thirty the next morning. Something was different.

He was punctual as usual. But this time his knock was a polite, almost timid tap.

When Phil answered the door, Helen saw the captain's sandy hair and sunburned face. But under his crisp white uniform, Josiah's shoulders were bowed.

This wasn't the same man Helen had said good-bye to at Port Everglades. Now Josiah carried a heavy burden.

Helen felt her stomach drop. Please, she thought, let me be wrong.

The captain greeted Helen and Phil, then sat in the yellow client chair. They took their black leather-and-chrome chairs opposite him. Josiah hesitated, then said, "You were right, Helen. Louise is dead."

Helen reared back as if she'd been slapped. "No!" she said. She knew it was true, but she didn't want it to be.

"Some Bahamian fishermen found her body yesterday," he said.

"She was wearing her uniform, including her *Belted Earl* polo shirt. The Bahamian authorities made a tentative identification and Louise's dental records confirmed it.

"I'd been expecting bad news since I got back from immigration yesterday. Her boyfriend, Warren, was waiting for her at the marina. He asked me where she was and I knew then that she'd never made it home. I checked with the dockmaster at the Miami Beach Marina. They didn't have a fishing charter called *Aces High*. The Bahamian officials confirmed they could not locate the charter."

"Mira killed her," Helen whispered.

"That's my guess," Josiah said.

"But there's no way to prove it," she said. "At least Mira will go to prison for smuggling."

"There may still be a way to convict her for murder, too," Josiah said. "A barrette with blond hair in it was found in Louise's back pocket."

"Then they may have the killer's DNA," Phil said.

"It's being tested now," the captain said.

Helen grabbed the arms of her chair as if she needed to hold something solid. "Poor Louise," she said. "I'd hoped she'd gone over the side unconscious. But she died alone in those wild waves, without any hope of rescue."

"She was determined to get her killer," the captain said. "She spent her last few moments buttoning her killer's hair and barrette into her pocket."

I hope they were only a few moments, Helen thought. In her mind, she heard the howling wind and felt the water slam the ship.

"Do you know what the chances were of her body being found?" Josiah asked.

That's when Helen started crying. I won't indulge in dramatics, she told herself. I knew her less than a day. But Louise complained about her job and I felt the same way, too. She was only twenty-three. Tears are unprofessional. They won't help her.

The harder Helen tried not to cry, the more she wept. Phil handed her his handkerchief and squeezed her hand. Helen mopped her eyes. Finally, her tears stopped.

"I'm sorry," she said.

"Don't apologize," Josiah said. "You should cry for her. Louise was a brave woman who died a terrible death. Now she deserves justice."

"I may be able to help," Helen said. "Was that barrette two-toned silver and about four inches long?"

"Yes. How did you know?" the captain said.

"Because Mira wore one and I admired it. She told me she bought it online at Head Games. The brand is Ficcare and the barrette costs about forty bucks."

Josiah pulled out a small notebook and wrote down the details. "Good," he said. "If she bought it online, there should be a credit card record. That will help the investigators. This is all my fault. I should have known."

"You should have known what?" Helen said. "That Mira was a killer? We had a nice girlie talk about hair. She helped me with the laundry and bawled me out for putting a wet bucket on a marble floor. I didn't have a clue she was a smuggler, much less a murderer."

"But still—" Josiah began.

"What?" Phil asked. "You didn't read Mira's mind? You think killers are easy to spot, Captain? The police don't. People get away with murder because they don't look like killers."

Josiah refused to take that excuse. "If I'd listened to Helen—"

"You still couldn't have saved Louise," Helen said. "Unless you saw her fall overboard, she didn't have a chance."

"But I could have prepared her father," Josiah said. "Louise is his only daughter. He's a widower and lives in Kansas City, Missouri. He didn't want her to work on the yacht, but she wanted adventure before she settled down. I had to break the news to him, then ask for her dental records. I've never heard a man cry like that before, and I hope I never do again. It was like I ripped out his heart."

"You did," Phil said. "And he'll never get over it."

The captain seemed to find comfort in Phil's blunt statement. He sat back in his chair and looked a little less tense.

"There is no way to tell a family their child is murdered," Phil said. "My first case was a young girl who ran off to South Beach and became a coke whore. I had to tell her father his daughter had OD'd. You don't get over it, ever. But you do learn to live with it.

"You didn't kill Louise. She's dead because *Mira* killed her."

"Is Mira going to be prosecuted in the Bahamas?" Helen asked.

"She's already in custody here for smuggling," the captain said. "The crime took place on a ship registered in the United States and was probably committed somewhere between Florida and the Bahamas. It will be treated as a U.S. crime."

"When is the funeral?" Helen asked.

"It will be in Kansas City as soon as her body is sent home," the captain said. "Her father made it clear he wants nothing to do with Fort Lauderdale. We'll hold a memorial service for her later."

He sighed, stood up and said, "Thank you, Helen, for catching Mira. At least she's no longer on my ship. I want my bill. Here's your stewardess pay."

Josiah didn't bother looking over Coronado Investigations' carefully itemized bill. He simply wrote a check for the full amount. Helen didn't charge him for the broken china cup. She figured she did more damage. She'd also dyed the crew polos pink.

Josiah shook hands with Helen and Phil. They stood at the door and watched his bowed back as he left the Coronado.

"I wonder how long he's going to carry that weight," Helen asked.

"A long time," Phil said. "He's a good man."

He glanced at the clock on their office wall. "It's eight oh three. Time to change into my Cabana Boy suit and work for Blossom."

Helen and Phil walked hand in hand across the Coronado court-yard on a cool April morning. They waved at Margery, who was skimming dead leaves out of the pool with a long-handled net.

"You're a great detective," Helen said. "Solve this mystery for me, Phil: How did Margery know we went to the taco truck last night?"

"Because we talked about it on the way to the Jeep," Phil said.

"Oh," Helen said. "That was no big deal."

"Once I told you, the mystery is gone," Phil said.

Thumbs greeted Helen at the door. "So I'm forgiven, am I?" she said. "Took you long enough." The cat flopped down on the floor and she scratched his thick fur.

While Phil dressed, Helen brewed more coffee. She took a cup into the bedroom and asked, "What will you do if you find one of the poisons at Blossom's?"

"Call you. That triggers the next phase of the investigation," he said.

"You can't call me from Blossom's house," Helen asked. "You're not supposed to know Arthur's minister. What if someone overhears you? You don't trust cell phones."

"I'll call you on my cell phone and pretend to order a new pool filter cartridge," Phil said. "Then you can meet me at the post office on Las Olas."

"The cute one with the blue awning?" she asked.

"That's the one. The whole neighborhood goes there. I can return a broken air conditioner part."

"I'll be home all day," Helen said, "catching up on my sleep and waiting for your call."

"There's no guarantee I'll find any poison today," Phil said. "I still have dozens of rooms to search."

"I have confidence in you," she said, and kissed him good-bye.

It felt good to be in her own bed. Thumbs curled up next to

Helen and they both fell asleep. She had no idea where she was when she answered her ringing cell phone.

"This is Phil Sagemont," he said, his voice impersonal. "Do you carry Intex type B pool filter cartridges?"

"Huh?" Helen said, still foggy with sleep.

"This is Phil," he said, emphasizing his name. "Mrs. Zerling's estate manager. Do you have Intex B pool filter cartridges?"

Now Helen was awake enough to remember his code. "I'm supposed to meet you at the post office, right?"

"Yes, that's right," Phil said. "I prefer the post office, not FedEx."

"See you there in twenty minutes," Helen said.

When she ran into the little post office, Phil was at the counter, mailing a flat-rate box. He turned and said, "Helen! Good to see you."

"It's been too long," she said. "Tell me what's happening."

"Got time for a short stroll?" he asked.

The post office was in Helen's favorite section of Las Olas, the part she thought had personality. Helen and Phil strolled past the old Floridian diner, where locals and tourists ate huge lunches. At an outside table, a brown pup sat at his owner's feet, accepting pats and praise.

"I know how Blossom killed her boyfriend," Phil said. "I found the poison under the kitchen sink: a jug of water with ten cigarettes in it."

"Why is that poison?" Helen asked.

"I think she made nicotine tea. Just add hot water to cigarettes and it creates a lethal brew. Seven drops are enough to kill a man."

"Does Blossom smoke?" Helen asked.

"No, but she can buy cigarettes. She left a four-ounce bottle of Angostura bitters on the kitchen sink. I unscrewed the cap and sniffed it. There was a definite tobacco odor. The bottle looks like the one I thought held hot sauce."

"So you think she put nicotine tea in Zack's salsa?"

"It would be easy," Phil said, "especially by the third or fourth beer."

"Why would she keep it in the kitchen?" Helen asked.

"She fired the housekeeper," Phil said, "and she has her meals delivered. No one else uses the kitchen. I have an idea how we can trap her, but I'll need your spiritual guidance, Reverend Hawthorne."

"At your service," Helen said.

"It's two o'clock. I want you to make a condolence call to the new widow about four this afternoon. That's when she has a perfect manhattan. She told me to go buy more Angostura bitters. She's been after me to make her a drink. So far, all I've made are excuses.

"When you're there, she'll suggest we have drinks. You ask for your usual white wine. I'll start making her a manhattan and tell her I didn't have to buy the bitters—I found a nearly full bottle on the kitchen sink.

"Then we'll see how she reacts when I pick up that little bottle of nicotine tea and pour it in her drink. Reverend Hawthorne will be there as a witness. I've tipped our friend Detective Mac Dorsey that we may have more information about that food poisoning case."

"Both of us working on the side of the angels," Helen said.

CHAPTER 36

Lightning flashes of panic streaked through Helen as she turned into Blossom's driveway. She and Phil were playing with fire. Worse—with a clever killer who used silent poisons. One misstep and Helen would be a widow.

This time, she had no trouble finding the Zerling mansion. Helen recognized the surreal sprawl of pink stucco towering over the tall ficus hedge. She parked the Igloo, gathered her courage and smoothed her prim gray suit. She was the Reverend Helen Hawthorne on a pastoral visit, pattering across the pink pavers in her sensible heels.

The valet and the black wreath from Arthur's funeral reception were gone. Today, Blossom answered the massive arched door.

Helen had to force herself not to react to the new widow's outfit. Her lacy black top clung like a cobweb and her red silk pants were tighter than a tourniquet. Red and black. Death and blood. The warning colors of a deadly spider that killed its mate. Blossom didn't bother toning down her extravagant beauty at home. Her hair hung long, thick and free, and her false eyelashes fluttered like trapped moths.

"Reverend Hawthorne, what a nice surprise," Blossom said, and showed a blood-rimmed smile.

"Call me Helen, please. I wanted to see how you were doing. I should have called first, but—"

"No, I'm glad you stopped by," Blossom said. "I've been meaning to call you. I need your help. Come have a drink. You do drink, don't you?"

"Definitely," Helen said. She followed Blossom through the gloomy corridors to a room that looked like a British club in *Masterpiece Theatre*. It was crammed with leather wing chairs, tufted hassocks and small, fussy tables. An inlaid table supported by eight husky, half-clad nymphs dominated the room. The nymphs held up the one spot of color: a pretty vase with a coy shepherdess and an ardent shepherd.

"What a charming vase," Helen said.

"Thank you. That's a porcelain potpourri vase," she said. "The shepherdess is French. Sevres. I love how she flirts with the shepherd."

Blossom gently lifted the gold-trimmed slotted cover. "Inhale," she said.

Could you inhale a poison and die? Helen decided to chance it. She took a deep breath and hoped it wasn't her last. "Heavenly," she said.

"Glad you like it," Blossom said. "It's lavender from Provence, cinnamon, sandalwood and more."

Behind the table, a magnificent rosewood bar sprawled along one wall, carved with lush nymphs, busty mermaids and other boozy dreams. The mirrored back bar glittered with cut-glass decanters and liquor bottles.

Phil was behind the bar, as they'd planned. With his silver white hair and white uniform, Helen thought he looked like a ghost in that cave of a room. Her heart was cold with fear. Suddenly, the plan they'd hatched together seemed foolish. She was glad the dark velvet curtains shut out the light. She didn't want Blossom to see her face when Helen was introduced to her own husband.

"This is my man, Phil Sagemont," Blossom said.

Helen felt her hackles rise at that possessive "my man." She politely extended her hand and said, "I'm Helen Hawthorne."

"She's a minister," Blossom said. "She conducted Arthur's service." She leaned forward and gave Phil a good view of her firm breasts. He stared. Helen wanted to kick him.

He tore his eyes away from the temptation and said, "I'm Phil, Mrs. Zerling's estate manager." His handshake was firm and dry. He slyly winked at her. Helen didn't smile back.

"I thought we could talk in here," Blossom said. "What would you like? Phil can make our drinks."

So now he's a bartender and an estate manager? Helen thought.

"White wine with a splash of soda," she said. She was too keyed up to drink a glass of wine. The alcohol would go to her head.

"Would you like ice with your spritzer?" Phil asked. "The wine is already chilled."

Helen saw the cold mound of cubes in the heavy cut-glass ice bucket on the bar, next to an old-fashioned seltzer bottle. "No, thanks," she said.

Phil took a tall glass from a shelf under the bar and began building Helen's drink. Blossom sat in a brown leather wing chair near the table and Helen took the chair next to it. The air-conditioned leather felt smooth and cool, but she had too much at stake to relax.

"Cashews?" Blossom handed Helen a silver dish.

Could you tamper with cashews? she wondered. "No, thanks." Helen abandoned them on a small, pointless table.

"Would you like a snack?" Blossom asked. "A sandwich?"

"Not hungry," Helen said. Those were the first honest words she'd spoken since her arrival. "I'm glad you don't mind me dropping in like this."

The prompt worked. "I needed to talk to you. As you know, Arthur died without a will," Blossom said, "and my lawyer says I'm entitled to his entire estate. I don't need all ten million and I don't want his daughter to be an enemy. Arthur wouldn't like that. Violet is well-fixed, but I want to offer her a settlement of two million dollars."

The same going-away present you offered your dead lover, Helen thought.

"Well, what do you think?" Blossom asked. She congratulated herself with a smug smile.

"Very generous," Helen said. "But why do you need me?"

"I want you to be the go-between," Blossom said. "Violet doesn't like me. She won't even talk to me."

"You both have lawyers," Helen said. "Surely they could negotiate this."

"Lawyers are so cold and formal," Blossom said. "I know Violet won't be my friend, but I'd like her to hate me a little less. There would be something in it for you, too. What do you need—a church van? A chapel? A vacation for yourself, so you can serve your flock better?"

Blossom might have been the devil herself, tempting Helen to forget her duties, weaving her into the plot to get rid of Violet. The widow was relaxed, almost languid, as she tried to buy Helen's soul.

"I can't take your money," Helen said, "but I will pass on your message and make sure Violet understands your offer."

Every last treacherous detail, she thought.

Phil brought Helen's drink on a scalloped silver tray and set it down on a linen cocktail napkin. "I'm ready to make you that perfect manhattan, Mrs. Zerling. I have all the ingredients—sweet vermouth, dry vermouth and bourbon."

"I hope you bought the Angostura bitters like I asked," Blossom said.

"Didn't have to," Phil said. "I found a nearly full bottle on the kitchen sink. We can use it. See?" He held up a bottle.

"No!" Blossom said, sitting straight up in her chair. She forced a smile and said, "I mean, I don't want a perfect manhattan after all."

"Sure you do," Phil said, and smiled. "You've asked for one nearly every night, and I've always said no. Well, tonight's the night. My manhattans are perfection on the rocks. It's all in the wrist." He waved the Angostura bottle at her. "A dash of these bitters and you won't be the same woman."

He's overdoing it, Helen thought.

"What's wrong? Don't you want my manhattan?" he asked. "I promise it will be good." He raised one eyebrow. He seemed confident and shy at the same time.

Helen had a hard time resisting Phil when he looked at her like that. Blossom was made of stronger stuff.

"I'd like one, but you've refused me so often, I've gotten used to making my own," she said. "I'll mix two manhattans, if you'll drink one with me. We'll try your recipe another day. You go out to the kitchen and get me the maraschino cherries. They're in the fridge."

She playfully shooed him out of the room, as if he were a bad boy. Helen sat frozen in her cold leather chair. She's going to kill my husband right in front of me, she thought.

Blossom stood up in a swirl of dark hair and red lipstick. Her clingy black and red clothes screamed a warning: The most beautiful predators were also the deadliest.

Helen picked up her drink and tried to follow Blossom to the bar.

"No, you sit there and relax, Helen," she said. "I'll make these in a jiffy and sit back down."

She doesn't want me to see her make those drinks, Helen thought. She watched in the mirror, never taking her eyes off Blossom. The woman could ruin Helen's life with one move.

Blossom took out two glasses. "Some people use off-brand liquor, but I like the best to make the best," she said. She added a healthy jigger of Knob Creek to each glass, then a half ounce of Martini & Rossi sweet vermouth and dry vermouth.

All that's missing are the bitters, Helen thought. She watched Blossom add a dash of Angostura to one glass—and not to the other. She set the manhattan without the Angostura near the ice bucket.

"Now, where is Phil with those cherries?" she asked.

"Is the kitchen far away?" Helen asked.

"On the other side of the house," she said. "He's sure taking his time."

Blossom picked up the glass without the dash of Angostura.

"You left the bitters out of your drink," Helen said, heading for the bar.

"I don't want them," Blossom said.

"But that's what makes a manhattan," Helen said. "Here. Let me add a splash." She reached for the small bottle.

"No!" Blossom said.

"I don't know why you don't want it," Helen said. "It's the key to everything. Just a little?"

"Stay away from me with that stuff," Blossom said. Her eyes were wild, her dark hair stood straight out and one false eyelash fluttered loose. Her cobwebby top caught on the edge of the bar and tore. Blossom didn't notice. The woman who'd killed two people was falling apart. She was terrified of a four-ounce bottle, the weapon that had murdered her lover.

Helen decided to help her unravel. "Can't imagine why you're so upset," she said. "What harm can a drop do?"

She unscrewed the cap. Blossom picked up the seltzer bottle and held it in front of her like a shield.

"I said stop it," she screamed, her voice frantic. "Stop it now!"

"What? Are you going to shoot me with that thing, like a Three Stooges movie?" Helen asked.

"Yes," Blossom said, and hit Helen in the face with a jet of seltzer.

Helen coughed and staggered back, wiping seltzer off her face. "You're upset," she said. "You've been under a strain because of Arthur's illness. But that's no way to treat your minister."

"I don't give a damn," Blossom howled.

There was no pretending now. This was a fight. Blossom waved the bottle of dry vermouth at Helen's head.

"Put that down," Helen said.

"Get out," Blossom said, and swung it at Helen. The bottle clipped her shoulder and landed on the leather chair, spilling out onto the seat. The fumes choked Helen, but she grabbed the cut-glass ice bucket and heaved it at Blossom.

She ducked, and the ice bucket hit the potpourri vase. It shattered, spilling its fragrant leaves and seeds on the tabletop. Helen heard something roll across the table and land softly on the thick carpet. She saw something brown and round. A ball? A wheel? A seed? It was rolling toward them on the carpet.

Blossom set down the sweet vermouth bottle, distracted by the moving brownish object.

Now Helen saw it clearly. It was a fat round seed. Blossom wrapped her hand around it as Helen whacked her on the head with the bottle of Knob Creek.

Blossom collapsed on the floor, still clutching the seed in her hand. Helen stomped Blossom's hand and she let go of it.

Helen picked up the seed. She was drenched with seltzer, stank of booze and was so bruised she could hardly move her arm.

Blossom did not move at all.

Phil strolled in with the jar of cherries, blinking in the dim liquor-scented chaos.

"Did I miss something?" he asked.

CHAPTER 37

H elen stared at the shattered shepherdess and wondered if Coronado Investigations' insurance covered Sevres smashed in the line of duty. She was still dazed from her unexpected battle with Blossom. Where was Arthur's widow?

Facedown on the rug, not moving. Not good, Helen thought.

Phil was still holding the jar of cherries and laughing like a loon. "You mean it worked?" he said. "The bluff worked?"

"What bluff?" Helen said. "What's so funny?"

"Blossom actually believed you were pouring poison in her manhattan," Phil said. He couldn't stop laughing.

Helen was angry—and wet. Water dripped off her seltzered hair. She brushed her drenched bangs out of her eyes and said, "I would have, too. Dumped it right in her drink."

"Still wouldn't have poisoned her," Phil said.

She didn't like his smirk. "That's the bottle on the bar," she said.

Four ounces of nicotine tea had created a path of destruction through the forest of tables and chairs and the jungle ropes of braid and tassels: The seltzer bottle was stranded on the floor. The dry vermouth bottle had glugged itself empty on the chair. The cut-glass ice bucket had gouged deep furrows in the inlaid tabletop as it skidded sideways and splintered the shepherdess. Two useless tables were toppled.

Helen's wine spritzer and the cashews had survived unharmed. So had the two manhattans.

"There is no poison in that Angostura bottle," Phil said, pointing to it. "I bought those bitters and pretended that was the poison bottle. I wasn't going to risk my life—or yours—playing with something deadly. The real poison bottle is still on the kitchen counter and the nicotine tea is in the jar under the sink. That bottle is safe as lemonade." His mouth tilted upward in a quirky smile.

Helen wanted to slap it off his face. Anger arced through her. "Phil Sagemont, I can't believe you let me think Blossom was poisoning your drink," she said. The fight left her with an adrenaline overload and she unleashed it. "And what were you doing staring at her breasts?"

"I was undercover," Phil said.

"Well, they weren't!" Helen flounced behind the rosewood bar and reached for the phone. "I'm calling 911. Blossom hasn't moved. She needs an ambulance."

"Good Lord, she's not dead, is she?" he asked. "I'd better check."

Blossom was still sprawled on the dark carpet, a study in scarlet, jet-black and corpse white. Phil knelt down next to the fallen widow and lifted an eyelid. "She's out cold, but she's breathing." He searched her scalp for a wound. "That's quite a lump on her head."

"They don't call it Knob Creek bourbon for nothing," Helen said. "I may have hurt her hand, too, when I stepped on it."

Phil winced. "Remind me not to upset you," he said.

"Too late," she said.

Phil finally realized she was in no mood for jokes. "I'm sorry," he said. "Truly, I am. When Blossom wakes up, she's going to accuse you of attacking her. The crime-scene techs should find enough evidence to support your story."

Blossom whimpered softly.

"Let's hope this is the seed from the suicide tree," Helen said. She set it on the bar. "We should get the police here."

"Let me make quick calls to Detective Mac Dorsey, our lawyer and Valerie Cannata," he said. "Mac may need a warrant for that poison bottle."

Helen handed him the phone.

"Her number's in my cell phone," he said. "Mac promised she'd wait for my call."

She did. Helen heard Phil give his report, quick and professional. Then his voice changed. He was explaining, then pleading. Finally, he said, "So it's okay? I'll see you here," and hit END.

"Something wrong?" Helen asked.

"Mac is just being cautious," he said. "She wanted to know how I found the nicotine tea and the poisoned bitters. She was afraid I'd been breaking and entering. She forgot I'm the estate manager here. Then she asked if I was working undercover for the police or the DA.

"Once I convinced her I wasn't a government agent, she said this was a lawful search. I have to show the investigating cops I found evidence in two murders. They can't even open that kitchen cabinet. I have to point and say, 'Lookie here, Officers.'"

"Why is Mac carrying on?" Helen asked. "She knows us."

"She also knows the laws about illegal searches," Phil said. "They're tricky. She doesn't want this evidence thrown out. Mac's on her way. Zack is her case, but this isn't her jurisdiction. We're in Hendin Island's."

Helen groaned. "Detective Richard McNally."

"She knows him," Phil said. "They get along fine."

"He knows me," Helen said. "We don't."

"We'll have our lawyer here for protection," he said. "We'll need Nancie when the police question us. After I call her, I'll give Valerie a ring. We promised her a scoop."

"Don't call Valerie," Helen said. "The police will check your cell phone. You can explain the calls to Detective Mac and our lawyer, but the cops will be furious if you call a reporter to a crime scene."

"I'll ask Nancie to call Valerie," Phil said. "Here goes. I hope our lawyer is easier than the detective."

She wasn't.

Once again Phil delivered his report, calm and professional. Then he grew increasingly upset. "She what! You have to get *her* permission? In writing? How long will that take? Okay, okay, I understand it's the law. Does she have to come here, too? Good. Yes, I promise. Helen will, too. Please, hurry. And don't forget Valerie." He hung up and sighed.

"What was that all about?" Helen asked.

"I should have known this," Phil said. "We'd discussed it in Nancie's office. Our PI work is privileged under Florida law. We need Violet's permission to tell the cops, or we can lose our license for breaking client confidentiality."

"Violet won't stop us, will she?" Helen asked.

"Hell, no. Violet will demand we tell the cops. The hard part will be keeping her away from here. Nancie promises she'll do it, but she wants Violet's permission in writing."

"I sure hope Violet's at home now," Helen said.

"Me, too," Phil said. "Nancie insists neither one of us talk to the cops unless she's with us. The police will probably split us up. We have to tell them that we want to help, but we will only talk with our attorney present."

Blossom moaned like something in a midnight churchyard.

"You took the words right out of my mouth, Blossom," Helen said.

"Is she coming around yet?" Phil whispered.

"Not quite," Helen said. "But soon."

"Brace yourself," Phil said. "I'm calling 911."

Helen found her wine spritzer and downed the whole drink. She needed fortification.

"Better eat those cashews, too," Phil said. "It's five o'clock. We'll be here until midnight, at least."

Helen was still munching when a wave of blue uniforms washed through the mansion. She and Phil were immediately isolated in separate rooms. Both recited Nancie's canned speech: "Yes, Officer, I want to cooperate, but I need my lawyer."

Both received Miranda cautions. Helen took comfort in the words the police officer recited: "You have the right to an attorney and to have one here with you during questioning, now or in the future."

Come on, Nancie, she prayed.

Detective Mac Dorsey arrived next. She'd been promoted to detective partly because of a case Helen and Phil had worked—and her colleague had bungled. Mac was a strong, sturdy woman. Since her promotion, she'd developed a knack for finding well-tailored pantsuits in resale shops.

She saw Phil first. "I'd love to talk to you, Detective Dorsey," Phil said. He didn't dare call her Mac in public. "But I have to wait for our attorney, Nancie Hays."

"Maybe Helen has more sense," Dorsey said, and stalked off to the sitting room where Helen was counting the tassels on the furniture, lampshades and curtains.

"Come on, Helen," Dorsey said. "You know me."

"I know the law, too," Helen said. "We can't talk until the lawyer gets our client's permission. She'll be here as fast as she can. Meanwhile, the crime-scene folks have lots to do."

Detective Richard NcNally was next. Detective McNally's sedate dark suit, white shirt and tie looked weirdly out of place in South Florida, land of sartorial outrage. McNally was even more unhappy with Phil than Detective Dorsey. His face turned the same shade of puce as his tie while Phil recited his speech.

"Hays can't be two places at once," McNally said.

"I'm willing to wait while she's with Helen. Then she can be present during my questioning."

"That could take all night," McNally said.

"I have nowhere to go and I'm being paid by the hour," Phil said. He smiled. McNally didn't smile back.

The detective had better luck with Helen. Actually, he had better timing.

She had counted forty-seven tassels and was estimating the yards of fringe on the chairs and lampshades when McNally interrupted her.

"Well, well," he said. "Ms. Helen Hawthorne. Again. This is like a family reunion."

The Addams family, Helen wanted to say. We've got the right decor. She congratulated herself for keeping her mouth shut.

Nancie Hays heard his remark as she flew through the sitting room door. The little whirlwind in a suit set the fringe flapping.

"Sarcasm is unprofessional, Detective," the attorney said, crisply. "Ms. Hawthorne and Mr. Sagemont are aware this is a serious matter and they are willing to cooperate with the police. They have the right to an attorney and I insist on being present during their questioning. Now, if you'll excuse us, I'll chat briefly with my client."

All night and a good part of the morning, Helen and Phil explained why they were at the Zerling mansion, why they thought Blossom was a killer, how she murdered first Arthur and then Zack. The police knew ten million good reasons for Arthur's murder. Phil supplied the rationale for Blossom getting rid of her greedy boyfriend.

The couple repeated their stories again and again, while their lawyer stood by in her dark-framed glasses like an owl in a brown suit.

Shortly after the first wave of police arrived, Blossom woke up. She was read her Miranda rights, and waived them. She claimed Helen attacked her. An ambulance took her to the ER.

Police officers sniffed the Angostura bitters bottle on the kitchen counter and detected a definite odor of nicotine. Phil pointed out the soggy cigarette butts floating in a jar under the sink. One cop gagged.

Even though the doctors believed food poisoning had killed Zack, samples of his blood and urine had been saved in case of criminal or civil liability. There was enough for further tests.

The brown seedlike object was bagged as evidence and sent to an expert for identification.

By eight thirty in the morning, Helen looked like she'd crawled out of the wreckage of an F5 tornado. Her eyes were red, her suit was torn and her shoulder was bruised.

She felt terrific.

Detective Richard McNally had applied for a court order to exhume the body of Arthur Zerling.

CHAPTER 38

Helen squinted at the glaring sun as she and Phil tottered out of the Zerling mansion. Nancie Hays marched beside them with a gunslinger's swagger.

The morning air felt cool and fresh. Helen did not. "I need coffee," she said.

"And you'll get it," the lawyer said. "At my office." Her brown suit wasn't even wrinkled. How did she do it? Helen wondered.

"Can't I go home and change?" she asked. "Please?"

"No," Nancie said. "My legal services come with a high price. We have to meet with our client in half an hour."

"But I can't—" Phil said.

"No whining," Nancie said. "Violet signed that release last night when we needed it. She cooperated. Now she has every right to know what happened. I'll stop for bagels and meet you at my office."

"I can't face Violet without at least eight hours' sleep," Helen said.

"I promise you'll be pleasantly surprised," Nancie said. "She is a changed woman."

"I could use a pleasant surprise," Helen said as she climbed into the Igloo. Phil followed behind her in the Jeep. They both drove carefully around the official vehicles scattered on the driveway.

Nancie's office parking lot was empty. Helen tried to comb her hair in the rearview mirror, but her bruised shoulder ached when she raised her arm.

Forget it, she decided. Violet should see I've been in a battle. Phil parked next to her, jumped out with surprising energy and opened her car door. Helen gingerly unfolded herself from the Igloo and leaned against his shoulder.

"It's over," she said.

"Almost," he said, rocking her in his arms. "I think that's Violet's Saturn parking under the palm tree."

Helen turned and stared. "That can't be our client getting out of it," she said.

This woman was fifteen pounds slimmer and more toned than the Violet they knew. Her hair was chic and the new color gave her skin a rosy glow. Either that, or Violet had had makeup lessons since they'd last seen her.

She didn't walk like Violet, either. She strode confidently toward them. "Phil? Helen?" she asked. "Are you okay? You look a little rocky this morning."

"I've been beat up by Blossom, then spent the night with the police," Helen said. "You look terrific. What's your secret?"

"Thanks," Violet said. "I was too upset to eat after Daddy died. I lost ten pounds and decided to keep losing weight. Now I'm working out at the gym four days a week. I feel so much better."

"But your hair is different and your clothes are new," Helen said.

"You like them?" Violet smiled. A sweet smile, with none of the old tension. "Clothes and hair were never my thing. My workout instructor sent me to a new salon. Neiman Marcus has a personal shopper. That was Blossom's secret, you know. She had the taste of a tramp, but she used a personal shopper to buy the right clothes to mix with people like Daddy.

"But I'm not going to waste time ranting about her. I'm seeing a counselor now. For"—she paused and lowered her eyes—"anger issues. I don't like Blossom and never will, but I'm starting to realize that some of my problems were caused by me. I can be my own worst enemy."

Blossom, Helen thought. She called her stepmother Blossom. Twice.

"But you were right," Phil said. "Blossom did murder your father. She had a lover and she poisoned your father with something from the exotic East, just as you suspected. Now that Nancie's here, we'll go inside and give our report."

Helen and Phil helped the lawyer carry in steaming cups of hot coffee, a tub of warm bagels, whipped butter, maple-honey spread and lox and cream cheese. They arranged the food on the conference room table. Helen burned her tongue on the coffee—she was that desperate for caffeine. Phil heaped a bagel with lox and cream cheese.

The little lawyer sat at the head of the long conference-dining table, savoring her triumph and a cinnamon-raisin bagel.

Violet sipped black coffee and listened to Helen and Phil. She cried softly when Phil told her about the seed of the suicide tree.

"Fran was right," Violet said. "It was the curry. It hid the taste. I hope Blossom goes away for a long time."

Helen heard a flash of Violet's old anger. But it was justified.

"I think she will," Nancie said, delicately picking a crumb off her brown suit. "Right now Blossom is in custody for the assault on Helen. But I expect further charges after Mr. Zerling's body is exhumed and tests are conducted on samples from her lover, Zack. Any more questions?"

"A couple," Violet said. "Why did Blossom use a different poison to kill her boyfriend?"

"I can answer that," Phil said. "She wanted to save the suicide tree seed for you. I heard her tell Zack that it would look like you'd had a heart attack, just like your father. She said she was going to try to mend fences with you. We warned Nancie, but she didn't contact you."

"I might have let her, too, as part of my therapy," Violet said.

"She was poisoning Zack while she talked about killing you," Phil said.

"Awful woman," Violet said. "Do you need to see a doctor, Helen, for your injuries?"

Helen started in surprise. Violet hadn't cared about anything but vengeance last time.

"No, just a bruised shoulder," Helen said.

"Your suit is ruined," she said.

"I never liked it anyway," Helen said.

"Is that it, Violet?" Nancie asked.

Violet nodded. They shook hands all around, but Nancie wouldn't let Helen leave yet. She pulled a camera from her desk drawer. "I'm taking photos of your injuries, including that shoulder. That bruise should be nice and photogenic this morning. Take off your blouse, please."

Helen finished the photo session yawning with fatigue. Phil swiped an onion bagel and they left.

The next two weeks passed in a blur of publicity and breaking news on the Blossom Zerling murders. Valerie Cannata seemed to have a new revelation on channel seventy-seven nearly every day. Each time, she mentioned Coronado Investigations. Helen and Phil were the stars of the six o'clock news.

First, a botanist confirmed that the oval seed in the potpourri vase was from the suicide tree, famous for its harvest of suicide and homicide in India and southern Asia, but hardly known in the West.

Next, Valerie reported that the medical examiner found traces of the exotic poison in Arthur Zerling's body during the autopsy. The samples of Zack's blood and urine showed evidence of nicotine poison.

Then Valerie broke the story that Blossom Zerling was charged with first-degree murder in the deaths of her husband, Arthur Zerling, and her lover, Zachary Crinlund. Now Blossom could no longer receive funds from the Zerling estate—or afford a high-priced defense team. Blossom waited for an ambitious defense lawyer to save her for no money, but the pin-striped sharks were busy rescuing other malefactors.

Blossom had to settle for a public defender with a bad haircut and a shiny suit. He saw Valerie's story about Arthur's kindness and contributions to the community, and advised Blossom to plead guilty to both murders and avoid the death penalty.

Helen and Phil cheered when Blossom was sentenced to life in prison.

The Zerling case ended where it began—in Nancie Hays's neat, practical office.

The new Violet sat in the lime green client chair. She was more attractive, less angry and definitely grateful. She examined her bill, wrote a check to Coronado Investigations with a flourish, then handed Helen and Phil a bonus check of fifty thousand dollars.

"Rich people usually look for ways to reduce bills," Helen said.

"Blossom won't get Daddy's estate, thanks to you," Violet said. "You've made me richer—and saved my life."

She handed Helen a pale blue envelope. "That's for Margery Flax, the woman who accompanied me to Daddy's funeral."

"We've already paid her," Helen said.

"She deserves a bonus for putting up with me," Violet said.

"We have something for you," Helen said. "Blossom asked me to go through your father's personal effects and give them to charity. I sent them to a resale shop that benefits people with AIDS. Do you want me to see if I can get his things back?"

"No, no," Violet said. "Daddy would be happy that his things will help people. That's the kind of man he was."

"We kept two personal items for you," Helen said. She handed

Violet her parents' wedding photo in the mother-of-pearl frame and the platinum Rolex Oyster that Honeysuckle had given Arthur.

Violet's expression softened as she read the engraving on the watch out loud. *"To my love on our first anniversary. We have all the time in the world—HZ. "*

"They didn't, did they?" Violet said, wiping away a tear.

"There's never enough time when you love each other," Helen said.

"Well, I'm sure you have places to go," Violet said, suddenly turning all business. She stood up and shook hands with the partners of Coronado Investigations.

It was five o'clock when Helen and Phil walked out together to the Igloo. "We'd better deposit our checks at the bank before they evaporate," Phil said. "Then we have one more place to go."

"Where?" Helen asked.

"It's a surprise," he said.

The setting sun was turning the Fort Lauderdale beach a tender pink when Phil parked the Igloo. The beachgoers were already a deeper pink. Tired, sunburned and sandy, they were folding their chairs and packing their coolers. Toddlers crying for naps clung to their mothers. Daddies gave their little girls rides on their shoulders to the family minivans.

Helen and Phil passed them as they walked at the edge of the ocean. Helen slipped off her shoes and let the warm water tickle her toes.

They walked as though they were the only ones on the beach.

"I know where we are now," Helen said. "This is where Margery married us."

"That's why I wanted to come back," Phil said. "I know you've been upset with me about that business with the Angostura bitters."

"No—" Helen began, then realized she had been. "Yes," she said. "You know me better than I know myself." She turned to face him.

"I was wrong," he said. "I should have told you what I planned." He kissed her forehead.

She ran her finger lightly along the bridge of his nose. She liked his nose. Like Phil, it was both noble and slightly crooked.

"You are my partner, Helen," he said. "My equal partner."

He kissed first one eyelid, then the other, while she held him close.

"In work and in love," he said. "Forever."

And then he kissed her on the lips, the way he did the night they married.

EPILOGUE

"Well, well, this is a nice surprise," Margery said as she read Violet's check. "Green. My favorite color."

"I thought it was purple," Helen said.

"It will be," Margery said.

The landlady bought a magnificent gold and amethyst necklace and a purple silk hostess outfit, then wore them to a party she threw by the pool. Phil barbecued chicken and ribs, and the Coronado denizens feasted and toasted one another.

"So, am I a member of Coronado Investigations?" Margery asked.

"You're an independent contractor," Phil said.

"Accent on *independent*," Helen said.

Violet Zerling sold her father's Fort Lauderdale mansion. "Too many sad memories," she said. Her real estate agent introduced her to a fifty-one-year-old corporate attorney named Gordon. They dated for a year before announcing their engagement. Violet knows her fiancé isn't marrying her for her money—Gordon is even richer than she is. She did insist that they both have wills and designated health-care surrogates. Violet and Gordon married at his Fort Lauderdale mansion and plan to live happily ever after.

Andrei, the fired first engineer on the *Belted Earl*, finally found work on a yacht called *Threesome*. That boat name is popular on porn sites and in XXX-rated movies. It is also used by some freethinking yachters. This particular *Threesome* was known to South Florida yachters as a perpetual party boat. Underage girls scampered about on the decks. Drugs were as abundant as boob jobs. Miraculously, the yacht was never boarded by the authorities. Competent crew regarded this *Threesome* as the last stop before the crazy train derailed. The owner made the crew miserable with his miserly pay and capricious changes.

Helen thought a stint on the *Threesome* was a fitting punishment for the Bulgarian engineer. Andrei was surrounded by lush, willing beauties who never noticed him. In the port bars, even the most naive stewardess would not go home with a man who wore a *Threesome* crew uniform.

Dick, the second engineer, was promoted to Andrei's job on the *Belted Earl*. Captain Swingle found replacement staff through a reputable Fort Lauderdale yacht crew agency, then hired Coronado Investigations to do background checks on the new crew.

HSI agents found an empty plastic tackle box and a duffel full of grimy evening gowns in a trash can near the car belonging to Mira's boyfriend. Kevin had parked his car in the Fort Lauderdale airport garage. Kevin said he didn't remember Mira ever having a tackle box. Mira gave him the gowns for his theater company's production of *Rain*, but the dresses were too damaged to be used as costumes. The company closed before the show's opening night.

There was not enough evidence to charge Kevin as an accessory to Mira's smuggling. Kevin missed his off-Broadway audition when he was detained for questioning at the airport. He went to New York three months later. He now works off Broadway—as a waiter.

Tests showed that the blond hair found in Louise's pocket was a DNA match with Mira's hair. Police produced Mira's credit card receipt for a silver two-toned Ficcare barrette purchased from HeadGamesOnline.com three months before Louise's death.

Faced with this overwhelming evidence, Mira confessed that she had seen Louise leave the bosun's locker after the head stew hid the tackle box of smuggled emeralds in there. The next time Mira checked the locker, the box was secured with a bungee cord. Mira never knew that the captain had found the emeralds and hired Coronado Investigations. She expected Louise to accuse her and Mira didn't want to get caught with the latest load of emeralds.

Mira saw the rough seas on the crossing as a way to end a potential problem. She lured Louise outside with a story that the boys had left a wicker sofa unsecured on the lower aft deck.

Mira got down on the deck, peered under the canvas cover and said, "The lower bungee cord snapped."

"Where?" Louise asked, as the shifting sea slammed into the yacht and knocked her off balance. That's when the much stronger Mira grabbed her ankles and tipped the hundred-pound Louise overboard.

Mira was charged with murder one. Her public defender reminded her that Florida is a death penalty state and Louise's cold-blooded murder would horrify a jury. Mira accepted a plea bargain for life without possibility of parole.

Shortly after the news of Mira's sentence, Captain Swingle held a memorial service for Louise at sunset on the Fort Lauderdale beach. Suzanne, Dick, Matt, Carl, Sam and Helen attended the service. The captain brought a dozen white roses. Suzanne set out a buffet table with appetizers that looked like the elegant, edible art Louise had served on the yacht, as well as the boys' favorites, pigs in a blanket and pizzas. Guests sipped champagne and drank beer.

Each crew member talked about how much he or she admired Louise, and tossed a white rose into the soft silvery sea. Sam the deckhand, fortified by several brews, was the last to speak at Louise's memorial.

He gave a less rambling version of his good girl/bad girl speech, then said, "Louise was a good girl. No, a good woman. And we were good friends. The best. She loved life and she loved the ocean and she even loved the pelicans. She said they were what pterodactyls must have looked like. I'll miss Louise."

Sam gently left a rose on the edge of the warm surf. Captain Swingle set the remaining flowers next to it. The tide carried the roses away as a squadron of pelicans glided above.

"Yay, Louise!" Sam shouted, waving his beer.

The crew lifted their champagne glasses in a final salute to her.

Helen watched the crew drift away after the service. She walked alone on the beach to the site where Margery had married her and Phil, and where her husband had pledged his love a second time. She had a pledge of her own to keep. Her sister, Kathy, had received the phone jack and the digital recorder that Helen sent her, and practiced daily, determined to catch the blackmailer. Kathy told Helen that she could slap the jack on the recorder in two seconds, even if Tommy Junior was teasing his little sister, and his father was asking if dinner was ready. Kathy felt prepared to record Rob, or whoever the blackmailer was.

Helen stood alone in the surf, watching the sun slip into the soft silken sea and the stars come out.

Then she said out loud, "I swear that I will trust my husband and tell him what happened to Rob. We will catch the blackmailer together. And then I hope that he will still love me."

.   .   .

Phil was waiting for Helen in their office when she came home, her hair tossed by the sea breeze. "I've been going over the books," he said. "Coronado Investigations is safely in the black. We could use Violet's bonus as the down payment on a bigger place."

"Do you want a house?" Helen asked.

"No, I like it here," Phil said. "But you used to own a big house in St. Louis."

"That was another life," Helen said. "A bigger house means more work. It would mean more cleaning. I did enough on that yacht. I can't see you pushing a lawn mower, Phil.

"We have enough room at the Coronado. If I need to be alone, I go to my apartment and shut the door. Same with you. Margery is our estate manager. If we moved, I'd miss our friends here."

"Me, too," he said. "What would we do without the Coronado sunset salutes?"

"I like our life," Helen said. "And I love you." She kissed his ear.

"I already have everything. Why would I want more?"